Hannah S

CHAPTER 1

I was twenty-two when I stepped onto the plane to London from Toronto. Going back to Britain seemed like the right thing to do. I was top of my final year in a tough business degree. I was ready to meet my future.

I'd finished university, endured the phoniness of graduation day with its forced photographs and fake, sad goodbyes. I thought I was ready to walk into any company I chose and begin a career full of challenge and success. Excitement was what I was looking for. That's really what I wanted. I went to university to escape the mundane in life, a place I thought would prepare me for the kind of life and lifestyle I dreamt of. I'd been to the financial district of London, its square mile and spent time in the stockbroker belt of Surrey and both had a big impact on me. I remember early in my freshman year in Toronto, a student asking me why I was studying business and what my inspiration was and I answered 'a flat in Chelsea'. He didn't know where that was and he told me he was studying to become a teacher because it had a good pension plan. He was eighteen years old and he was thinking about a pension. It depressed the hell out of me. I wanted to poke him in the chest and shout 'how about living a bit? How about having a life of risk and adventure, one worth living?' I didn't of course but I did think to myself, good luck as you count down 45 years of your life waiting for your little pot of gold and live out your sorry little existence of no ambition. I came to understand later that most Canadians do have ambitions to live a comfortable life of two cars, two kids and two houses, one being a summer holiday home by a lake somewhere in the north of the Province they live in and a hefty retirement fund to live out the rest of life on. He fitted the profile and he doesn't know where Chelsea is.

It was the summer of 1980 when I finished my degree and returned to Edinburgh, the city I grew up in. I knew nothing about Margaret Thatcher's government or the social and economic revolution taking hold of the country. Graduates were battling to find jobs and companies were firing instead of hiring. Hundreds of thousands of hard working people were being laid off. Two months later I bolted to Greece where I spent the autumn into winter picking oranges with a group of foreign nationals from around the world. Americans, Swedes, Australians, Canadians, Brits and South Africans made up the bulk of our orange picking team and hard work every day was followed by bottles of retsina, ouzo and beer in the local tavernas late into the night. It was great fun but eventually I had to face the reality that holidays for me were over and that real life and the real world had to be faced head on and said my farewells to the finest group of people I'd ever met and to Greece.

This morning I was about to start work in a health food shop stacking sacks of flour, beans, split peas, lentils and oatmeal and make sure customers were happy. That was my job description anyway and it wasn't exactly how I had pictured my leap from student life into the business world. This was not part of my plan at all but I'm home and employed.

After looking out my window at a dull and grey sky above Edinburgh Castle, I showered and dressed and was pouring myself a mug of Earl Grey tea when my elder brother, Neil, came into the kitchen and asked me to make him one too. "Is this the day the world has been waiting for, for Tom to show his face?" He laughed and said I was wasting my time, wasting my years at university and should have stayed where I was. "Edinburgh's screwed. If you wanted to come back to this part of the world, you need to go to London where the jobs are, well what jobs there are. You've come back at the worst possible time and the country's full of unemployed graduates. I'd have even forgotten about London, Canada's the land of milk and honey. Mum told me you had job offers in Toronto, most people would swap what they have for what you had. This job is not what you're about."

"I know" I said "but I've got to do something and the interview somehow sold me. I've got a good feeling about this and it's just for a little while. It'll be a good way of meeting people and I think I need that."
"Up to you" Neil said and we spent the next few minutes drinking our tea and listening to the news on the radio. Neil was a journalist working in North Berwick and at 25 he'd had enough of reporting on cats stuck up trees and being rescued by the local fire brigade, holiday makers being rescued from sand banks off the beach and he wanted out. His dreams of reporting for the BBC and travelling the world had been replaced by the idea of being a freelancer barely getting by and his conviction that he had peaked and achieved all he wanted in life by the age of 23. It was a ridiculous claim of course but he stood by it and agonised at the stupidity he saw in politicians he met in his job and the sheer idiocy of most of the stories he covered. He was a deep thinker, had been as long as I could remember and told me he'd once fallen into what he described as a catatonic state after a drug fuelled London party with an actor friend of his and for five days could only remember his name and his height as both appeared on his passport. He said he slowly regained his memory and wits but he was left with a clearer impression of the futility of what much of life is about and what really matters. He had no time for power driven egotistical maniacs or celebrities and their lust for fame. Neil was the kindest person you'd hope to meet.

Nature's Foods was about a three mile walk away from my dad's flat where I was staying near the Usher Hall and I decided to walk the length of Princes Street, past Edinburgh Castle, Princes Street Gardens, The National gallery, where I'd spent days filling in time admiring the art and the Scott Monument, the sixty metre towering Victorian Gothic structure, before turning up St Andrews Street by Waverley Station amongst a sea of commuters arriving from their train journeys and along London Road. Maybe not the city of London but on London Road I'll be working I said to myself, all the time thinking that Neil was right and that any kind of future for me would be down south. Anyway, any time I'd been to London I felt good there and although visits were brief, I never had a bad time and never tired of the sights, the nightlife and theatres, the sheer size of the place. I loved walking alongside the Thames and watching people from almost every country in the world doing the same, taking photographs to take back home, holidays of a lifetime in action around me.

I arrived at the shop just before eight o'clock and had been told that a woman by the name of Janet would meet me, she was the manager of the shop floor and she'd introduce me to the staff and briefly tell me what I was to do for the first few hours until Ian Roberts arrived. Ian was one of the founding members of the business and was one of the three senior managers who had interviewed me ten days earlier at the company's head office and warehouse complex and had seemed the friendliest. I thought he was the decision maker to my less than remarkable appointment to a position which probably no one else had applied for. The entrance to the shop was bright and almost cheerful. There were hanging baskets of fruit and flowers of all colours, pictures of farm workers from countries with sunny climates picking all varieties of crops, all smiling, all looking happy. This was a place for people to come and shop who cared about their health.

A woman of around 40 approached me and asked if I was Thomas. I said I was and she introduced herself as Janet. "Follow me Thomas and I'll show you around before we open and let you know what I'd like done this morning. Ian has told me a little about you and we're all excited to meet you and welcome you." I walked into the shop itself and was surprised to see so many large wooden barrels on the shop floor, filled with different types of food. There were barrels filled with rice, with beans, oats, barley, muesli, all kinds of grains and shelves behind with jars of honeys and jams and dried fruits, peanut butters and marmalade. "You're going to love working here and I'd like you to know that all the young ladies here are here to help you get settled in. There is so much for you to learn and you're going to be asking lots of questions. Ian said you've got a good brain." Good brain, I thought, strange way of putting it.

"Nina," Janet called out and a young woman in her early twenties came towards us from the back of the shop. "This is Thomas, Thomas, this is Nina. She's been with us for nearly three years and knows everything you'll need to know and is our top sales lady, has been for the past two years."

"Pleased to meet you Nina" I said. "I'm looking forward to starting and working with you." Nina told me she was still learning and there was always something new from a customer every day. Nina went back to whatever it was she was doing earlier. There were two or three other women chatting amongst themselves, tying aprons around each other and laughing and Janet introduced me and we spoke briefly, I said how glad I was to be starting and the younger one told me she'd just finished a course at Edinburgh University and that this was her dream job, working with people, helping them find new and better ways of eating natural foods from around the world and that living healthily was what it's all about. She'd studied languages and loved it when French or Italian tourists came into the shop. She was wearing a pair of dungarees and had short blond hair and struck me as someone who was trying her best to hide her natural good looks.

"Hannah," Janet called out. A young woman, quite tall I thought for a woman, she had short brunette hair, very slim in jeans and a tight fitting schoolboy rugby shirt behind her apron approached us. "Hi, I'm Hannah, Hannah Swann, you must be Tom. I'm very pleased to meet you." I heard Janet mention the name Thomas and Hannah replying she'll be calling me Tom. Hannah had held out her hand to shake mine and I felt her warm soft skin, unsure how long to hold her grasp. Maybe it was a second longer than normal or usual but it felt longer before I released my

hand from hers. "Thomas" I said "but my friends call me Tom. Tom Miller."
Hannah smiled and then supressing a giggle looked down at my shoes. "Polished your shoes this morning, did you, just for us?"

My heart wasn't beating, it was thumping. Hannah was impossibly pretty, slim to the point of almost too slim , faded jeans and a simple shirt, not a hint of makeup, yet a red blush to her face, hair way too short for classic beauty I thought and she's wearing a pair of slip on shoes. Not an effort of any kind to impress anyone. She didn't need to, she was simply perfect. She had the most beautiful eyes I'd ever seen. Beautiful eyebrows, cheekbones, her mouth, her lips, her nose, the shape of her face, everything and the body of a model. I glanced at her hands, no ring, unattached I thought, no chance, accent not Edinburgh. I feel like we've met before but know we haven't. We were looking at each other and I was wondering if she was going to say we have met. Her smile made me smile. There was a strange familiarity but anyone I had seen this beautiful would have been at the front of my mind, not the back and I'm now staring, I've got no words, I'm just standing there speechless. I wanted to look away but couldn't and was beginning to feel a nervousness building up, a deep sense of uneasiness. I hadn't prepared myself for this. At last Hannah laughed and I pretended it was about my shoes and looked down but I sensed that she laughed to relieve me from my awkwardness. "You don't mind me calling you Tom, do you?" I laughed and said no and Janet asked Hannah to unlock the front door and shouted out to the rest that the shop was now open and the day beginning.

Downstairs was to be my main working area, beneath the shop floor and next to the small staff kitchen. The accounts department and the floor where the jars of jams, oils, peanut butters and dried fruits were mixed was on the first floor above the shop and all staff used the kitchen to prepare snacks, have lunch or cups of tea or coffee. When anyone took a break from working, they usually did so in the kitchen. Janet took me to the kitchen and prepared tea for us both. She showed me where the stock for the shop was stored and pointed out that this was my area of responsibility. No one other than me or management had authority over the stock and no access was allowed to customers. Rows and rows of stacked sacks everywhere I looked. "You need to be strong for this job" Janet said to me.
"I see that" I replied. The sacks were almost all marked 50 Kgs and I quickly calculated that at 110lbs these were on the heavy side to be lugging up the stairs we'd just come down. Ian had said I'd be gaining quite a bit of muscle and that the guy before me had quit due to a back injury. Why so bloody heavy I thought.

Janet told me that I'd be spending the morning filling up the wooden barrels upstairs on the shop floor and that whoever was stationed closest to the top of the stairs would be coming down and letting me know which sacks were needed. A delivery was due later in the morning and I would be helping to offload from the truck and taking some of the order to the first floor, some to the basement we were in and that now was the time for that cup of tea. Janet struck me as a kind lady, a motherly figure to her staff and cared for or looked after her figure. Actually all the women on the floor were slim and attractive and I was wondering to myself if this was part of the deal for working here or if it was due to a lifestyle of healthy eating. Maybe I could learn a lot about food here. I'd never really given it much thought other than the eating an apple a day thing and a bit of exercise.

"Any questions so far?" Janet asked as we sat by the kitchen table drinking the finest cup of tea I'd ever had. "Not really, I'm sure I'll get the hang of things quickly and I'm up for this," I said. "Who's stationed closest to me by the steps?"
"Funny you should ask because that's been Nina's place for months and Hannah asked to swap with her on Friday. You'll be working with her quite closely and she'll be a great help to you. I adore her, well everybody does. The customers just love her. She's made such a difference since she started working here and it's her friendliness which wins people over. She learned very quickly and gives out very good advice on which foods are best suitable and she has a sense about people which I just can't put my finger on. She came in on Friday morning and told us all that you'd be starting today and that we weren't to ask you if you were American. We all laughed and the girls

were still at it this morning when you arrived. You do know that she lives with and shares a house with Ian and Simon who interviewed you?"
"No. I didn't," I replied.
"Ian's going out with her older sister, Susan and they all come from the south of Scotland and Hannah came up to Edinburgh about six months ago. Well, not Simon, he's from here as you probably know."
"Yeah, Simon I know, he went on about the school thing a bit and made a couple of jokes. The American thing I'm having to get used to. The thing is I lived in Canada for four years and I wasn't aware of any change in my accent. In Toronto, people I met always asked if I were Scottish, sometimes I'd be accused of being Irish but no one thought I was Canadian and never an American. I come back to Edinburgh and suddenly I've got this American tag and I don't know why. I haven't tried to change the way I speak and if it has changed I'm not aware of it" I said.
Janet smiled and said I sounded a bit American to her and we finished our tea as a few of the accountants and bookkeeping staff arrived and made their introductions to me. All well dressed, the men in buttoned up shirts and ties, the women stylish and me in my faded jeans, t-shirt and shiny shoes.

I spent the rest of the morning answering calls from Hannah at the top of the stairs to bring up sacks of different types of rice, all marked from India or Thailand, beans, black and white lentils, brown, green and red and muesli, a customer favourite I learned before Ian arrived to surprise me with an offer for a quick lunch at the local pub.

Ian was 28 years old, he was smartly dressed in black trousers and open neck black golf shirt, he had a thick matt of red hair with red stubble. He wasn't the tallest of blokes and had arms like Popeye covered in thick hair. I'd never managed the hairy arms bit. He'd gone to Edinburgh University and after graduating, travelled the world for two years before returning with the idea of importing the finest raw, natural foods from the Far East and South and Central America and opening his first shop in Edinburgh designed to cater for people who chose a healthy lifestyle, many but not all vegetarians. No time for lunch I discovered, two draught beers were ordered. He asked me how things were going, how helpful Janet had been, if there were any questions I had. As I was thinking about the question I had he said that I wasn't to look at this as a dead end job and that he wanted me to cut my teeth in the basement and shop floor and that he believed I had a future to look forward to with the company. He wanted and saw me as a potential buyer of produce for the company and that learning from the bottom up was the best way forward for me. I sat there listening, still with my question in mind, when he told me that Simon hadn't really given him as much support as he'd hoped for in recruiting me and that he thought it was just down to silly schoolboy rivalry stuff from years back. "Yeah, I got the hairy rotter bit at the interview, heard it a million times" I said. There were always big rugby clashes between our schools, mine Heriots and his Edinburgh Academy but I'd never got into that side of things and although we didn't play the sport of my choice at school and had to play rugby, my passion had always been football.

"Well, hopefully I can prove him wrong and prove you right. I want to thank you right now for your support and I'm happy with the way the morning has gone. One question I have and it's really none of my business I know but I heard about you and Hannah's sister, Susan and Hannah, who I've obviously met now all coming from the south of Scotland."
"Ah yes" Ian replied with a wry grin on his face. "That didn't take you long, did it? I'm seeing Susan and she asked if we could find a place for Hannah when she finished school last year, get her away from the clutches of her father, show her the big city life, unclip her wings, let her fly. She's a fabulous girl, she's settled in well and is loving life in the shop, in Edinburgh, meeting new people every day. She's the middle of three daughters and the most molly coddled of the lot. Her father dotes on her and she is his favourite, though he would deny he has any such thing but she's one of a kind and Susan worries about her constantly. I suppose I'm quite protective of her too. Sometimes, no all the time, she never sees the bad in people, she's quite naïve and trusting to a fault. Hannah seems so full of self-confidence and she charms and captivates people who meet her for the first time and I don't want her getting hurt or taken advantage of because of it. That's why I'm telling you all of this Thomas. I need

you to watch out for her in the shop. She's had a couple of bad experiences with customers and Janet's not exactly the most intimidating person you'll meet when staff needs protecting. She's brilliant, an absolute gem, she's like an uncut diamond waiting to be polished and I'll be a lot happier knowing you're there to sort anyone out if it's needed. The sad thing is she's got a boyfriend from our home town and the guy's a brute and she's totally under his spell. No chance there Thomas, I'm afraid. Let's drink up and get back to work."

"I wouldn't assume for a second I had any chance. She sure is good looking isn't she?"

CHAPTER 2

I arrived back at the flat knackered. The truck delivering 100 sacks of rice and flour had arrived late, around half an hour after I got back from the pub and all the flour had to be carried upstairs, not down, to an area where the flour is carefully emptied from the sacks, weighed and poured into small branded plastic bags. My legs and back were aching. I had little time to chat to the women on the floor and made sure when I was called upon to refill stock into the barrels that I did it quickly and kept any small talk to a minimum. Neil was busy on his typewriter knocking out a story about sea gulls stealing food from holiday makers brave enough to face the fierce winter winds off the North Sea hitting the beaches of North Berwick. I needed a shower.

Neil asked how the day had gone and if there was anything news worthy. I told him that everyone seemed friendly enough and that the lunchtime beer was cold and that that was about it.

The evening with Neil was uneventful, the wine good and we rustled up a couple of omelettes. He mentioned that his girlfriend, Marion, was smoking too much weed, she might drop out of her classes at Herriot Watt University where she was studying accounting and go travelling. He didn't seem too concerned and if he was, he hid it pretty well. I remember asking him about his girlfriend for the first time when I was still in second year and asking if she was a looker. Nice bum was his reply. She had an interesting hippy look to her and always seemed happy. Maybe the weed helped. That and the fact that she came from a very wealthy family and her grandmother owning a massive tract of coastal land in the Western Highlands didn't hurt. An estate so big it gobbled up a few dozen hills and valleys, an enormous forest and a small village.

"Travel where?" I asked.
"India. She wants to go there for six months and get away from the cold. She says she's sick and tired of the wind and the rain, mostly the rain. You probably don't feel it after Toronto but it still gets too bloody cold here at this time of year" he replied.
"It's a different type of cold here," I said, "Canada's a dry cold but this wet cold here gets into your bones. It's worse in some ways. It's bleak, it's dark and it's depressing. I got a letter from mum and she says the divorce will be finalised by the end of the month and that dad's taking up a new position in St Johns. She also said Ben and Samantha were doing well at school and coping with the divorce okay. Not great but better than she hoped for and Sam says she misses me more than dad. I told her when I left that this was just an adventure, a sort of experiment and that I'd see her soon, here or there. You know, not to worry sort of thing." I was starting to worry that my sister was worrying and at 12 years old she had enough of that to deal with at her new school. Saying goodbye to her at the airport was the hardest part for me and her tears and hugs didn't help. "It's hardly surprising that she misses you

the most" said Neil. "She's had you wrapped around her little finger since the day she was born and played you like a banjo ever since. She dotes on you because you're always there for her."
"I don't know about the banjo but hey, I'm the one who always ended up on babysitting duties, reading to her, teaching her how to ride her bike, helping her with her homework and watching her favourite cartoons. Where were you and Ben when you were needed?"
"letting you do all the work" Neil laughed.

The next morning at the shop started slowly but by eleven o'clock I was beginning to get run off my feet. Hannah was constantly calling out "Tom! We need more oats! We need more muesli! More brown rice!" more of everything it seemed. The sacks were getting heavier as the morning wore on. The barrels weren't even half empty but I thought this was the way it's supposed to be and who am I to argue? Hannah always smiled when I saw her and always said "thank you so much" when I'd topped up the barrels. There were a lot of shoppers and it occurred to me that Ian had a bit of a gold mine on his hands. The guy goes backpacking around the world and comes back with a business idea of pure genius.

By lunchtime a lot of the staff were tired and some taking a break in the kitchen. I decided I'd work through and avoid what was a bit of a rush hour in the basement. I was restacking one of the racks of hazel nuts when Hannah tapped me on the shoulder and asked if I wanted a bite of her sandwich. "Feta and avocado, it's delicious" she said. "No thanks, I'm not that hungry," was my reply and she seemed genuinely disappointed at it. "Alright, thanks, I'll have a taste" I said and she was right about it.

"I'm going into the kitchen to make you one and I'll be right back. Don't go disappearing on me now. If you do I'll find you." I had no intention of disappearing and when she returned we sat down together on one of the sacks and ate lunch together. "Where did you go to University" she asked and I replied "Toronto." She asked how far away it was and when I said I thought about 3,000 miles she looked down at her flexing ankles and giggled. I started laughing too, at what I don't know, what can possibly be so funny about the distance between Edinburgh and Toronto? Nothing. Hannah I discovered was 19 but despite appearing so grown up and stunningly pretty she was almost childlike in her behaviour. "What's so funny?" I had to ask.

"Just the way you say it" she replied.

"Maybe a bit more" I said. "You know, when you fly you don't really think about the distance, you think more about the time it takes and the flight's about seven hours if you fly out of London. I've done it three times and I try and sleep through it. It's boring."

"Is Toronto different to Edinburgh? What's it like being back?"

I thought about Hannah's question for a moment and answered "it's like travelling 20 years into the future, arriving in Canada. It's big, it's modern, the streets are

wide, cars are longer and wider, like you see on all those American shows on TV. I never saw a mini or beetle on the streets. It's quite spectacular, the architecture is different, most peoples' houses are built from wood and you've a choice of dozens of TV channels from America. The restaurants are different, people eat out more and there's an overall feeling of more space. They're big into suburbia, trees lining the streets, lawns meeting the pavements. Coming back at first was difficult. The buildings here are old and dark. You know, grey and black. Everyone here dresses in dark colours, never bright and colourful. Here you've got a choice to dress in any colour you want as long as it's navy blue or black. There it's green or yellow or red, orange or blue. White too. On the streets, they smile and laugh a lot more than here. They're more talkative and friendlier. You don't see poverty like you see here, council house estates, things like that. Canadians are optimists. The drizzle and clouds here got to me a lot for the first few months but I'm getting used to it now. Winter's better here. Months of a white snowy landscape get to you too."
"Do you miss Canada?"
"Do I miss Canada?" A good question I thought. I missed my mother and my little sister but I didn't want to tell Hannah that. She meant the country. "I miss Toronto in the summer is the best way I can put it. I don't miss the winters. I miss the ice hockey. I miss watching the New York Rangers. I used to catch the train to New York and watch them play. I miss America being nearby."

Hannah asked about my family and I asked about hers, where she went to school and if she missed her friends. She told me about her close school friends who still lived in the small town she grew up in and said she missed her mum most of all but she was making some new friends in Edinburgh and loving her new life. The best thing she ever did was how she put it and her sister was like a rock in her life. Although only four years older, she acted like a mum to her. We chatted away for the best part of three quarters of an hour and not once did she mention or come close to mentioning the presence of a boyfriend, the brute as Ian had put it to me.

By the end of the day and closing time I finished what I was doing, said my goodbyes to the girls on the floor and to Janet and left. Fatigue was setting in and I decided to catch the bus home rather than walk. Two days in and I'm hopelessly tired and I'm 22 not 42.

The next two days passed with each one seeming to get busier than the day before and I was busy taking inventory of stock and advising Jim in accounts on the first floor of orders from the warehouse I thought he would need to be making. Nina was getting friendlier with me and had ditched her jeans for a flowing floral pink and green dress. She had a bubbly and happy character and the shop floor was a nicer place to be with her on it. A couple of times she came downstairs with orders she needed help with and I was happy to do whatever was needed. Sometimes she sold an entire sack of what I'd call stuff to a customer and I had to lug it off to their car or van parked down the street or around the corner. How they got it out at home was their own business.

I was looking forward to tomorrow being Friday and although Saturday was a work day just like the rest but busier I'd been warned, to me it still meant the weekend and I was hoping that my old school friend Harry, would catch the train down from St Andrews where he was repeating a year in his economics degree and we could go out for a few beers. Harry had a huge crop of ginger hair and had been short for his age at school. The combination meant that he was often marked for bullying and I sort of took it upon myself to look out for him. Plenty of scraps and blood noses were had. Now he was a six-footer, looked a lot like a young John Lennon and even sang in a band with some of his university mates for beer money, as he put it. Plus he could now look out for himself. He went through more girlfriends than I could keep up with and I never knew who I'd be introduced to as the next. It was hard keeping up with his lifestyle of chaos but we were close friends and had a shared history which cemented it. We supported different football teams but lived with it.

It was getting late into the afternoon, it was dark outside and the shop was fairly quiet. Hannah had asked me to bring up a sack of rice and I was half way up the stairs with my 50kg haul on my left shoulder when she appeared at the top. "Do you like wine" she asked.

"I drink it at times" I said "but not too often and dry, not sweet. Why do you ask?"

"Have you ever been to Calton Hill?" Hannah replied.

"Once but is it okay with you if I slip past and put this sack down?" Having relieved myself of that weight off my shoulder I told Hannah that in all the time I've been living here, I'd only been to Calton Hill once and that was when I was about 12 years old. "I thought I would bring a cork screw to work tomorrow and if you are interested we could buy a bottle of wine after work, walk up to the top of the hill and drink a couple of glasses together, look out over the city lights and you know, talk a bit. You've only just come back to this country and maybe you're a little lonely. I don't know, maybe you've got lots of friends still here and it's a stupid idea."

"That's a very kind thought of yours. I wouldn't say I feel lonely but if you're up for a glass of wine without me feeling that way then I think it's a great idea. Not stupid at all and not one I'd have ever thought of. I'd love to share a bottle of wine with you on Calton Hill" I said.

"Good, it's a deal then" Hannah replied before saying, "you buy the wine because I'm not very clued up on it and might choose the wrong one and I'd hate to get something you don't like. I put on my favourite top for you today."

That night I'd thought of writing a letter to my mum and a note to Sam. Ben was Ben and too busy with his life right now to care about what his older brother was up to. We were four years apart in age but close and didn't need to check up on what the other was up to. I was thinking instead what the wine and the favourite top being worn for me meant. Surely it's an obvious sign. A signal's a signal and it's not that it was even that subtle. Then again Ian had said she has a boyfriend and she's under his spell and hinted that if I was interested in Hannah that I'd be wasting my time. No chance I think he said. Why the wine tomorrow? It's a deal, is that her way of saying it's a date? My mind was beginning to race and thoughts of us kissing under the stars came into my mind. Are we talking a girlfriend here? I hadn't been involved with anyone since leaving university and that was over six months ago. I'd only ever had one real girlfriend and two very casual flings but no one who came within miles of Hannah. Every guy who I saw come into the shop eyed her up, a few chatting to her probably asked her out while they ordered their bag of mixed nuts from her. She was so far out of my league, probably the most beautiful woman I'd seen in real life and yet there was that familiar feeling when we met. Yes I felt that nervous feeling in the pit of my stomach and a racing heart- beat. I tried all I could to keep my cool, but something very deep inside was telling me it's okay, you're on the same wave length. There was some kind of freaky déjà vu thing going on connecting us.

My mind was flying and I decided against writing the letter. Maybe best in a day or two. When I have some good news for mum or can give Sam a good laugh. This time tomorrow I think my life will be very different than it is this time today.

CHAPTER 3

It was Friday morning and I had no idea what the day had in store for me and wondered if Hannah was thinking the same. I woke with less enthusiasm than I had falling asleep and was beginning to think this visit to Calton Hill was probably nothing more than a kind hearted gesture from an angel in a human form who had taken pity on me and my lonely, single, pitiful path through life and thought a glass of wine would cheer me up. I remember saying to mum while I was preparing my final Canadian barbeque in our garden in Toronto that I envied people who had someone to share their life with and who could always count on them, who took away that chronic feeling of always being alone. Not in a way that a parent, a brother or sister or friend could, something far deeper where you don't have to pretend anything to that person and who loves you for all of you and despite all of you. Mum's response was that she certainly didn't get that feeling from the man she married and that kind of ended the discussion. I dreamt of having someone to laugh with, to really laugh. I could hold conversations with people but never really shared what I was thinking, the big things in life, my worries and sadness and even at times surrounded by those closest to me I could feel a crushing sense of being totally alone. Someone had told me you're born alone and you die alone, both being things you have to do on your own and hopefully you'll have some fun between the two. I hoped to find someone to share that fun with and who'd understand me and somehow comfort me in moments of my despair or doubt about myself. Real life was a heavy burden at times and a load I couldn't carry alone for a lifetime.

I arrived at the shop and the first person I set eyes on was Hannah. I could swear she was wearing a bit of makeup around her eyes, maybe a bit of light pink lipstick. She hadn't worn a drop all week and she still made the world's top models look plain. She was wearing a short black skirt with black woollen tights and a tight black top. When God made her he was in one almighty good mood. This was nature at its finest in every way, in every detail and I had to say something, but I had to stay cool about it, I needed to be able to save face if I was indeed seen as a sorry soul who needed an arm around his shoulder for comforting, a whisper in his ear that life would turn out okay after all.

"Morning, Hannah. You're looking great." My God, was that too much, too over the top, maybe too little? So much for keeping my cool.
"Morning, Tom, thanks" she replied with her beautiful smile. She seemed genuinely happy with my comment and I made my way downstairs to my domain and to the kitchen for my Earl Grey tea. Now time to act normal, just be myself for the rest of the day and treat today just like any other I've had in my life, nothing more, nothing less. She's just flesh and blood like you I thought, she's wearing that outfit because she's trying to impress me, she's wanting me to want her, she's deeply unhappy with her brute of a boyfriend who probably has no class, who

doesn't understand her, who doesn't deserve one inch of her. She's temporarily stuck with an imbecile who she met in a one horse town. I'm going to save her, not her me.

The day was a busy one, the shop breaking at the seams with shoppers and barrels needing topped up all the time. Clients parked almost quarter of a mile away needing me to haul sacks of rice and beans, some even offering a tip, one guy offering me some money if I nick the stuff, which obviously I refused to do. Lunch came and I decided to use the time to get to the nearest off license and buy that vital bottle of dry white French wine. Once in my possession and at a cost double what I'd normally buy if I had to, I returned to the shop and put it into the kitchen fridge. Jim and Mark from accounting both set eyes on it and asked whose it was, what the special occasion was and I said that it was a friend's birthday and I was stopping off at his flat after work. There was a raised eyebrow on Mark's side which I took as thinking I might be gay but hey, what the hell, I had things to think about, keep my focus on the closing door at five o'clock and beat a hasty retreat with Hannah without being seen together with my bottle of wine. It was wrapped in a brown paper bag and no big deal carrying it out in public.

Five o'clock arrived and I said to Hannah that I'd wait for her at the top of the block. I didn't want Janet to see us leaving together. She had a bit of a mother hen way about her when it came to Hannah and I was told she was a gossiper. Keeping things private seemed a good idea to me. Calton Hill was about a twenty minute walk, pretty close to the centre of town on the east end of Princes Street and has an Athenian acropolis built on it. It's known as Edinburgh's shame because it was never completed in the 1820s, but it's a nice place to hang out and a great view of the city. It was a perfect venue, a perfect choice of Hannah's other than that it was dark and bloody cold. And the wind blows a bit up there. As I was harvesting one or two doubts about this date of a life time and visions of Hannah catching the bus to her home, wherever it was, I spotted her through the crowd of pedestrians coming my way. She hooked her arm around mine, didn't say a word and we headed along London Road. I asked her if she was okay, not too cold and she showed me her jacket, the thickness of the lining and said "soldier on, you lead the way."

We arrived to a beautiful view of the city lights and the castle lit up and out came two glasses borrowed from the kitchen and her cork screw. I pulled the cork and we sampled our first drink together. She was cold and huddled up next to me, her arm firmly intertwined with mine and we sat there in silence for a couple of minutes. "The last time I was here was with my whole family. It was a lot different then, a warm summer Sunday afternoon and everyone together. You don't think of it ending. It was a pleasant surprise, you asking me to sit and sip some wine with you here" I said. Hannah laid her head on my shoulder and shivered at the cold. The wine was beginning to take its effect and a feeling of warmth was seeping through me and I really had nothing more to say as we stared out onto the lights of Princes Street. Looking across at all the great historic and iconic features of Edinburgh in the dim light, I knew that getting that flight from Toronto was the best thing I ever did. I'd forgotten how beautiful the city was and how old and rugged it looked after the newness of Toronto. Pure silence with a woman I met five days ago and no awkwardness to accompany it. She must surely feel the same. Eventually I broke the silence and said that the monument, the pillars we were next to were built to commemorate the defeat of Napoleon and that it's a memorial to all the soldiers who died in the wars against him. I told Hannah that my grandfather had fought in the first world war and that he was shot in the head at the Battle of the Somme and carried out alive on the same day that every one of his friends in his regiment was killed and how, when I was fifteen, he told me about his experiences in the war and how horrific it was and that his two great pieces of advice to me were never to join the army and always dry my feet after I bath. Trench foot was awful, the wet, the cold, the dirt, the rats, mutilated bodies and their smell, the endless fatigue were all unbearable and there were many times he wished a German sniper would end it all for him. "Is he still alive? Was he not brain damaged?" asked Hannah.

"No, he died four years ago but he lived a long life. He used to joke that he must have been brain damaged because a year after he was shot, he proposed to my grandmother but he'd always crack that joke in front of her and they'd both laugh. The surgeon told him he was less than half an in inch away from death. It's crazy when you think about it. Half an inch of that bullet hitting and I wouldn't be here. All his childhood friends from his school and neighbourhood fought next to him and he was the only one to survive and he never had any really close friends after that. He had my grandmother and my mum and uncle in his life. He became a teacher and he taught at the same school for forty years. When I told my mum some of the stories he told me, she said he'd never mentioned a single word about the war to her. I don't know why he felt okay to tell me but I did ask him a lot of stupid questions about being a soldier and killing in war which made him laugh and maybe he wanted someone to know what it was like and what he went through and that person was me. He was a great man and we'd talk about things I've never spoken to my dad about. He was more like a friend than a grandfather. Then again, he's the only grandad I knew so maybe that's what they're all like. I asked him once if he was afraid of dying and he said no, he'd just miss our silly talks." There was still wine left in the bottle and I poured it into our glasses and Hannah just looked up and smiled. "I've never been to the zoo" she said. "Will you take me there?"

"Sure" I replied.

Hannah said "okay, Sunday. Let's go on Sunday. Let's sit here till we finish the wine and you tell me all about your family and I won't say a word. I just want to look at the city lights and listen to your voice. I don't remember much about my grandparents. They all died when I was young. You're lucky."

Thirty minutes later we packed up our things and Hannah asked if I'd like to go back with her to meet up with Ian and Simon where they all lived. There was some beer in the fridge. The house was a fifteen minute bus journey and was a beautiful three bedroomed double story building overlooking the sea of the Firth of Forth she said. On the journey there she asked me how tall I was and what my dad did seeing as I had spent the last half hour only talking about my mum, brothers and sister. I told her I was six foot and that my dad was a university professor who lectured vet students. She said she was 5 foot 8 and her dad built dry stone dykes for the local town council and he was a soldier in his younger days.

The bus arrived close to the house and we went up a flight of stairs past a tiny bedroom on the right which she briefly opened the door to show me before turning into the living room on the left to be met by Ian and Simon slouching on a tartan covered couch drinking beer. Hello there they both boomed out. "What a pleasant surprise this is" said Ian. "Come in, come in, take a seat, you're not driving are you, make yourself comfortable and I'll grab you a beer." I thanked him and cracked open the can of lager and said "cheers to you both and thanks for the warm welcome. I didn't know I was coming until half an hour ago so I hope you don't mind this unexpected visit."
"None at all" said Ian "cheers to you too." Simon stayed quiet and shouted at Hannah to get him another beer

while she was up and in the kitchen and she arrived with a beer in hand for Simon and a cup of tea for herself and sat down next to me.

I can't even remember what we were all talking about but there was lots of laughing going on and Ian was proving to be a real entertainer with his stories and he was clearly enjoying his beer. I was feeling the weight of the can in my hand and aware that I was close to empty and should hide the fact and make ready to beat a retreat and call it a night when there was a sound of a motorbike engine, closely followed by a loud knocking at the front door. More like a thumping sound. Hannah jumped to her feet and went downstairs while Ian's voice fell silent and Simon shuffled a bit on the couch. He looked nervous. Seconds later Hannah walked in next to a tall, well-built man, wearing leather motor cycle clothing and a helmet under his arm. She unzipped and removed his jacket, all the time looking uneasy. What's up I thought, don't tell me this is the bloody boyfriend. The guy's built like a brute alright but he must be ten years older than her and he doesn't look happy. He had a big well defined jaw, too big, a rather large nose, dead eyes and short, curly, sandy coloured hair and far too ugly to have anything to do with Hannah.

Ian got up and shook the man's hand, followed by Simon who didn't. "That was quick" Ian said. How long did it take you to get up, the traffic okay?"
"Aye" he replied, "two hours."

Simon nodded at him and said to him "this is Thomas by the way. He's just started with us at the shop."
I was about to get up off my seat but hesitated when he turned to Ian and said "we're off to bed. I'll see you in the morning."

Hannah and he left without saying another word and the door was closed behind them. "That's Jimmy for you" Ian sighed.
"Yes" said Simon, "that's Jimmy alright."
I was aware that they had both glanced across at me for any reaction but there was none coming from me. I was pretty stunned by the whole thing, shocked is the right way of putting it but I was aware that I had to appear not the slightest bit bothered, act unaware that I had just witnessed an almost violent emotional abuse of a woman. I mean he could have been slightly more subtle about the whole thing rather than broadcast the fact that he had nothing of value to say to any of us present and without her obvious consent not to finish her cup of tea first, was about to bed her within seconds. She didn't even say goodnight. I'd glanced into the room when Hannah opened the door to it and it just fitted the bed and no more. Not like there were arm chairs or a TV going. Nope, just pure sex is going on there right this moment, right now. I felt sick to my stomach but thank God for the can in my hand and the dregs of beer left in it. I could pretend I still had a way to go to finish, act in no hurry to leave as that could now be seen as a reaction on my part to the brute's behaviour and seem cheerful. I carried out that

charade for a good ten minutes, told them I had to be on my way and that I had a great time.

It was only about nine o'clock when I drifted quietly past the bedroom, down the stairs and into the night air. I needed that air and I needed to get away from that house. I had no desire to stand waiting nearby for a bus, I wanted to get as far away as I could, as quickly as possible and I started walking briskly, brisker still as I made my way in the general direction towards central Edinburgh. It took me nearly an hour and a half to get back to the flat and I'd calmed down a bit by the time I got home. This was her boyfriend. I was someone she shared a bottle of wine with, a bloke she's known for five days after all. I had no right to feel offended and no right to judge another person. He lives 150 or so miles away and hasn't seen her for a week and is horny as hell, needs to get the leg over with urgency and she's happy to oblige. They're playing out beauty and the beast because he's got to be one of the ugliest men I've ever seen.

The next morning I arrived at the shop, said my good mornings to all and headed for the sanctuary of the basement. I have authority down here and I've developed a need for my Earl Grey tea. Is an addiction possible and if so, well there's worse things to be addicted to than a cup of tea I thought to myself. I got a shout from upstairs calling for muesli with 'urgently please' attached to it and grabbed a bag and made my way upstairs. I was half way up when I noticed a figure standing at the top and blocking my way. It was Hannah. Not looking as great as yesterday, clothes not so revealing. She was angry and stood with her hands on her hips. "I'm sorry about last night. Jimmy was awful. I feel deeply ashamed."

I said it was okay and none of my business, it was her life after all and I enjoyed the beer with Ian. She said she heard me leave and hadn't slept all night.

"I suppose you won't take me to the zoo tomorrow, will you?"

"I'll take you if you still want to go" I said "but what about your boyfriend? Does he want to come too? To the zoo I mean."

"I told him that I had work to do and he's leaving first thing in the morning. Are you joking? That's not funny. I really am sorry about what happened. It was the worst night of my life. We can meet at nine if it's okay with you. I can catch a bus to the zoo and meet you at the entrance."

"Okay, nine o'clock at the zoo it is" I said. "Kind of you to apologise but you don't owe me one. We shared a bottle of wine together and I talked about my grandfather. No big deal. I've got to ask though. Why did you ask me back to your place for a beer? The early evening was great and maybe a better idea if we ended it there."

"He didn't tell me was going to be there. He told me on Tuesday his bike was in for repairs. He lied to me."

CHAPTER 4

I woke at around 6:30 on Sunday morning and got ready for my day at the zoo. Harry had got hold of me on Saturday evening and said he couldn't make it down from St Andrews as there was a big student party going on and his band was playing and getting paid the highest fee they'd ever had. It was too good an opportunity and he'd met someone new anyway and wanted to spend Sunday morning with her. I'd see him in a week or so.

I had to catch the bus in time to get to the zoo early as I didn't want Hannah waiting for me, maybe arriving and leaving, thinking I wasn't going to pitch up. Friday hadn't worked out as I had expected or hoped for and I thought today might be the day. I'm not and have never been in the business of stealing another guy's girlfriend and to me that was always a line I wouldn't cross but this time it was different. He'd over stepped the mark with his crass behaviour and if he didn't know any better, well then that was his fault, his loss and anyway, Hannah was way too good for him, she needed saving from the brute and I was the one going to do the saving. Then again I thought maybe she did enjoy the night, maybe she didn't sleep through it because they were too busy having sex and sleep was the second best option. Why the hell did she ask me back to her place when she must have known he'd be arriving on his revved up bike, must have known the awkwardness that would follow, why the hell did she want me to see him or him see me? The thought troubled me.

We should have cut short our evening at Calton Hill and ended a perfect day there and then but she chose to take it one step too far, one line crossed that should never have been crossed. She must know I'm keen on her at the very least, she must know that I'm falling for her and yet she got her calculations wrong. I've never spoken to a soul outside of our family about my grandad and never shared our personal conversations with anyone. I opened up to Hannah and let her in a bit and maybe she didn't see it. I've got some pride and I felt a sense of humiliation that night and I wouldn't put it past Ian and Simon having a good laugh at my expense when I left. I mean what would they have been thinking? They might have seen it all before, every week even but I was there this time and coming to think of it, they're thinking why was I there anyway? What the hell was Hannah thinking?

I got to the Edinburgh Zoo entrance at quarter to nine and stood at the nearest point to the ticket booth and was surprised at how many people were there. It was mid-winter and not exactly the perfect season for the zoo. At five to nine Hannah arrived walking alongside another young woman. Hannah was smiling and seemed excited and put her arms around me with a big hug. "This is my sister Susan, this is Tom" she said.
I shook Susan's hand and we said hello to each other. Susan was slightly shorter than Hannah, a bit thicker set but you could see they were sisters. She was attractive but had none of Hannah's prettiness.

"Susan just came to make sure I got here okay. I wasn't sure of the bus stop. She's going into town and has things to do there." Susan told Hannah that she'd see her that evening and we said our byes.

Hannah looked at me and smiled and I paid for our tickets and into the zoo we went. Our first stop was to see the penguins and Hannah was smiling and laughing at the way they walked. She thought they looked like toy soldiers marching and we spent twenty minutes just sitting on a bench watching them. I told her that I wanted to see Sally the elephant, who I hadn't seen in years, and we made our way through groups of people towards the elephant enclosure. She had never seen wild animals in real life and was giggling at the sight of them as we passed one enclosure after another. The bears and the lions, she loved, Sally not so much, a bit boring she thought. The parrots she wanted to see and we were walking along a narrow path when she suddenly put her hand in mine. I was walking holding Hannah's hand and in seconds acutely aware that my body was functioning in overdrive, blood pumping through my veins at speed and filling a part of me to overflowing. I looked down and thought bloody hell this can't be happening, it's never happened like this before and it's just her hand in mine. What do I do? I told her I needed to sit down on the nearest bench for a while and just rest for a bit and I was hoping no one passing us by could see the bulging part of my anatomy going on. Some adjustment of my jeans was needed but how do I do that discreetly and even then, will the evidence of my excitement be hidden from view? I managed to get to a bench quickly and sitting down together, still hand in hand, I thought to myself, give it a few minutes and it'll all calm down, all get back to normal.

We talked about the animals and how lucky or unlucky they were to be kept in a zoo. They get food but they lose their freedom and Hannah kept going on about the penguins and how she wanted to go back to see them again. "Okay, after the parrots" I said "but let's just sit here for a couple of minutes." The chill in the air and the passing of time wasn't having one effect on my condition and the blood flow wasn't diminishing. No wonder Jimmy needed her there and then I thought to myself. I tried an old trick I used to use with Kristen in Canada when I wanted to calm things down a bit, but that was naked in a warm bed, not sitting on a bench in the freezing cold. I replayed in my mind a football match I'd been to, analysing and remembering the formation of play, a goal about to be scored. Take my mind off everything happening to me at this moment in time and replace it with images and thoughts of something past which have nothing to do with sex. I was quiet for a while as I went into an altered state of thinking and listening to Hannah going on about the penguins. My plan wasn't working. My body was in too excitable a state and not listening to my brain. Switch off, for God's sake switch off, you're not being called into action right now I was telling it, but nope, it wouldn't pay any heed to the instructions.

"Are you okay" Hannah asked.
"I'm fine" I said, "I just need to settle down a little. I think I'm warming up a bit, too warm and need to take my jacket off."
"It's cold" she said.
"Not to me," I replied. "Remember I've been in Canadian winters these past four years and this is warm." I unbuttoned and removed my jacket, stood up and quickly let the jacket hang in a loop over my right forearm covering the front of my lower body to my knees. I could walk in crowds like this and no one would think a thing. Hannah immediately took my left hand in her right and was none the wiser to my plight and we headed towards the bird enclosures.

We spent another two hours walking, watching the animals, passing people of all ages, married couples, families, singles, kids, you name it, everyone looked at Hannah. Most couples would stare at her and then glance at me for a second, me with my strategically placed jacket in hand and her with her radiant beauty. She really didn't belong here. She belonged on the cover of the world's greatest women's magazines selling fashion or riches. she was out of place walking through Edinburgh Zoo on a cold January afternoon with a man like me. What have I got to offer someone of her beauty, her classiness I thought and I admit I felt a bit of a fraud, a thief who had nicked a valuable national treasure and I was thinking that the people we passed were thinking the same.

We eventually made it back to the penguins and were lucky enough to catch the last few minutes of feeding time by the zoo keepers. Of all the great animals to watch here, she loves the penguins. The good news from my part was that my heart beat had begun settling down and my nervous system had got used to the feel of Hannah's hand but I couldn't help but think that if that's what her hand does to me, what the hell is the rest going to be like. It was unimaginable.

We caught a bus into Princes Street and I had said I'd buy her a beer in one of the pubs on Rose Street. She wanted a half pint of shandy and I ordered a pint of lager and found a quiet table in the corner. I wanted to tell Hannah that I thought she was extraordinarily beautiful and that she could have anything she wanted in the world. Not just her looks but her being. Then again it wasn't about what I thought, it was a fact and my thinking had nothing to do with anything. It didn't alter or change anything. Factually no one could argue against it and she as the holder of it must know herself anyway. What am I going to do? State the bloody obvious and expect to get points for it? We looked at each other and Hannah then looked around the room and said how beautiful it was and that we should keep it as our secret place, a special place for the two of us to come and that no one else knows about. I agreed and then stupidly said that thousands of people already know about the pub. I knew what she meant of course and my attempt at humour maybe dampened the moment a bit.

Not the mood though and Hannah turned to me, "do you want me to be your girlfriend?"

I was caught off guard for a split second, didn't see that one coming. "I'd like that" I said. "Do you want me to be your boyfriend?" As I said that, it seemed to be a childish reply and not something that would flow from my lips, but it did and did without my thinking about it.
"Yes" Hannah said "I do want that."
"Okay" I said "but what about the one you have? I wouldn't want to share you or anything like that. I mean, it would have to be just you and me."
"I've thought about it" she said, "I'm phoning him tonight and telling him that it's over between us and that I never want to see him again."
"Bloody hell, I can't believe this is happening" I said, "Hannah, you're probably the most gorgeous thing on the planet, are you sure about me? I think the guy you're with is completely wrong for you but why me?"
She smiled and she leant across and took my hand and held it tightly, she squeezed tighter and tears rolled down her face, she bit into her bottom lip and said "I am not and you know why." She was to me and I didn't.

"One thing I need to tell you is that I won't want you from this very moment eyeing up another woman and you can start with Nina on Monday. You're mine, not hers and not anyone else's." I hadn't given a second's thought to Nina but I kept quiet, not really knowing where that came from and said "you know that anyway. I'm going to order another round for us to celebrate this" and leant over and kissed her for the first time. Not a long lingering one but a proper kiss and that was that.

CHAPTER 5

I'm sitting in my room staring at a blank piece of paper with pen in hand and can't even start the letter to mum. I'm thinking too much about the day and what just happened. It's been the biggest day, the biggest week in my life and I should be happy, no I am happy. Shouldn't I be happier with a smile on my face or something but then again I've never been one for smiling a lot in life. I remember years ago, I must have been about seven, just arrived in Edinburgh from Kenya where my dad was stationed working for the Overseas Development Agency for the British Government and two or three times I'm standing with my mum in a shop or at a bus stop and old women would come up, pinch my cheek and say 'don't worry wee dear, it might never happen' and I'd be embarrassed and mum would laugh. I was too serious even then. Mum told me I smiled and laughed a lot growing up in Kenya and lost it when we got to Britain. We arrived in London and we lived for a year in Surrey before my dad got his professorship and then took up a position at Edinburgh University.

I used to dread the first day of the next primary school year when the new teacher would ask us to stand up in the classroom and I would have to say I was born in Kenya and there were four children in our family and I'd be asked why I wasn't black. I remember one teacher in particular who laughed so much that my classmates were in stitches. I told him, with my voice trembling, that my godparents were black and he asked if I meant my grandparents and I got teased a lot about it at school and it caused me a lot of anxiety when I was younger. I stood out and was different because of my accent. I was always accused of being English. Most of my friends at school in Kenya were black and all my schoolmates in Edinburgh were white and I never understood the joke or the laughter. No teacher I had in Kenya ever did that to me.

I am happy but I'm not yelling it out for the world to hear, or Neil for that matter and he's in the room next door. I'm wondering to myself what love feels like because what I'm feeling is not something I've ever felt, but then again I only met Hannah a week ago. Is it possible to happen so quickly? It's a good feeling but an uncomfortable one and it's already tinged with sadness.

After seeing Hannah onto her bus, I came back to the flat and made myself something to eat and fell asleep for an hour only to be woken up by the phone ringing. Neil answered and it was Hannah asking for me. I'd given her my number at the pub. She said she'd phoned Jimmy, broke the news to him and that he hadn't taken it too well. Not well at all in fact. She sounded upset and I knew now was not a good time to go around and comfort her and she needed a bit of time on her own. Now I'm processing my role in all of this and thinking that I stole her from him, broke the rules of nicking another bloke's girl and blown up his and maybe her worlds and if so I did so without thinking about the consequences. It's not sitting that well with me but then again I'd do it all over again if that's what it took to be with Hannah.

I can't really write to mum and say I've got a girlfriend even though according to Hannah I have. We haven't had sex yet and that's a marker. I hardly know her and don't even know what she's thinking or going through right now. She should be happy too and doesn't sound it on the phone. Her voice was trembling, not full of joy. We haven't said we love each other or anything like that. We're nowhere on the scale of a relationship and it's only a few hours old anyway and coming to think of it, where will it go? One thing I know for sure is that I adore her. She's everything and more than I could ever ask for and already I'd hate to lose her. My God, that guy must be feeling awful. He must be going crazy, any man would and I'm to blame for his anguish. I wonder how badly he's taken the news and I wonder how Hannah broke it. Nice and gentle or full on brutal and blunt? He must be wondering or asked her why and did she mention me? 'You know Jimmy, that guy sitting down at Ian's place that you didn't say hello to, didn't shake his hand and introduce yourself to like a gentleman would have and just before you announced to all present in the room that you were about to screw me in sixty seconds time and would see Ian and Simon in the morning. Yeah, that man. He's the one I'm dumping you for, the one who pinched me from you and the one I'm going to be having sex with from now on'.

I shuddered at the thought and suddenly remembered Ian's description of him as a bit of a brute. A fighter no doubt and he certainly looked the part and maybe crazy enough to seek some form of vengeance. You read about these things, of some deranged maniac who snaps and decides to kill and they end up in jail for twenty years and it's all over the papers. Maybe Neil will be covering the story in a few weeks, front page headline stuff. Madman murders famous journalist's brother in broad daylight and pleads insanity. It happens. Nope, it won't happen to me, I can defend myself, that's one thing I can do, learnt the best way from the best teacher in Toronto and I haven't forgotten. Might not be a fighter but defending myself I'm pretty good at.

I needed a break from my crazy thoughts and phoned Marion and headed out to see her at her flat near Haymarket. It was a ten minute walk. Marion always listened to nice music and although I wasn't really into weed, it was good to share a joint with her and a beer. I arrived there and it was exactly as I pictured and within minutes was taking a puff and drinking a cold lager. The mood was relaxed and cheerful and we talked about the job market, about politics and about Marion's favourite subject, Margaret Thatcher and the Royal family, her usual stuff. Although Marion came from extreme wealth, she was a Labour supporter and I'd been out of the country too long to care to get involved in opinions about whose policy was better than the other but I was always a good listener in her company and more so when she handed her joint around.

Now feeling very relaxed, better than earlier in the evening, Marion said that a friend of hers, whom I met once, Linda, was quite keen on me. Linda was a couple of years older than me, an attractive woman with long brown hair and a single mum to a five year old boy and that I should call her and ask her out for a drink. I was in a pretty good mood by now and told Marion that I think I may have that base covered and would tell her all about it when the time was right but that I did think very highly of her friend. Marion handed me her joint for a puff and I held it in my hand, staring at the burning tip and said "does this stuff just make you feel more relaxed or do you experience something deeper?"
"More than just relaxation. Yes, deeper I think. Why do you ask?"
"I knew a lot of students who smoked in Canada and of course I tried it a few times at parties but I never really got into it and once or twice just felt the kind of relaxation I'm feeling right now. I had a friend, Mark, who was pretty big into it. Probably a bit too much. Two years ago the two of us decided to go on a crazy trip to the mid- west on a two week break in the holidays. It was a spur of the moment thing and we packed two bags, jumped into my car and headed off. I won't bore you with all the detail but we did the whole Utah, Arizona, Nevada thing and we spent a couple of nights in the New Mexico desert. I told Mark I wanted a proper shower and we drove into Santa Fe and a

bit of civilisation and checked into a motel. We met a bloke at the bar and he said we must visit Mexico as we had come so far and that we'd carry a regret with us for life if we didn't. So the next morning we're off to the Mexican border and after the border crossing drove to a small coastal town called San Felipe which he told us is the place to hang out. It was like something from a wild- west movie with a main sand road and the only thing missing was Clint Eastwood with his cowboy hat standing in the middle of it.

I parked on the edge of the beach and we got out and couldn't believe the beauty of the place. The heat was overwhelming. This will do for a few days I thought and when I told Mark that, he agreed and said 'let's do this'. The beach was set in a peninsula and the water temperature was like something from a warm bath. There was this portly elderly local with long shaggy grey hair and a beard and he was wearing a red t-shirt with white lettering on it saying 'clams make you horny' and Mark and I started laughing as he approached us. He called us gringos and showed us a cutting from a Mexican newspaper. He was in it with his t-shirt and he was surrounded by all the finalists for a Miss Mexico pageant. I told him it was great advertising and he explained he ran his own business selling clams to Americans and that we must buy some and he'll arrange the cooking as we were unlikely to have packed a suitable pot to cook in and we'd have to light a fire on the beach and look for drift wood and there wasn't much around. I asked him what the point of us wanting to get horny was all about as there was not much we could do with it if we were and he said he could organise that too. It was bloody hilarious and we were all laughing. Anyway we took him up on the offer of the clams and declined the after action part and that evening ate one of the best meals we'd ever had.

There were a few tourists camping along the beach, travellers more than what you'd think of as tourists. On our second night two girls about our age asked if they could join us and hang out. They were Californian and yes they were both blonde and tanned and slim and looked the part and they had a bottle of tequila they said needed sharing. We were all eating from our pot of clams and drinking tequila and staring in wonder at the sheer scale of the vastness of stars we could see in the sky. I was thinking these girls have been pretty forward in joining us and was wondering where the night could lead to. One of them brought out a huge joint and said 'let's have a smoke', lit it, took a massive inhale and passed it around. I don't know how much time had passed but I was lying on my back, staring at the stars in the sky and started laughing at my sudden realisation. Everything, absolutely everything in life made perfect sense. It was bloody obvious and I hadn't been aware of it before and I couldn't believe I hadn't. It was like a spiritual awakening and I understood why I was alive and what the whole point and purpose of living was all about. I knew I was experiencing the strangest moment in my life and it had to do with the truth and life was no longer some great mystery. I passed out.

It must have been around six in the morning when I woke up. Mark was asleep and the Californians gone and I was completely alert. No hangover, no drowsiness, nothing and I recalled everything of the night except the realisation I'd made. I couldn't remember what the bloody breakthrough in consciousness I'd made was. I should've written the damn thing down at the time. When Mark woke up I asked him if I had shared any of my thoughts and he said no and that if I had, he probably wouldn't have remembered it anyway as he was too stoned. He did say that whatever we smoked wasn't any marijuana he'd known before and let me tell you, he knew his stuff. To this day I can't retrieve the memory and it's driven me nuts at times. It's like it's almost there, just about to get it and then nope, it's gone. Anyway, I walked along the beach looking for the girls and I couldn't spot them anywhere. They'd disappeared into thin air. Mark and I spent another night on that beach and headed off the next morning towards the California border and about five miles out of town amid rocks and sand and cactuses we see a man about our age standing on the side of the road and he's holding up a piece of cardboard. I slowed down thinking he's a hitch hiker. As I approached him I could read the sign saying 'have you lived in the light'. I pulled over and reversed back to him and asked if he wanted a lift. He said he didn't and I asked him why he was holding up the sign and why was he alone in the middle of nowhere and why it was written in English and not Spanish. The guy had long hair and a beard, looked like a hippy and he said he was on a mission in life to spread the word and wished us a safe trip. 'In life or to the border'

I asked and he replied 'both'. To me, the whole Mexican experience felt unreal. Mark thought nothing of it and just wanted to get back to the USA. He couldn't wait for coffee, Disneyland and San Francisco on the way back. And it was a long way back. My time in Mexico freaked me out a bit. I don't know if parts were real or not. The two girls, the guy with the card, the joint. Have you ever had anything like this?"

"I can't say I have, exactly that. It sounds quite profound. If the Californians were there you must have been smoking something very different to what I know of and if they weren't then I'd wonder what was in your clam sauce" laughed Marion.

I was about to get up and leave when she told me she needed to tell me something and wanted to know what I thought about it. "I'm all ears, no hurry to go anywhere" I said.

"I remember when we first met, it wasn't that long after Neil and I got together and you visited for a few weeks before your final year and we talked, well I argued about your spiritual beliefs. Do you remember that night?"
"Yeah, not in great detail but I recall your strong doubts and you saying 'where's the proof?' Asking me why I was so intrigued by the whole thing. You couldn't believe that I believed and me telling you that it wasn't about religion, any one and that, no, it wasn't about a fear of death. Have you changed your mind?"

"I've been doing part time work at a care home for the want of a better word, the mentally challenged, a place where the entry requirements are an IQ of 60 or below."
"Is that the requirement of the care worker" I joked.
"Shut up and listen Tom. I do the work after my classes and have been for almost two years and one of the people I looked after was a woman named Sarah, not much older than us. I got to know her very well and she grew to rely on me quite heavily, heavier than I hoped for. Well, just before you came back, our doctor discovered she had advanced cancer of the ovaries and didn't have long to live. She and I talked about it and obviously the subject of dying came up. I thought of phoning you in Toronto but I knew you were in mid exams and didn't want to distract you and so spoke to a friend of my mum. She always claimed she was clairvoyant. I didn't want to but I did because Sarah asked me one afternoon when would she wake up. I spoke to the lady and she just said that I must tell her that she'll see a very strong bright light but not to be afraid of it, her eyes will not be blinded by it and she must face the light and not turn her back on it. She must walk towards it. I told Sarah and a week later I went to see her in the evening. She was lying in her bed and I was standing between her and the door and she said that her mum was standing next to me and had come to fetch her. I swear I felt an immediate presence close to me and I turned around and looked at the picture she had of her mum on the wall. She died when Sarah was 15 and I asked if she meant she was looking at the picture. She said no, that the woman standing next to me was her real mum,

not the one in the picture and she told Sarah to thank me for everything I had done for her daughter and that she could feel my love for Sarah. She didn't sound like herself at all, the way she spoke. She always spoke simply and childlike and now she's sounding like a grown up adult. I was in shock. Well, Sarah died that night and yes I was very emotional about it and troubled by what Sarah had said about her mother. I spoke to the lady in charge of administration and she got hold of Sarah's file and we went through it together and discovered that she was adopted when she was 18 months old. Her real mum as she put it, the one who gave birth to her was only 18 when she gave her up as she couldn't cope with Sarah's mental handicaps and slow development. She was a single mum as well. Sarah never knew she was adopted. We went through the registrar of births and deaths and it wasn't easy to find but we did eventually and her real mum died 21 years ago. Sarah and I got to know each other well and she remembered very little of her childhood and she never mentioned her real mum. She confided in me about everything, absolutely everything about her life, always told the truth and she was an amazing but simple person. Very childlike and vulnerable and would never have survived on her own without the care home. I knew everything about her up until two hours before she died. What do you think of that?"

"What an amazing story" I replied.

"It gets better. The day after I discovered all these hidden facts, I went into the courtyard of the home to sit and view the garden and say a little prayer for her and I'm five minutes into thinking about Sarah and a tiny fluffy white feather fluttered down and landed right next to my feet. I just burst into tears at the sign from an angel."

Marion was in tears and I went over and hugged her. "All your years of searching for the truth Tom and here I get an experience you'll probably never get in your lifetime. I'm sorry I argued with you before and I've been waiting for the right time when we were alone to tell you. Neil knows but I wanted to share it with you alone."
"Marion, I believe it. Trust me I believe you. The white feather though?"
"I promise you Tom. The white feather fluttered to the ground right in front of my face. I looked up for a bird, a noise in a tree, nothing but a bright blue sky."

After thanking Marion I left and took a deep breath of the cold night air and suddenly felt overjoyed about the thought of life with Hannah. What on earth did I do to deserve this I thought to myself and started back on the ten minute walk back to the flat.

I was feeling pangs of anxiety as I made my way along Princes Street on what was the first week anniversary of my new job. The work was better than I expected and I was actually enjoying it and the physical challenges that came with it and I wondered how to go about the next step. It couldn't be kept a secret from the staff at the shop. Surely with Hannah's sister going out with the owner, word would get out. How was Ian going to react? He was the one who said I had no chance and maybe he meant hands off. Perhaps there was a company policy that says don't date staff.

When I got to the shop any anxiety had disappeared when I arrived to be met by Hannah with open arms and a hug and a kiss and the girls on the floor clapping and Janet grabbing my hands and saying 'lucky you'. Hannah was looking her beautiful self and there was no sign of any sadness. I was worried about that phone call and the sound of her voice last night but this morning she looked overjoyed and full of happiness. A week ago today I was standing near speechless in her presence and now we're standing, facing each other in more or less the same spot, her hands in mine and smiling at each other. Looking into her eyes, I knew she was feeling what I was and I was no longer alone.

The rest of the day passed pretty uneventfully and quickly. I tried as best I could to be professional and do what I was paid to do. I have to admit my mind was elsewhere for much of the time and I had to find the right words to put it to Hannah that I think we should go back to my place after work and the rest would be obvious. Well, without me saying it that is. When I thought about things, Hannah had asked me to Calton Hill, to the zoo, did I want to be her boyfriend. She'd made every single move and it was my turn to be brave and take the lead to take things further. The next step felt more like a leap. The question was, was she expecting that step to be the one I was and right now

I'm literally dying for the moment. The coward in me was half hoping that Hannah would initiate the conversation. With time approaching closing time I had to broach the subject. Be as casual about the whole thing as possible. Anyway maybe take it down a notch or so and just do the fooling around bit for a while and see where it takes us, doesn't need to be the full blown thing. That might be more Hannah's style. A virgin, I know she's not but she might be quite conservative about things like this and expect a bit more time to pass, a few more dates under our belts. That type of thing. I was hoping not.

I saw Hannah taking off her apron and reaching for her jacket next to the kitchen and thought for a second she was just about to head home and this day was somehow just as normal as any other when it was anything but. "Hannah, I hope you're not heading for your bus. I want you to come back to my place, see the flat, spend some time together, you know, maybe meet my brother later, have a bite" I said.
"About time" Hannah replied smiling and we put our jackets on, she put her arm in mine and we headed out the shop into the cold dark night.

Once we arrived at the flat, the first thing I did was show Hannah around the rooms, the castle view and put the kettle on. We had a cup of tea together and, sitting next to each other on the living room couch, we started to kiss. Deep, deep kissing and the touch of her lips was like something I'd never known. It was like being wrapped in a warm blanket with her as we held and felt each other. She wanted to kiss so badly and passionately and as I put my hand under her top she said "let's do this naked." We undressed, her breasts were beautiful, her long legs perfectly toned and her hips accentuating her slimness, she was quite simply too beautiful to believe possible and we embraced and lay down on the couch. I was kissing her breasts and caressing her body all over when the thought of my brother arriving back sprung into mind. The first place he comes is the living room and it's only ten or so steps from the front door. I can't stop now I thought and I can't afford to get caught like this by him, a sight he'd definitely never let me forget. Potential humiliation or ecstasy, what's it to be? I just had to enter Hannah, couldn't not and the hot moist sensation was just too much. Too damn much. I didn't last long and this time it worked in my favour. I quickly jumped up and said, "oh shit, put your clothes on, my brother will be here any second." Hannah and I dressed as if we had a fire to escape, her giggling all the time and me stumbling and fumbling. I'd just tied my left shoe lace when the noise of the front door opening was heard and Hannah gasped. We sat there, shuffled apart from each other to leave a bit of a gap, I grabbed my tea cup and Neil entered.

"Hi Neil, Neil, this is Hannah, Hannah, Neil." Hannah jumped to her feet and extended her hand to my brother and he took it, all the while staring at Hannah and then said "what are you two up to?" He looked at me, looked down at my one untied shoe, looked at Hannah and said "it's like a sauna in here. Tom, you're beetroot. Been busy? Hannah, welcome, pleasure to meet you, are you a model?"

Hannah laughed and I said "Hannah, Neil's a journalist and doesn't miss a thing. He's like Sherlock Holmes and sounds like he's saying you should be modelling." There was an awkward silence for a moment before I said to Neil, "Hannah works at the shop, she's from near Stranraer and been here six months."

"Oh, I see. Are you two getting together?"

Hannah replied, "Tom's officially my boyfriend as of yesterday and yes, we are together and you're going to be seeing a lot more of me?"

"I hope so" said Neil "and Tom, are you going to be seeing a lot more of Hannah?"

"Lots of her" I said and Hannah started laughing loudly.

Neil said he had some work to do in his bedroom and Hannah and I headed out the front door on our way to an Indian restaurant around the corner for our first proper meal together. "Your brother's interesting" Hannah said as we sat down for dinner, "there's no shyness there and I like that" she said smiling at me.

"He is, he is that, he's interesting all right. I'm sorry I came so quickly but it was just as well" I said.

"You can say that again on both accounts" and we were laughing at that remark and its spot on accuracy. Hannah had only had Indian food once before and she was intrigued by the menu and had many fascinating questions for the waiter and he was very obliging and friendly and I ended up ordering a mixture of dishes I'd never tried before. I ordered a bottle of wine and asked Hannah to tell me about herself, hoping she'd miss out the Jimmy part, when the meal arrived.

"This is delicious, absolutely delicious. Try some. Me? Well you know I have two sisters and you've met Susan and Caroline's two years younger than me and she's very pretty and I get jealous of her sometimes. My dad spoils her. I didn't do too well at school but I was good at running. I won all the hundred meter races I ran in and have the medals and I got involved with the wrong person and I suppose screwed things up a bit for myself. And then I met you."
"Why did you get involved with the wrong person" I asked.
"It's a small town. I was 15 and he was the big guy around. A lot of the girls fancied him and he chose me and I thought I was lucky but although he was good to me, he stopped me doing a lot of things I wanted to and the worst thing was my marks dropping at school. I didn't do well enough for university and I disappointed my parents."

I was sipping my glass of wine, mesmerised just by looking at Hannah. I was glad we had just had sex together and the boyfriend title had a bit more substance to it I thought and here I was with my girlfriend in a dimly lit, warm restaurant eating great food and drinking a good wine. Hannah's wearing jeans and a jersey, no makeup, she has a natural prettiness which I doubt makeup could enhance her beauty any way, I mean how could she possibly be

better looking than she is right now. And it's not just her face. You slip off the clothes and it's God given perfection. How must she feel about herself and coming to think of it, why isn't she modelling and making millions? Hannah clinked her glass against mine and smiled and her smile did just make her prettier still after all.
"Well there's still time for university if you wanted" I said.
"I know I could Tom, I could go to college and get the marks I need but I don't know if I want to. I was silly, I listened to Jimmy and he didn't want me to do well, didn't want a posh girlfriend."
"How does that make you posh" I asked, "has nothing to do with it, I don't get that one."

Hannah looked up from her plate and said "I can't answer that. What about you anyway? What was it you told me last week you studied, business or something?"
"A business degree yes, a lot of accounting I don't like, marketing I enjoyed and the advertising side of things, sales, that sort of stuff. I'd like to get into the sales side of business but I don't mean door to door selling, more like finalising business deals on a company expense account, wining and dining kind of thing. I like the personal interaction in business, I think a lot of business is based on relationships that you can develop. People do business with people they like. Well, like and trust. You've got to have trust as well but I wouldn't like to work for a company where I'm stuck in an office doing the whole nine to five bit. I wouldn't like that. I think Ian's onto something

great and he must be one happy man. By the way, did you tell him last night?"

Hannah grimaced a bit and said "he heard me on the phone. Jimmy kept phoning back and Ian had to have a word with him about it. It was horrible and not what I expected. I didn't think he would react like that. He was so angry. He was yelling at me and telling me I was stupid as usual and didn't want to listen to what I was saying, the usual things, that no one else would have me, I'm not good enough, I think I'm pretty but I'm not, he felt like killing someone. He calmed down a bit and said he was going out to the farmer he's friendly with nearby with his torch and shoot some rabbits. He always does that, always goes hunting when he's angry. "

I refilled our glasses with the wine left in the bottle and asked "kill who? You said someone and he's got a shotgun has he?"

Hannah laughed and said "don't worry Tom, not you. He doesn't know about you. I told him he was wrong and that I was seeing someone else and am good enough and I'm not going to listen to him anymore. I'm yours now, all yours."

I called the waiter, settled the bill with a better than my normal tip for his great advice on the menu and we headed back to the flat to continue where we'd left off, but this time in my bedroom.

CHAPTER 6

The next few days passed and Hannah and I were getting into quite a good routine of finding moments in the basement of the shop to kiss behind the sacks of hazel and walnuts and it became our own private meeting place, in its own way, far from the madding crowd of shoppers above us and we were getting to know each other better and more intimately behind those nuts. We went back to my place in the evenings and once took a quick bus trip to her place at lunch time, getting back to the shop just before the hour's break. Nobody at the shop seemed to notice or at least seemed to mind and the only dampener on the mood of the shop floor was the appointment of a boss for Janet, a lady by the name of Alison who took an office on the first floor. She was in her mid-thirties and I had no direct contact with her and gave the matter little thought. I didn't think Janet needed someone to report to, she was by all accounts a very competent lady and knew everything that needed to be known about the running of the shop. But hey, I'm just the bloke in the basement who fills up oak barrels of oats and beans and fetches and carries.

On the Friday Hannah seemed particularly chirpy and chatty with the shoppers, seemed in one hell of a good mood. While I was emptying a sack of brown rice into one of the barrels near her, she whispered into my ear that we should steal our lunch break at her place. We timed our departure just in time to catch the bus, no waiting time and fifteen minutes later were in her bedroom undressing. She had a small record player in her room on one of the wall shelves and put on her Joan Armatrading album, a sound I would become very familiar with. Why her favourite, I have no idea and never asked and we were soon wrapped in each other's arms in her bed, the same one of course that the brute had taken her into a week ago. Yes it was my second time in her bed but the Friday bit stuck at the back of my mind. I found a better angle for me to be on top of her with which I could feel the inside of her pelvic bone as we made love. When it was over I lay on my back next to her and waited for my heart beat to calm down. I had tried but I couldn't last any longer and once the point of no return is reached there's no holding back. Hannah had turned her back to me and I gently touched it with my fingertips, running my hand down her spine when I noticed her almost convulsing and then I heard her softly cry.

Hannah's crying gave me a sudden gut wrenching thought that it was all over between us, that she was thinking about the brute, as I now called him, his name sounding too friendly if I used it and her tears were those of regret and sadness. "What's wrong" I asked quietly.
"Nothing," she said, "just leave me alone for a minute."
I lay there staring at the ceiling and the sounds of Joan Armatrading sounded very sad. Hannah turned around and wrapped her left arm and leg around me and squeezed my body tightly. I don't get this at all I thought to myself, daring not say a word. I've never experienced anything like

this sadness and tenderness both at once. I just lay staring at the ceiling, my breathing and heart beat back to normal wondering what's wrong with Hannah, what thoughts are going through her mind. She had stopped crying and kissed my shoulder and said "I never climaxed with Jimmy and I just did."

Now that's sort of a double edged sword when you hear that. It invokes thoughts immediately of someone else on top of your girlfriend. Surely this is good news to hear and she's very emotional about it. Hannah didn't want to break up with me and all is well with the world. She pulled herself up a bit and looked into my eyes and said "all this time I thought there was something wrong with me and I couldn't orgasm making love. I know you don't want to hear it but Jimmy always said it was my fault and he never wanted me to bring it up. I never told anyone about it and I thought it was me, I thought there was something wrong with me and I'm not like normal women. Tom, what did you do to me? You've made me the happiest girl in the world right now."

By the time we arrived back at the shop we were almost an hour late and Janet was evidently unhappy about our lengthy disappearing act. She mentioned something about half empty barrels to me and I went downstairs and back to work. I worked harder that afternoon and the barrels were restocked and I had to offload a large delivery on my own as the driver claimed to have a strained back despite the fact that I saw him running up and down the stairs to the first floor, seemingly happy and without a care in the world. His laughter, I thought, had to be at me emptying his truck of a few thousand kilograms of rice and beans whilst he flirted with the office staff and drank tea.

I was thinking about Hannah all the time, her words to me in bed and couldn't get it out of my mind, the thought of her lying there with Jimmy the week earlier. I had a very uncomfortable feeling about it and was thinking to myself that I had wished I'd never set eyes on the guy because now I could put a face to her having sex with him. It wasn't so much the thought that she was involved with someone else just a week ago but the thought that she was involved with him, the brute. She smiled at me each time I passed her on the shop floor, she busy with customers and me with my 50kg sacks over my shoulder. The sheer physical challenge of the job was actually helping me take my mind off Hannah and what she might now be thinking about me, about herself now that she knows there's nothing and never has been anything wrong with her and I needed a bit of a rest. With the offloading complete and the truck and its very happy and healthy looking driver on its way back to the warehouse I sat down in one of the chairs at the entrance to the shop. I had picked up one of the brochures on Nature's Foods and its special offers when I noticed a man about my age, maybe mid- twenties picking through some of the baskets on promotion next to me.
"Do you work here?" he asked me.
"I do," I replied, "is there anything you're looking for?"
He said that he was looking for cheese and I told him there was a fridge cabinet full of a variety of them on the shop

floor and that he should have a look there. "I'm looking for cheese without rennet" he said.

"I can't help you there" I said and told him I had no idea what rennet was and that there were plenty of good cheeses stocked and that he should ask one of the sales ladies to assist.

"You work here and have no idea about rennet. What kind of a health food shop employs people like you? I'm vegan and can't eat cheese made with rennet" he said.

I stood up and said "I'm not employed here to sell any of the food and frankly don't care if you're a vegan or not and there's a whole lot more serious shit in the world happening than for me to care about what goes into making cheese. Who cares? Cheese is cheese. If you like the taste, eat it."

He was getting angry by this stage and I thought it best to call Janet to come and sort the guy out with his dietary concerns when he said "I want to speak to your manager." It occurred to me that that person must be Ian and I dismissed the thought of phoning up head office and pandering any further to this fool and called Janet to help. Janet came to my aid and I went back to the basement squeezing Hannah's hand as I passed and didn't give any more thought to the encounter about cheese and rennet.

It was around seven o'clock in the evening when Harry arrived at the flat with his latest partner, Rachel, an attractive petite brunette with beautiful green eyes. They'd caught the train from St Andrews earlier in the afternoon and done a bit of shopping on Princes Street and were keen to hit a couple of the west end pubs. I introduced them both to Hannah and to Neil and we headed out, the four of us, into the cold and windy night.

Harry was at his talkative best and full of stories about the wild student parties and how he and Rachel had met and that they planned on travelling down to Norwich to spend the next term break with her family. Rachel said she wanted to be a teacher after graduating and that Edinburgh was high on her list of places to live and that it was full of good schools and would be a great experience for her. I listened to her talk about her chosen career and her certainty about what she wanted its direction to take and found myself agreeing with everything she said. She was a confident and happy person and seemed to have her life planned out. Rachel turned to Hannah, "and you Hannah, are you happy where you are?"
Hannah blushed and said she was. "I just fell into the job, I didn't know what I wanted after I finished school and I like working with people, getting to know customers, helping where I can. I don't think I'm a career sort of person, I'm just taking it day by day but yeah, there are days I love what I'm doing."
I sensed I was next on Rachel's radar and had hoped Harry had told her enough about me and that there was no real need to quiz me about anything. Harry and I just hung out together when we met up for a beer and we'd talk football, a bit of politics, old school mates, never the future.
"And you Tom, is this a career for you?" Rachel asked.

I laughed and replied "working in a shop doesn't sound like what I planned but there's more to it than there seems. I've got a few ideas what I'd like to do and I'm learning something new every day. It's not long term but it's a business and that's what I want to get into, what I studied for. Business is about people and their interaction when you think about it and I'm meeting people, something I wouldn't be doing if I were sitting in the flat unemployed. Right now it's just a job and the best thing that's happened to me. If it weren't for Nature's Foods I'd never have met Hannah after all."

Rachel smiled at Hannah, Hannah's blush now more noticeable and Harry went up to the bar to order more drinks. As they were chatting to each other I was thinking my last remark was maybe a bit over the top. I'm making my feelings for Hannah too obvious too soon and Harry was sure not to let that one go and let me know about it later and if he did he would be right, it was right out of character for me. I was watching Hannah with Rachel and here she was, smiling, laughing, chatting away as if she'd known her for ages, the most natural and beautiful woman I'd ever seen and thinking how right now, right this moment, this very moment is the best I've had in my life and how Harry, in his own way was helping in being part of it with Rachel, a pretty, charming and sophisticated woman who seems full of joy. I never had this in Toronto, no best friend, no girlfriend I felt like this about and no Edinburgh pub scene. I'd made the right decision to come back and I felt like I had everything I needed in life right now. The only part of the future I was giving any attention to was Harry arriving back with beer in hand.

CHAPTER 7

Hannah and I toasted our first month together with a glass of wine, her sitting on my lap, the two of us staring out at Edinburgh Castle. It was a typical dull and grey winter's day and the rain had just stopped, the castle looking less like a tourist attraction and more the imposing fortress it was. We'd spent every day, every evening and most nights together and a lot of time in bed. I don't know who wanted or needed it more but it was a close tie either way and sex seemed to be the most important thing tying us together. There were nights we barely slept and days at work we were totally mentally and physically exhausted. It was becoming like a drug and we both needed a fix regularly. I was wondering if this was normal, the way most relationships are or at least start out as and it's not really the type of thing you can talk about with others to gauge what normality is. I certainly wasn't going to ask Harry for his opinion and family, well that was out of the question. Hannah didn't bring it up and I wasn't about to either. Part of me thought to push more of it onto her and the whole orgasm thing but I knew I'd be lying to myself because I wanted it and my body needed it just as much.

One night lying with her head on my chest and our arms around each other she told me all about the brute. He was ten years older than her. He decided what she could wear and who she could speak to. He had to have sex three times a day, every day before she came to Edinburgh. He constantly criticised her, told her she wasn't good enough and no one else would have her. I lay there feeling a numbing pain like a knot in my stomach twisting itself tighter and tighter but said nothing and let her talk. I listened to her every word in almost disbelief and yet believed every word she said. When she finished she was crying and I held her tightly against me, almost feeling tears myself and said that at fifteen years old she must have been too young. Surely he could have been locked up with the age gap between them and her being underage. I asked her why she wasn't allowed to wear makeup and Hannah said Jimmy told her it was for tarts and made her look like one when she tried to put lipstick on once . I told her that Lady Di wears makeup, my mum puts on lip stick, hell, the Queen herself. Did he think the Queen's was a tart?

I told Hannah that I couldn't believe she went out with him once but that at the best part of four years together it was purely staggering and I wished I could wish it all away, for her and for me. I explained that he wasn't good enough or good for her in any way, that he stole her education from her with his own crass stupidity, his labelling good marks in class as a sign of being posh was his inferiority complex at work, that when he said nobody else would have her he was really talking about himself and nobody else would have him and that if I didn't dislike him so much I'd feel sorry for him. Hannah's first taste of beer or wine was in Edinburgh. He told her anyone who drank was an alcoholic and that he'd shove the whole glass down her throat if he ever caught her doing it. She went along with the whole thing to keep him happy, never dressed up, never talked to boys at school or in the street, only once tried a touch of lipstick until the week she met me and later that was from Nina's handbag in the kitchen at the shop, but the thing which bothered her most was her loss of friends and her marks at school. The funniest thing she told me was that she passed Higher French with an A. I didn't know anyone who got an A at that grade in French and she laughed when she explained the whole thing to me. She had told him that she wanted to do well in French and he was okay with that because even five year olds in France could speak French and it was no big deal, didn't mean a thing. She had fooled the fool.

Staring out the window together I asked Hannah if there was any part she missed of the brute.
"Well, he is huge but that didn't do any good did it" and she looked at me and laughed.
"Oh he is, is he? I didn't mean part as in body part" I replied.
"He had the biggest in the village" Hannah said laughing some more.
"Well, how many men live in the village?"
"What's that got to do with it?" asked Hannah.
"A lot. If it's ten then it's not a very big contest and if it's 10,000 then it is and if it is that, then what kind of village is it where all the men walk around looking at each other's dicks. That kind of thing doesn't happen in Edinburgh. Do they all wear kilts where you come from and flash each

other in the streets as they greet each other a good morning?"

Hannah was staring directly into my eyes as if she was giving the question about the population size of the place they came from a lot of thought. All I had meant when I asked my stupid question was there a part of her life she shared with the guy which she missed. Maybe she did like the control thing he had over her or maybe all this freedom was too much for her. She can wear anything she likes, dress as she wishes, do makeup and have fun with it, have a cold beer or a glass of wine, talk to whoever she likes, go to college and redo her exams. Dream of becoming whoever she wants to be.

Eventually Hannah spoke. "I told Simon the same thing and he didn't take it well."

"What the hell? Simon! What's it got to do with him" I asked, realising the answer to my question mid-sentence.

"What do you think?" Hannah replied. I shuffled uncomfortably in my chair and Hannah got up and walked towards the window. Looking out she said "it was only once. It happened one night. I'd had a row with Jimmy on the phone and was upset and Simon spent the evening listening to me and comforting me and we had some drinks together and we ended up in bed. I swear it was only the one time and I didn't want to do it again and he did and he's been bothering me about it for weeks saying how much he wants me, how you're not the type of person I need, that you have no friends and that's why you spend all your time with me, that people without friends

have something wrong with them and that's why they have no friends. He says all the time you're a loser."
I was in shock. I didn't know what to say, how to react. I just knew I felt as if I'd been hit in the gut with a cricket bat. "I can't believe it. Simon, the same guy that doesn't like me and all this time I thought it was about school. It's because he wants to screw you and can't and blames me. He says I'm not good enough now and what does he know about me or friends or any part of my life? I haven't said more than a few words to him. He knows nothing about me at all. Of course, Jimmy didn't know any of this, did he?"
Hannah was looking at me and there was sadness in her eyes.
"No, I never told him. He never knew. It would have crushed him. He liked Simon. I wanted to tell you that the reason Simon doesn't like you had nothing to do with which schools you went to, who had the best rugby team. He told me all about Heriots, the Herioter and the hairy rotter joke and it never had anything to do with any of that. He's even told me he's in love with me and waits every night till I come home, hoping I'll change my mind. It only happened that one time and I was wrong to do it and stupid and I'm sorry. I'd only ever been with Jimmy but it was still wrong and it's not me. Then a few weeks later I saw you in the shop. You hadn't seen me, you were looking at the basket of flowers and I knew you had to be the Thomas we were expecting. As soon as I saw you I knew I wanted to be with you. I knew it had to be you and it was and you might not believe it but when Janet called

me to meet you, I was shaking, I was so nervous. When you held my hand, I thought I was going to faint. We're together now, the rest doesn't matter."

I now had another face to put lying naked with Hannah and although marginally better or more acceptable than the brute, just and this one I'd be seeing from time to time. Simon, I couldn't get my head around that and I needed to say something, anything that wouldn't make things worse. "I've got no need to defend myself against Simon and I'm not surprised he's attracted to you. You can have any man you want but what he says about me and his view on me is way off the mark. I've got friends, you've met Harry and there are two others I'd like you to meet. Okay, they're old school mates but in my defence, not that I need one or looking for one, I've been away for four years. I made friends in Toronto, still got them but that prat you live with knows nothing about me or what friends I do or don't have. I wouldn't dream of judging the guy and good luck to him in his life. He's never left Edinburgh. Of course he's got a bunch of friends here, who cares, but for him to play the clever psychologist about the importance of friendship to the character of a person, that's just a joke and you should tell him. Tell him you told me about the whole thing. That should be interesting. Tell him you want him to fight me and the winner gets the girl. I'd love it."

Hannah was smiling and held out her empty wine glass and I took both ours to the kitchen for a refill. When I came back into the living room Hannah said "what do you mean I can have any man I want?"

"You can."

"I cannot and you're just being silly" Hannah said. "You're just saying that. I know Jimmy made me feel I was worthless at times but there's nothing special about me."

I said, "looks wise, you score ten, emotionally and all the other stuff that goes with it, you're one of a kind, good, difficult, in between, mostly sensational, in bed, ten. Okay not any man but most. Let's take off the gay ones, the really old geriatric ones and the seriously devoted, heavily religious married ones but certainly not many of those married. Let's put that total together and say that's ten percent of the adult male population over the age of 16. There you are. Ninety percent of all men would want you."

Hannah was laughing as I finished my calculations and said "I don't believe a word you're saying and if you're just trying to get me into bed then you don't need to. That's yours anytime. Anyway, so what if you think that's true. I don't want them."

I was looking into my wine glass in hand and said "I've got an idea. You know that jumpsuit or whatever you call it, the tight black one that you pull yourself into? Put it on, we'll walk down the Princes Street hand in hand and I'll give it a squeeze when I think you're being given the eye. If you get ten of them by the time we reach Jenners, I win. If not, you win and the loser buys lunch. Hannah was laughing loudly at the thought and said "deal. You're going to be dead wrong. Just because you think those things about me doesn't mean anyone else does. I'm doing it for me, not you and only because I'm starving and lunch out sounds great."

Half an hour later we were outside the flat, Hannah in her tight black one piece jumpsuit, ten minutes of putting on a bit of eye makeup and lipstick and a quick spray of perfume. We walked hand in hand a few blocks to the west end of Princes Street and as planned, started the test outside the House of Fraser. The street was busy with shoppers and those out for a walk or just window shopping. I must admit that I was concerned that there may be too many women shoppers and not enough men on Princes Street and at the end of the first block by Castle Street my count was nil. Onto the next block towards Frederick Street and two men passed without a glance, then a third and a fourth, looked at her yes, but not eyeing Hannah up. The fifth guy looked and my count was one. By Frederick Street it was up to four and the third block took us towards Hanover Street. I was aware that because the pedestrian traffic was so busy my experiment could be compromised by virtue of the fact that a lot of passing people couldn't get a good view of anyone approaching, let alone a great looking woman. Two guys passed together, the definite eye, up to six. A minute or so later and it was seven, eight, nine and ten. I said "test over. I won or should I say you won."
Hannah smiled and said "what do you mean?"
I replied "shall we pop in and have a look around Jenners and then lunch on you? I won in that you got the ten and quicker than I thought and you won in that you should feel

good about yourself. You've just made the day for ten guys out there." Hannah smiled and said "do you honestly think I need you squeezing my hand as some part of a silly experiment to feel better about myself? I feel good about myself by being with you."

"No I don't think that. I don't need it either. My point was to show to you that the brute is the biggest idiot on the planet and lied to you."

The weeks were ticking by in the shop and every day I could swear Hannah was looking more and more vibrant, happier, always laughing and joking with customers. She was like a magnet to people and everyone who met her fell in love with her in their own way, young, elderly, men and women. There was a lot of talk in the shop of the summer wedding of Lady Di and Prince Charles and July 29 had been pencilled in as a very special date. Although a bit shorter in height with short brunette hair, Hannah had a very Lady Di way about her and I used to tease her about it. She had the beauty, but that touch of shyness and the blushing and her ease with people of all descriptions made her Diana-like.

One morning when I was sipping my cup of Earl Grey tea in the staff kitchen, Hannah came in looking a bit tense and a little out of breath. I hadn't seen her last night, one of our rare evenings apart and one I'd spent writing letters to mum and Ben and had posted on the way into work. I'd been telling them both how great things were and had enclosed a photograph I'd taken of Hannah to back up my claims about her.

"I've spoken to my doctor and I've made an appointment to see her this afternoon. I've told Janet and she said I can take rest of the day off after that and I'd like you to come. I spoke about us and the doctor agrees that it would be good idea if you came with me."

I was stunned. "What's wrong" I asked, "are you okay?" Hannah laughed and said "don't worry, I'm not pregnant. Will you come?"

"Of course I'll come. I'll phone Ian and tell him I need a couple of hours off" I replied.

We got to Doctor Caroline Scott's office at two o'clock and waited. Hannah was quiet and hadn't spoken on the bus and I was wondering what awful news was in store for us. Why the secrecy, why wasn't she telling me what was going on? I thought there must be some concern for her health but she seemed okay and she hadn't mentioned any worry to me about it at all. When Hannah was called she went into the doctor's room on her own and closed the door. Twenty minutes later the door opened and Hannah asked me to come in. Dr Scott was a young woman in her late twenties or early thirties and welcomed me with a firm handshake. "Thomas, I want to thank you for joining us. Sit down and make yourself comfortable." I sat down, feeling anything but comfortable.

"I want you to understand that this is not about you, it's about Hannah. She's a very young woman who's coming to terms with adulthood and responsibilities and decisions and all the complications which come with making them. I'm putting Hannah on a mild medication to treat her anxiety and it will help her sleep a little better. I need to ask you a question and please be honest and forthright about your answer and I'll understand completely whichever way you reply. Hannah has been suffering what I would simply call feelings of guilt. Feelings which I don't believe have any guilt attached to her whatsoever but nonetheless are very personal feelings which are affecting her mentally and physically. As you know, she has recently split up with her boyfriend of a number of years. Years going back to when she was fifteen and she has told me she is very, very fond of you and happy to be with you. She needs to confront her feelings and I've advised her to see and talk to Jimmy and deal with her problems openly. It's the only way I see her resolving this crisis she's experiencing and Hannah has said she agrees but she only wants to do it if you're okay with it. Are you okay if she meets with him and discusses things with him?"

I sat there listening to every word and heard 'she's very fond of you'. Fond of me, is that it? I had told Hannah I was in love with her weeks ago and she had said she had close feelings to mine and I thought with a bit of time she'd feel the same. That we were on the same wavelength but fond isn't on it. Is it?
"Of course it's fine with me" I said, trying my best to keep a bit of dignity about myself.

"I didn't know but of course I want the best for Hannah and if this is the best way of helping then yes, I can go along with it."
The words were coming out of my mouth but this was the last thing I expected when I walked into the room. I didn't see this coming at all and I was wondering if this is this a GP or a psychiatrist I'm talking to. I know she's not a psychologist by prescribing medication but this doesn't seem like a regular doctor talking to me. How bad is Hannah's health and what on earth is she feeling guilty about? He must have been phoning her in evenings when she got back from the shop or late at night and she didn't let me know. I know he can barely write so he won't be sending letters. I was beginning to feel like I needed some of that medication the doctor was giving to Hannah.

Dr Scott went on, "that's truly kind and caring of you Thomas. I immediately thought when you walked in that you are that kind of person. It's not about ourselves, it's about recognising how we can help others and you're showing great understanding and caring. Hannah wanted to talk to you about it but I advised that it would be best if we discussed this together. I'm sure Hannah is relieved and delighted to have your support during this very trying time for her."
I looked at Hannah and she was looking down at the floor. She didn't want eye contact with me and I felt a sense of separation between us immediately. Is she still my girlfriend I wondered, have we just split up and what's she going to talk about with the brute. He's not one much for

talking that's for sure, screwing, yes, foreplay, no, straight into the action with no joy on her side, yes. Was I or am I that bad that she's having or had second thoughts about me and what of all those nights she's confided in me about how bad he was to her. Am I worse? Every moment together we've been happy or just dealing with all those things that come with new relationships developing, we've had sexual intimacy off the scale and I'm sitting in a doctor's office and it feels like I'm giving my consent for my girlfriend to go to bed with another man? I'm living a nightmare here I thought.

We left the doctor's rooms and waited for two buses, one to take Hannah home and one for me back to the shop. The silence between us was awkward and I wanted to show Hannah that at 22 I would be mature about this and understand that 19's a young age to be coping with all the suddenness and earth shattering changes she's going through. I put my arms around her and we stood there in silence until her bus arrived.

I didn't speak to Hannah that evening and the next day she was off work having phoned in and spoken to Janet. The day dragged on and the shop floor felt empty without her and all of the staff seemed a bit subdued. It just wasn't the same place without Hannah and I was glad to get back to the flat and be on my own. Neil was away on a piece of news he was covering near Dunbar and I decided against making anything to eat and would get into one of the books he had been raving about for weeks. I was thinking back on our middle of the night talks and the hours I spent listening to Hannah describing her years of anguish with the brute and lost count of the times she cried, describing the life she had and things she had missed out on and couldn't make any sense of the talk with the doctor or the anguish Hannah was feeling. I would understand if she decided to cut short our relationship for another man, a better person than me, better looking, rich, better prospects but to do so to go back to what made her so unhappy in the first place made no sense at all. Maybe Dr Scott got the wrong end of the stick and doesn't know what she's just done. Maybe she's not qualified to give out the advice she did and I like a complete dummy bought into it hook, line and sinker. Maybe the whole thing is a dreadful mistake and there's still time to fix it. But then I recalled the words from the doctor that Hannah was very fond of me and those words weren't from someone in a loving relationship. I mean you can be fond of your aunt or a cousin or a dog or a cat but it's not a word I thought she'd use for her feelings for me. She can be fond of her postman or milkman or her teacher but not me, not fond of. It means and says nothing but 'I like Tom, he's okay'.

I had to turn this bad moment into a positive one and immediately thought of London. I could pack things up here, jump on a train to Kings Cross Station with my CV and start knocking on doors. There are lots of companies the type I'm looking for in London and there's always Stamford Bridge to look forward to. I'd only been to see Chelsea once but they were my team in England and that's a positive move. No friends or family but a new start is nothing for me to be afraid of and thousands of people take a leap into the unknown every day and why should I be any different I thought. The phone rang and I expected it to be for Neil. It was Hannah and she wanted to see me right away.

Two buses and thirty minutes later I was at her door. Both Ian and Simon were out and she was alone and we went straight upstairs to her bedroom.
"I'm sorry about the whole thing Tom. I needed to see you again and talk to you. I phoned Jimmy and he's coming here but it won't be for another two hours. It's not what you think, I've not changed my feelings for you, the exact opposite, and it's just that I feel so bad for Jimmy. He's asked me to go back to him so many times, he's been crying, he's banged his head against a wall and cut himself badly, he says he wants to kill you. He won't listen to anything I say and I worry about him a lot. I didn't mean for any of this to happen and I never expected him to react like he has. It's as if he's lost his mind and he's admitted he was wrong about me, that he wants another chance and he just needs to see me, that's all."
"Did you have to see him at night? I know I said I support you seeing him but did it have to be at night? He could have come up this morning. You could have gone out for lunch or met for a coffee. It sounds ominous to me. He'll be spending the night here, won't he?"

Hannah was sitting next to me on the bed with her head in her hands.

"I don't know. I don't know what's going to happen. I still have feelings for him you know. It's not like I can just flick a switch and they all go away, it's not that easy. I didn't think any of this through when I met you and I've made a terrible mess of my life and I don't know what I want. You've taught me so much and believe it or not, I've listened to every word you've said. I can't believe you're 22and you're so wise and so clever and everything about you I love. You've freed me from my biggest fear in thinking there was something abnormal about me and you've made me realise that some men do find me attractive. I don't know what I would've done if I hadn't met you. I want you to make love to me."

We did, there and then. I was getting dressed when there was an almighty thumping at the front door. Just like the one I heard the first time I was here and there was no mistaking who it was. Hannah was in a panic and started dressing, straightening the bed sheets and covers and whispered that I have to go. We went quietly down the stairs, me expecting to see the letter box open and the brute peering through before breaking the door down and Hannah tip toeing down, holding my hand. Once down she led me to the back garden door and let me out without saying a word. At the top of the garden there was a road and once on it, I looked back up towards her bedroom window curtains to see if I could see any shadow of a man, but there was nothing and I left.

It was Sunday morning and Neil and I were reading the papers and drinking tea. Hannah hadn't been to work for two days now and yesterday was one of the busiest the shop had seen. Most of her regular customers had asked after her and some genuinely worried they might never see her again. A worry I shared. The phone rang and Neil jumped up expecting a call from the newspaper. It was for me and it was Hannah. She said she was going to spend the day with Susan and that she couldn't wait to see me again and she'd be at the shop tomorrow and had lots to talk about. She had told Jimmy that it was over between them and that she was moving on in her life. Some of what she told me sounded like the doctor speaking but she did sound very happy and excited. After the call I went back to the newspaper and my tea and sat looking at a picture of a duck in a park and words about spring. I was thinking to myself what is Hannah so happy about, how did she spend one, maybe two nights with the brute. He had to have stayed the night because he was obviously there yesterday and he doesn't do a lot of talking. They must have had sex straight after we did and now I'm supposed to be happy about her happiness and the news that it's over between them. Over between them again? In my own way I was party to this whole thing and had agreed that it was okay for her to meet up again with the brute but right now it just felt like a betrayal and I was the one on the receiving end of something bad. It was good news, great news I just received and yet I was feeling as miserable as I'd ever felt.

CHAPTER 8

We were well into spring and the looking forward to summer and July 29, the great wedding to be of Charles and Diana. There were pictures and reminders of the Royal family in all the papers and much of the economic gloom of the country was being replaced with a sense of optimism, if not about jobs then about hope. Lady Di had captured the imagination and heart of much of the country surrounding the wedding and interest in it was largely about her. The people loved Diana. Hannah and I were practically living together at my dad's flat and she spent very little time at Ian's. She got on great with Neil and the two of them often went shopping for groceries and odds and ends we needed to keep our home and ourselves clean. She had become good friends with Marion, often shopping together and popping into a pub for a shandy or a glass of wine whilst going about their business and met up with my two old school friends, Jeff and Ron, both of whom had taken a real shine to her. We went to the Usher Hall, a block from us, for concerts and joined the library which Hannah loved, though I found myself reading newspapers instead of books.

I had decided weeks ago to put the matter of the weekend of the Jimmy visit to the back of my mind and face the future with the cards I'd been dealt. I could dwell on the thoughts I had and let them eat away at me or brush them aside and face the reality that whatever Dr Scott had advised had actually worked and Hannah's happiness was all that mattered. She wasn't on any medication and if she slept any better I swear she'd be dead. In fact there were times at night I'd put my ear against her breastbone to listen for a heartbeat such was the lightness of her breathing in her sleep. I'd always have to wake her with a cup of tea ready and if I didn't, she could sleep till midday. It was a warm sunny morning when we arrived for work and when I entered I was told that Alison wanted to see me upstairs. I'd had very few exchanges with her since her arrival and she tended to keep herself in her office most of the time.

"Come in," Alison greeted me, "have a seat."
I thought it odd that she wanted to talk as we didn't have anything to do with each other on a working basis and if a promotion was in mind, that would be coming from Ian and I had been waiting to hear from him for some time and word about me as a potential buyer for the company. Maybe travelling to exotic sun baked parts of Asia or Central America, places with white sandy beaches and palm trees. I knew I could be a good negotiator, could knock prices down a bit and handle the shipping side of things, build up valuable business relationships and put my degree to good use. At least use it and make my mum happy.
"I've had a few complaints about you" she said. "Your job is to ensure complete efficiency on the shop floor and make sure all our stock is looking at its best for customers to want to buy. I don't need to tell you about the bottom line and profit, you've got a degree in business. I've asked

around and there are times when the barrels are looking awful, they're practically empty and customers think we're sold out of what's supposed to be in them. If they're not buying and the stock is lying downstairs in the basement because you can't be bothered to restock, that affects our profit margins and by all accounts should be deducted from your pay. Janet has said there have been one or two occasions when the girls on the floor have complained about sore backs from having to bend over so far to scoop up from the bottom half of a barrel. She also said you were very rude one afternoon to one of our customers who was asking about vegan cheese and you belittled his lifestyle choice in front of staff. On more than one occasion you've been late back from lunch. It's unacceptable from a shop boy."

Did she just call me a shop boy and if she did, what exactly is that? It sounds hellishly insulting whatever it means and I hardly make enough money to deduct from. I thought I had been doing a fine job and doing more than asked or expected. I'd carted tons of sacks over the months, I'd gone out of my way to help customers carrying their purchases to their cars or vans parked blocks away, I'd changed the whole storage system in the basement, improved the way we did stock take and only once or twice let the barrels run down because I thought that looked better from a shopper's point of view, that the stuff is selling and that when they see it topped up and almost overflowing there was perhaps less reason or at least need to buy there and then. Rightly or wrongly it was part of my marketing and advertising campaign and I only ever did it to the black beans barrel.

"What are you going to do?" asked Alison.
"Quit" I replied. "I'll leave now or work through to the end of the day if you like. You don't have to pay me for today but I quit."
"Quit?" she shouted at me, "that's rather defeatist isn't it?"
I was looking directly at Alison and registering her shocked look and trying to control my anger, my breathing getting heavier and all I wanted to do was walk out. I had nothing further to say, no defence against her unwarranted and inaccurate accusations and the blistering reference to me as the shop boy. I thought of myself as the stock controller or manager, something quite elevated sounding, someone carrying a bit of authority and responsibility.
We were looking directly at each other, Alison gripping her pen tightly in her right hand when I said "actually, let's just do it right now. I'm sorry but I can't serve a day's notice. You'll have to call the warehouse and get someone sent up here to help out. Maybe Simon can carry for a day. "

I walked down the stairs and noticed Janet looking rather sheepishly at me. What have I ever done to her I thought. Hannah asked me what happened and I told her I quit and would see her later. I walked out the shop, took a deep breath and walked back in the direction of the flat. Half way along Princes Street I decided I'd cross into the gardens and sit on one of the benches and take in another view of the castle. It would give me some time to reflect on what just happened and why I was ambushed like that. It was not something I ever expected could happen, I didn't even report to the woman and she acts as if she's my boss and her attacks were stinging. I got on with every single customer I met in the shop and helped in any way I could but for one guy who wanted cheese, caught me on an off moment and was the one having a go at me for something I knew nothing about. Actually when I thought back to the time, it did make me laugh a bit but he had it coming. The girls never complained to me about sore backs and if they did, I'd have changed things straight away. As for being late back from lunch, I knew how late most people were from their visits to the kitchen and that attack was unjustified. I'd developed real biceps from lugging those sacks just as Ian had said I would and I wouldn't have these if I hadn't been working hard. Coming to think of it, why wasn't this criticism coming from Ian? Did Susan know and why didn't she let Hannah know?

The thought that I was incompetent did creep into my mind and I wondered if I did in fact quit or jumped when I was about to be fired. I'd worked at half a dozen summer jobs in Canada to help pay my way through university and never got fired or come close to it. I always prided myself on learning quickly and doing a good job and this one was no different. Somehow I managed to mess things up and I'm now sitting on a park bench unemployed in the middle of a beautiful morning. I was disappointed in myself but more so in Ian. He owns the company, we know each other socially, there have been dozens of times he could have spoken to me about the job and my performance in it and yet there was never an inkling of anything wrong, any disappointment on his side. There was no sign at all. It felt good sitting on the bench, watching the world pass by, seeing the flowers in bloom and I decided I'd come to this very spot more often and maybe sit and read a book or just watch people pass on by. It looked like a lot of people weren't working and I was now one of them.

When Hannah arrived back at the flat in the early evening she was clearly angry. I'd never seen this expression on her face before and hadn't pictured her look of utter fury. "What happened" she asked. "No one in the shop knows what's going on and everyone is angry. Janet says she was tricked by that woman, Alison."
I had decided I wasn't going to tell Hannah the embarrassing parts of the interaction but ended up telling her the whole thing. She wanted to phone Susan about it and wanted to have words with Ian, wanted to hand in her resignation but I asked her not to and that it was probably for the best and a sign I needed to do something different.
"We're not going to London, we're not. You get a job in one of those advertising agencies or banks and the first thing you'll be doing is eyeing up the women in their fancy offices and short skirts and I'll lose you" Hannah said.
"That's not going to happen and you know it" I replied. "You're a hundred times more likely to be nicked from me than me from you. I'm not thinking about London at all so you can relax about that. The job's too good for you to

consider leaving, the customers adore you and I don't want any of that to change. I thought I was doing a good job but obviously not good enough for someone and that's that. We leave it at that and move on. Harry mentioned an idea of his the last time we were out and maybe it's something to think about. I don't want to sign onto the dole, I don't want to go down that road if possible but then again, hey there are better people than me on it. Nothing wrong at all but it's just something I decided before I came back here that I wouldn't do. I don't want you to worry about me. I can look after myself and there will be plenty of doors opening when I put my mind to it and really start giving a proper career some thought and doing something with my degree."

"Please, please, just not London. I panic at the thought and I love Edinburgh. No one can steal me away from you and you know it. I can't bear the thought of losing you and I know London's full of beautiful women and I won't stand a chance. I want us to live here, just exactly as it is" Hannah said and wrapped her arms around me and began crying. I held her tightly in my arms and whispered "you're mad, absolutely mad. I adore you and there's no one else in the world I want. London's not in the picture but I'd love you to see a Chelsea match one day. Just for a day trip."

Hannah was showering when the front door opened and Neil and Marion walked in unexpectedly. I thought my brother was still reporting from an oil rig in the North Sea. "Finished for a couple of weeks," Neil said, "and I just want to sleep for a few days but Marion wants to come over and shoot the breeze a bit with your model girlfriend. Where is she?'

"In the shower" I replied, "she'll be out in few minutes. Want a beer? Marion, some wine?"

We were sitting talking about my sudden departure from the workforce when Hannah walked in. She joined us with a glass of wine and she and Marion started talking to each other about friendships.

Neil turned his back slightly to them and said "I've been in touch with dad and he's worried about you, says he never hears from you, no call, no letter, nothing. He says he's settling in well in St Johns and has a beautiful view of the sea and four empty bedrooms for us to visit any time we want. Don't know why he bought such a big house but it's his life and he's always done it his way anyway. He's going to post some pictures and sell us on the idea of spending holidays there. I don't suppose you're in any rush to get back to the country but I said I'd pass them on and I'd speak to you about keeping in touch with him. Anything wrong between the two of you?"

"No, nothing" I replied. "Nothing at all. He accused me of taking sides in the divorce, which I probably did, but no not really. I just find when he drinks he can become a bit of a bore and he keeps digging up the same old stuff, things I don't really want to talk about, you know. It's always mum's fault, she spoilt us, I wasted my time at university and should have been a vet, should have done better at sport, how much better my life would be and could have been. He thinks I was dead wrong to come back and I only took that citizenship at the last minute to get him off my back. You spent a bit of time there, Canada's a great place and it's modern compared to here and I get it when he says there's a fantastic future there and I can build a life there but he doesn't once give me any credit for anything I've done. No, that's not right, he does and he cares but could have done better springs to mind. I'll write to him, been meaning to do it for a while and keep coming up with excuses for myself. It's not that he doesn't understand me, he doesn't listen to any of us and he blew it completely with mum. He screwed around and paid the price for it. I don't hold that against him, look I'm grateful for this flat he's got and I've told him but when he drinks he goes into that regret and blame everyone else mode and nothing is ever his fault or his doing. It pisses me off and yeah, I do get angry about the whole thing when he gets going."

"Great," said Neil, "so you're getting on just fine."

We helped ourselves to another beer from the fridge and poured Marion and Hannah another glass of wine.

Marion had lit a joint and Hannah was having a puff between fits of coughing when she said "I think Hannah is wasting her talent. I've told her she's far too beautiful to be stuck at the back of a shop on London Road. She needs to be on front covers of magazines or ramp modelling, she needs to get some photographs taken and sent to agencies. Tom, you can organise that now that you aren't working."

"I've said as much to Hannah," I replied, "but she just says she's not pretty enough or that I'm half blind. Glad to hear you saying that, Marion. Coming from you, she might listen."

Hannah was lying back in her chair looking at the ceiling and said "you don't seem to understand that I'm not that type of person. I couldn't do it. I'm too shy to stand in front of people and do that kind of thing. I'd faint with fear. I just don't have the confidence to do that and I really don't think I'm pretty enough that anyone would want my picture in a magazine or in the papers. There are a lot of things that frighten me."
"Give me an example" I said.
"Okay I'm afraid of ghosts. I'm absolutely terrified at the thought."
Marion looked at me and said "what about you, Tom? Are you afraid of ghosts? I know you believe in them. We both believe what Sarah said she saw."
"I'm not afraid of a ghost. Of course not. I don't disbelieve in them, no. In fact I'd love to see one. Think about it, it would be a bit mind blowing to experience it. I read all the Castaneda books when I was in Canada and it got me thinking. I'm not saying a hundred percent believing but it made me think about spiritualism and the soul and to me it's more believable than not. Our religious education class at school was right after maths where our teacher encouraged us to ask as many questions as possible. 'Don't bottle the thought up' he'd say. 'Don't leave the class wondering. I'm here to help you master mathematics'. A minute later in a different classroom, I'm discouraged from asking any question on religion and believe me, I tried. I

think the whole idea of discovering the truth about the soul and of God and I'm not meaning a God with a long white beard. Marion, you know what I think. You look up at the stars on a clear night and think where did that all come from and I've known a couple of physics students, astrophysicists in fact in Toronto and they think they know everything. The Big Bang explains it all, or at least will when it's proven and I told them, so what, where did the atoms colliding come from? They said that's not the point when to me that's the only point. Or they said, well there's theory they could have come from nothing and that can't be proven but it's a theory. One of the top student's whose dream was to work for NASA said they'd never know, it was unexplainable, couldn't be proven or disproven. I said to one of them, take an ant and throw it down the back of a television tube and expect it to figure it out. It's got to understand the question first and then make sense of all the wiring and the switches, the transformers, the whole mechanism and the way everything interacts to make the television work. After a million ant years and thousands of generations of ants, one crawls out of the back of the set and says, 'yes, I've worked it out'.

'Good' the questioner says, 'now who pressed the on button'?"

"And you're just having a beer" Neil asked.
"Let's go to St Cuthbert's grave yard and spend the night,' I said.

Marion was too relaxed she said and she and Neil had other plans for the night.

I said "Hannah, let's make a flask of coffee and we'll take a blanket and lie in the burial site tonight and check out any night time action. They say face your fears to overcome them and when the sun comes up you'll have no more ghost ones."

Hannah was feeling the effects of the weed she and Marion had been smoking and smiled at me and said "let's do it. As long as I'm with you I'm fine."

The graveyard was two blocks from us, lying at the bottom of the castle and it was half past one in the morning when we got there. There was a half-moon in a clear sky and enough light for us to see and climb over a fence into the burial site. We sat next to one of the headstones in what I reckoned to be about the middle of the graveyard and I put the blanket around us and my arm around Hannah. Hannah began giggling and I whispered to her to keep quiet. We sat there in silence for over an hour before we decided to open the flask of coffee to keep us warm and keep us awake and quietly spoke about what we'd rather be doing back at the flat and what a stupid idea of mine this was. Both of us were getting a touch uncomfortable on the cold stone chamber we were sitting on and Hannah was fighting her urge to fall asleep with her head resting on my shoulder. There was a bit of an eerie feeling to the place and not one I'd like to visit again in a hurry but I thought that if we could get through this night, it would be something to remember for us both, something we could

share together. I couldn't see the time on my watch clear enough but it must have been close to four o'clock when I was aware of something moving close by, maybe twenty yards away.
Hannah was looking in the same direction and was squeezing my hand and whispered "what's that?"
I was straining to see or make out the figure but it was still now and it seemed to be a man, quite a tall man. The figure moved again slightly and it looked like a man in a top hat wearing a long dark coat. "I think it's the undertaker," I whispered.
"What? Why would he be here at this time of night?" replied Hannah.
I was beginning to feel uneasy about the sighting and it didn't make a lot of sense to me that an undertaker would be working in the middle of the night. "He might be the night watchman" I said. "Maybe something's planned for tomorrow, some memorial or event and we've just come on the wrong night. It's not the undertaker. Nobody'd been buried here for a hundred years."

We sat in silence staring out towards the figure which appeared completely motionless and unaware of our presence. I was waiting for him to make a move before suggesting we did but nothing was happening.
I turned to Hannah and whispered "let's get out of here now."
I quickly folded the blanket, grabbed the flask and took Hannah's hand. When I turned round to see where the man was he'd gone. He could be heading our way I

thought and we're trespassing and we better get out of here quickly. We were ducking down between the gravestones and towards the western edge of the property, I climbed over the fence first, Hannah threw the blanket over and I took her hands as she clumsily tried to scale the railing. On her way down her jacket caught the fence and she was stuck, couldn't move, couldn't free herself and started panicking. I told her to put her legs around my shoulders and she managed to untangle her jacket and we fell towards the road. We got to our feet and started walking quickly towards the street lights.
With her hand safely in mine I began to laugh and said "that was a bit crazy. What the hell is someone doing in the graveyard at this time of night?"
Hannah was dead silent and said nothing.
Back at the flat we were getting undressed in the bedroom when finally Hannah said "that was a ghost, wasn't it?" I was sitting on the edge of the bed thinking who or what we just saw and said "it can't have been an undertaker and I doubt a night watchman would wear a top hat but wouldn't it be strange for a ghost to have a top hat and cloak too?"
"I don't know what it was but it wasn't very scary was it? You were great. You didn't seem that afraid to me. So there you are. You faced one of your great fears and look at you. You're smiling at me. I bet you enjoyed it, didn't you?"
Hannah held out her hand for me to hold and said "Tom, I loved it. Thanks for taking me. I feel so safe with you. Oh my God, I just love the fact that you make me feel so safe.

It's not just the graveyard, your family and your friends I love being with them, you're such a lucky man to have them in your life and now I feel I have them too and they're all such wonderful and kind people."

As days go, it was one of the stranger ones in my life. It was becoming clear to me that with Hannah in it, boredom wouldn't have much space.

CHAPTER 9

It was a warm and sunny Sunday in mid-June and Hannah had asked me to take her to Holyrood Palace for a visit as the build up to the Royal wedding was beginning to affect a lot of people who liked the Queen but had little interest in the daily affairs of the Royal family. It seemed that Diana had changed the attitude of many towards the monarchy and she had become everyone's favourite. July 29 would be a public holiday and the wedding broadcast live across the nation and we all knew it would be, if not a celebration, memorable.

Hannah had spent some time after work getting measured by Nina, whom she'd become good friends with, for a knitted dress. It was supposed to be a surprise for me. Nina had been given a knitting machine by her girlfriend and was practicing her skills using Hannah as her subject. I knew nothing about it, other than I was in for a surprise and that it would be well worth the wait. I wasn't expecting anything of it and actually not waiting at all for anything and I was just glad to hear Hannah was having so much fun working with Nina on the dress. Ben had finished high school in Canada and had applied for university entrance in Ontario and at St Andrews and had just arrived for a visit to Edinburgh and was staying in the spare room. It was great to catch up with him again and hear how mum and Sam were doing without wondering what parts were being left out over the phone or in a letter. Ben was frank and blunt and didn't leave any parts out. He'd just turned nineteen and now the same age as Hannah and it was hilarious seeing his reaction to her when they met. He basically just said she was mad to be going out with me and should reconsider her options. The two of them hit it off straight away and the three of us were planning on taking a whole spool of amusing posed photographs today to send back to Canada. Ben had turned into a real Canadian and if anyone sounds American here, he did and even though I hadn't been back that long, I was picking up on the accent thing I was exposed to when I first arrived.

Ben was into his coffee and we were sitting in the living room having a cup together talking about his now favourite sport, ice hockey and the New York Rangers when he said "what's your plan with Hannah? Are you two going to get married? You'd be crazy not to."
"She's only nineteen" I said. "She'll be turning twenty in December. She's a teenager still and don't give me the Diana story, yeah, she's nineteen and getting married I know but come on, it's far too young. It's 1981, not 1931, people aren't getting married at that age anymore. What's wrong with living together and if you need a ring on your girlfriend's finger to feel secure then there's something wrong anyway isn't there?" I replied.
"Maybe" Ben said "but everything you wrote to me about her in your last letter is true, she's gorgeous and you're not going to do better are you and it's clear as daylight that she's crazy about you. You should think about it."
The truth is that I had been thinking about it for the very reason Ben said but it was too soon, we were still getting

to know each other better and there were times I enjoyed being away from Hannah. I hadn't been out on my own with a friend for a beer since I met her and I'd thought about that too. Not to be away from her for the sake of it but I missed talking about other things with friends, like football or stupid jokes women wouldn't find funny. It's not that Hannah had ever said to me that she didn't want me hanging out with friends without her anyway. It's just that it hadn't happened and it was great having her with me when we all did get together.

Hannah arrived back at the flat with a parcel under her arm and said she'd be ready in ten minutes. Ben made another cup of coffee and I poured some hot water into the tea pot and we continued talking about life back in Toronto.
Hannah walked in, stopped in front of us, did a twirl with her arms above her head, turned to us and said "what do you think?"
It hadn't occurred to me what a knitted dress was like and I understood now when she explained to me days ago that it could be a bit unforgiving if you got it wrong. Well Nina sure didn't get an inch wrong. It fitted tightly against her body, there were black and gold hoops from top to bottom and the bottom part was half way between the top of her legs and her knees. It was near as damn a mini skirt or mini dress or mini something. She wore black tights underneath with her flat black shoes to finish off. I surveyed this work of art as if I'd just seen the person for the first time and looked at Ben. His face said it all.

"Wow Hannah, unbelievable, that's what I think. Bloody hell, you look sensational that's all I can say. You're going to be turning heads like crazy today. Good job we've got the camera. Ben?"
"You look beautiful" Ben said, "I hope you don't sting because you look a bit like a bumble bee but Tom's right." Hannah was smiling, standing on her tip toes and hands behind her back. She sure did look like a model.

We spent over two hours at Holyrood Palace taking the photographs we promised ourselves, me with Hannah, Ben and Hannah, me with Ben and lots of just Hannah. There was still a lot of light left in the day and Ben asked Hannah if she'd ever been up to the top of Arthurs Seat, Edinburgh's extinct volcano, nearby. Hannah hadn't and we headed off from the palace and up the hill Ben and I had done many times in our youth. At the top we paused to take in the view and waited for a young couple to enjoy theirs before making their way back down and leaving us alone to finish off the film left in the camera. I got Hannah to joke around in a couple of modelling poses and with the perfect light I knew we'd captured something pretty special.

We decided against buses and meandered our way back towards the flat as the evening set in and ended up at a small Italian restaurant near the Meadows, one of the city's most beautiful parks and sat down for a light meal of pasta and wine, talking about the royal wedding and the merits of St Andrews University and life generally in

Scotland against Ontario. Ben was interested in studying accounting and wasn't sure where he wanted to study. He didn't particularly like the idea of a career in accountancy but he liked the idea of making lots of money and some friends of his from school had influenced his thinking and right now he was having more difficulty in deciding which country he wanted to study in. I said he should consider Edinburgh as well as he'd have some family around and still a friend or two from years back he'd kept in touch with. Hannah said 'her too'. It was a warm evening and we were in no hurry to get back to the flat when Hannah mentioned that Nina and some friends had planned to spend the night at a club not far from where we were. It might be an idea just to pop in and have a beer there. It didn't really appeal to me but Ben was right up for it and thought it a great idea of Hannah's.

It was a night of dancing and I'd never danced with Hannah and she could dance. She had a natural rhythm which seemed to flow with the music and the beat and it was almost as if she was in a zone and world of her own. It was mesmerising watching her and I was okay with dancing but just okay. I left her with Ben and Nina's group of friends and sat down for a beer at the bar to rest and take in the scene from a distance. Ben joined shortly after and as we sat not needing to say a word to each other watched as a succession of men in their twenties went up to Hannah and danced with her, sometimes talking, sometimes the gentle touch to her arm and all the time Hannah just kept on dancing. She'd pause between the music being played to wipe her brow and chat to the guy she was dancing with, sometimes gesturing in our direction to them, always laughing and smiling, at times giving us a wave and the two of us sitting there watching the scene unfold. One of the guys she was dancing with came up to me and called me a lucky man before leaving the club and it was close to midnight when I gave her a wave and tapped my watch wrist and shrugged my shoulders to say are you done yet? Hannah had been dancing away without taking a proper break for nearly three hours and was ready to head home. I wish she could have seen what I had seen. She would have no doubts at all about herself and her effect on men. She might have looked like a bumble bee in her dress but she was the queen bee without a shadow of doubt.

CHAPTER 10

The sound of crashing thunder and ringing woke me out of a deep sleep. I lay still, trying to make sense of the noise. There was thunder all right and the ringing sounded faintly like the telephone in our living room. Hannah and I had had a late night and she was sound asleep and it felt as though I was living in the twilight zone, uncertain if I was dreaming or awake. I ignored the ringing sound until it was clear that it was the phone and I was awake. I got out of bed and answered it. "Hello" I said.
"Good morning. Is Hannah there? Can I speak to her?"
"Who's calling?"
"It's her father. I tried her house and there was no answer. My wife gave me this number."
"She's asleep. Would you like me to wake her up?" The phone went dead. I knew there and then there was trouble. Hannah and I had been together for over six months and I'd never spoken to her dad, her mum a couple of times but never him.

It was the week before the royal wedding of Charles and Diana and I knew of Hannah's plans for her parents' visit and thought he may have wanted to ask her about arrangements for the day. The abrupt ending of the call was ominous and I had to tell Hannah. I wondered why her dad was calling at such an early hour when I looked at the clock in the kitchen. It was half past nine. We'd probably had a glass or two of wine too many and I could feel a slight throbbing in my temples and a thirst I needed to quench. Drinking from the kitchen tap, I was thinking to myself I didn't even have time to tell him who I was and ask him if his call was urgent. I was still half asleep.

I thought of leaving Hannah alone to sleep for a bit, but woke her anyway and told her about the call and its sudden ending. "Tom, what exactly did you say?"
"That you were asleep."
"Why the hell did you say that?"
"Because you were."
"For someone clever, you can be a complete idiot at times. I know why he hung up on you. My God, you can be a fool." She phoned back and spoke to her mum and was told that her dad was too distraught to speak to her and that they might not be coming up to Edinburgh to see Hannah and watch the royal wedding on television with us as planned. His fury, I was told, was the news I bluntly broke to him that his middle child, Hannah, was no longer a virgin.

Hannah told me that her father hated me and that at that moment she did too and I sat at the kitchen table with my hands behind my head trying to grasp the severity and the stupidity of the situation. I let Hannah talk and dump all her anger on me, waiting for her to calm down and realise that there was an overreaction of an epic scale going on. I was supposed to have told him she wasn't here, that I'd get a message to her and at least introduce myself to him and show a little respect. At one stage, with Hannah in a flood of tears, I thought she was inconsolable and would pack up her things and leave. She needed a shower and I needed a cup of tea.

I was looking out the window and the dark clouds and torrential rain didn't help my mood when Hannah came back into the kitchen, wrapped in a towel, with a pen and her diary in hand and told me she was going to list for me all the things her dad could object to me about if I were to meet him and actually have a proper conversation. "I need to ask you a few questions. I'm worried that you might say something to my dad and clash with him." "Clash" I asked. "I don't go around clashing with people and I have no intention of having a disagreement or argument with him. I'd like to meet him and get on with him. And your mum. I've been waiting for the day too you know. Don't worry. I'm not going to tell him it wasn't me."

"Very funny. You've got to take other people's feelings into consideration you know and not just think about yourself" Hannah said.
"I wasn't bloody well thinking about myself" I replied.
"You just weren't thinking. That's the problem."
"I was half asleep, I've got a bit of a hangover going on and some bloke I don't know phones out of the blue and wants to talk to you. Okay he said he was your dad but I thought he knew about us, I'm your boyfriend. What the hell does he expect? I didn't say you were too tired from too much sex, just that you were asleep. He can interpret that how he damn well wants."

I put her cup of tea down on the table in front of her, my hand was a bit shaky I noticed and I think she did too. It was anger I was feeling and I knew I had to do all I could to control it. Her accusations hurled at me felt like an enormous injustice, as though this sudden family revelation I'd exposed was done with some kind of sinister intent on my part. I had been thinking of her family as dysfunctional and I'd told her all about my family's own dysfunction months ago. I had nothing to hide and as chaotic as things got in my family over the years, there was never any pretence of anything else or hiding the truth from each other. I was furious at the sheer injustice I was facing. How was I to know that her father had to be sheltered from the idea that his grown up daughter might have a sex life? She thinks I did this deliberately.

"Before you start" I said, "there are a couple of things I want to say. I've listened to you and a lot of what you say is pure and utter rubbish. You should hear yourself speak. It's unbelievable. First of all and you may not have noticed but I've had to live with the thought of you having sex every day since you were 15 years old with one of the biggest idiots I've ever had the misfortune of meeting. Yeah that brute boyfriend you had, you've told me before that your dad likes him because your words, not mine, he's a man's man. That, I doubt of the guy very much by the way. He's a moron, he thinks clever people are posh, thinks a man with a beer is an alcoholic, beats up people he doesn't like in your village, shoots rabbits when he gets angry, controlled your every bloody action as some kind of

deranged control freak and I on the other hand am the villain because I stole your virginity a few months before your 20th birthday. I love it, just bloody well love it. And your dad hates me as you say and you do too now. Hate's a very strong word and now you want me to sit down and take a quiz to see if I pass or not. Maybe I should just treat you as badly as that lunatic did, make your life completely miserable and your dad would like me. That's what the whole things sounds like to me. Why didn't you tell him the truth? Is it so bad? Yeah the truth is you lost your virginity four years ago and I was in Canada at the time and it couldn't have been me you lost it to, could it?"
I was getting angrier as the words came out of my mouth and nothing made any sense. Hannah was the woman I loved. She was everything which made any sense to my life, every reason to wake up in the morning. I had my say and sat down on the table stool and took a gulp of hot tea.

"I know you're angry with me. My dad's in pain and I kept things a secret from him to make him happy. He'd never have allowed me to see Jimmy or let him in our house had he known."
"It couldn't have just happened in his mother's house, not over so many years. What did your dad think the two of you were doing in your bedroom, playing scrabble? Hardly seems plausible with him barely literate. Your dad must be a blind man or a fool. Why's your virginity so important to him? Your mum would be bound to know. Women know these things, especially mums. She'll know all about this absurd family secret or lie. Does she hate me too? You've

told me that for the first time in a long time that you're truly happy. Why doesn't your happiness make them happy? What the hell's going on here?"

"No she doesn't hate you and I don't hate you, you know that and you know how happy you've made me. I'm happier than I ever dreamt possible. I just wanted to keep my dad happy, that's all. I want them to come here and I have the whole lunch planned and I want my dad to like you. They're crazy about the Queen and were looking forward to watching the wedding and it was going to be such a special day for us all. There are things about my mum and dad I think you should know and they're going to ask questions about you and I just want to know you won't blow it or offend my dad."
"I'll tell them that I'll take offence if they get offended. Okay" I said, "what's on your list?" I started to laugh.
"What's so funny?" Hannah shouted.
"You are. This whole argument is."
"There's nothing funny at all."
"The fact that we're talking about your virginity is what makes it so funny."

Hannah looked down at her diary, paused and then looked at me, "my mum and dad go to church every Sunday, it's a big part of their lives and you don't believe in God."
"There's no way I'm going to bring up religion Hannah, never, you can tick that off, don't worry about that. They say never talk about religion and sex with strangers and here we're on both subjects straight off. Yes Mr Swann,

your daughter's great in bed and I don't believe in God, my name's Tom, pleased to meet you."
Hannah laughed and I must admit I was quite relieved to hear her laughter again.
"It's not that I don't believe in God, I'm not arrogant or foolish enough to say that because I do believe anyway. I've never told you that I don't believe in God. I think there is a God. I don't know what form God takes. Fair enough, I don't believe in religion, well religions exist but I don't believe all of their stories. I don't knock people who do believe and I envy many of them and I respect them. I'll tell you a story, a very odd one. I knew a lot of Christians in Canada, not like your mum and dad, young ones who believe I'll go to hell. Hang on a second, maybe they are like your mum and dad. They were all very happy people, happier than me anyway and their happiness I thought was free. All the problems I carry, all my worries and troubling thoughts of should I do this, should I do that, should I turn right or maybe left, they didn't have. Put all your worries in God and Jesus they would say and you live a happy life."
"Why did they believe you'll go to hell?" Hannah interrupted.
"Because I'm not a born again. Having sex before marriage didn't help. Sound familiar? Anyway I met a woman in Toronto and she was probably about 85, maybe older and she had been a nurse her entire career, never married and she nursed badly injured and sick people when she was younger. Those in the emergency ward who had bad accidents or illnesses. The last 35 years of her career she

nursed the elderly she said, people who were on their deathbed and had sat holding the hands of thousands of patients at the very moment of death. I asked her if any of them had any visions of death and how they reacted to dying or knowing they were about to die. She told me that those with faith, as she called it, were the happiest and let go of life the easiest. She said they were more at peace with it but she did say that a lot of her patients, religious or not, said 'what a beautiful meadow' just before they died. It's stuck with me, those words. What a beautiful meadow. They saw a field or a garden, spoke those four words and then died. She did say that there were plenty who just passed away with a smile and not a word. So there you have it, you live happier and die happier with religion in your life and it's free and I can't afford it. Her name was Pattie by the way."

"What if she just made it up?" said Hannah.

"I believe every word she said. She had no agenda or reason to lie and she spoke from the heart and couldn't care less what I thought. It's funny how you don't ask if stories from the Bible were made up.

I'd love to believe the Bible stories but I can't. I'm sure some are true. You know, how did the kangaroos from Australia get onto the ark, how do you survive in a whale's stomach for three days when its acidity breaks down your flesh and there's no air to breathe, the wine from water. Do you know what a miracle is? Nature, that's a miracle enough for me. I think our souls survive, well the mind that is, the soul exists and we're all connected to a great mystery with a God or infinitely massive intelligence or love or something greater still. Does that help?" I waited for Hannah to say something.

"It sounds like a lecture" she said. "What if you're wrong? What if every word in the Bible is true, because that's what my parents think? What do kangaroos have to do with it?"

"Not a lot I suppose. Or it is a lot. Australia's a long way away. I could have said polar bears and the North Pole." I replied. "I'm not lecturing or trying to convince you of anything. It's just what I think and I've thought a lot about what I'm saying. Hey, to each their own. Some believe, some don't and no judgement given."

Hannah had written a few things down as I gave my version of going to church on Sundays. "So you believe in life after death, heaven and hell?" she asked.

"Life after death? Yes. I thought you knew this. I remember dreaming of sitting in a meadow when I was about eight years old. I was sitting talking to a girl my age. She had long blonde hair, we were talking and laughing together and were suddenly interrupted and I stood up and she asked if I had to go and when I replied yes, said she'd catch up with me. She told me to look at the beautiful flowers in front of us and never forget. I remember the daffodils. My mum woke me up for school, not in the dream and it's the only time I can recall being really pissed off being woken up, it's the only dream I can clearly remember and I believe it was the same meadow those old people saw on their deathbed. Heaven, yes, the meadow's there, hell, no, just a scare tactic of religion to

make you follow their rules. I believe there's a dark place for souls, a lower spiritual realm, but it's not eternity and there's hope in time. Maybe that's hell enough. When I say I believe, it's more like I'm saying I think it's probably the truth. I don't think we're here by accident."
More scratching of the pen on paper.
"Okay" Hannah said, pausing for a moment with a bit of a frown, looking thoughtful, "what are the most important traits in a person and what are the worst?"
"Easy one," I replied, "kindness and compassion to the first and arrogance and selfishness to the second."
"I knew you'd say that" Hannah continued on, "do you support the Queen, are you a fan of the Royal family?"
"Yes to the Queen bit, no to the family bit. I think the Queen's great, a great person, my mum's a year younger and looks a bit like her but I don't buy into the worshipping of the monarchy, only because the whole class system here sucks and they hold it, the whole thing up, give it the oxygen to keep going. In Canada, they're all more or less middle class, no one asks or talks about working or middle or upper class. It's total bullshit, the class system here. Hey look at me, I'm this class or that class, what kind of society needs that going on in it? Listen to the news every day. They say Prince Charles is marrying a commoner in Diana. There's nothing common about her. How the hell does it sound, a commoner? It's demeaning, sounds like common as muck. Does the guy professing to be upper class talking to me assume he's better? Sounds better, doesn't it? I saw it at school. It was a joke. There were two guys in my year and they found out that you

have to earn respect. You're not born into it. But I'm not part of any group of left wingers shouting their mouths off or demonstrating and waving flags. I just think we're all just trying to get by, do our best while we're alive. So you see, I can tell your mum and dad if they ask, I believe in God and I like the Queen and I'm being dead honest."

"You're right about the honest part," Hannah said, "almost done. Do you support your team because you hate Catholics and do you drink too much?"
I let out a deep breath and said "are you sure you're asking me these for your parents or are they for you? Rangers, well when I first came to Scotland, my grandad took me to Ibrox. It was a game against Falkirk, I was seven, I was told Rangers played in blue by my dad before and I was supporting the team in white, like everyone else. At half time grandad told me the team in white was in fact Rangers and Falkirk were in blue, Rangers won two nil and the bug had bitten. I don't hate anyone I can think of and I had a good Catholic friend who went to matches with me years ago and he was a Rangers fan. I don't even understand the difference between the religions and don't care. I don't judge people by these kinds of things and if I get asked too many stupid questions like this I might need a beer. Don't think I do about the drinking question but yeah, it's a good one because my dad went down a bad road and I know I won't because I saw what it can do."
Hannah had put her pen down and was sipping on what was left of her tea and said, "my dad doesn't follow football but he hates your team, just thought you should

know, be on your guard if he brings it up. He might not even talk to you if they do still come, he doesn't talk a lot. I think that's why he liked Jimmy so much, neither of them talked and when they did it was about carpentry or the garden. He's a big man and he doesn't drink, mum neither. You're so different to him in every way imaginable and I can't see the two of you getting on. You've read a thousand books and he's probably read one, you've been to university and he left school when he was 16. He joined the army and had some tough friends, all yours are graduates and couldn't hurt a fly. He's a simple working class man who's getting old. He doesn't hold any opinions and doesn't give any thought to the kind of thoughts you give to life. I didn't learn anything from him in life and I learn from you every day. After Susan was born he wanted and was sure the next would be a boy and of course I came along. I've done everything my whole life to try and please him and make him happy."

"Are we done?" I asked Hannah. "Have I passed your quiz?"
"You've passed mine, you might not pass my dad's but I still want them to meet you. It's time they did and I want them to see how happy you've made me. I can't believe how much I've changed in six months, how I see things differently and you've opened my eyes to the real world. I know my mum can hear it in my voice when I talk to her and she's a lot calmer about things now. She got so worked up when she heard I broke up with Jimmy and she thought you might be a bad influence on me but she's

seeing that's not the case and she's always known the truth about me. She didn't approve but she's the one who took me to see the family doctor and insist I go on the pill."

I held Hannah's hand and said "I think your quiz forgot to ask me if I believed in the Loch Ness Monster."

Hannah laughed and said "you better."

I said, "I went up there once and can you believe it but all the way up I looked out over the loch in case something bobbed up out of the water. I was on a bus and it was full of tourists from England and they wanted to sit on the right hand side, everyone looking to spot the elusive creature. I'd never been to Inverness and when the bus stopped and we got out in the town centre I saw all these tourist shops with windows full of gimmicks and the bus emptied into the shops. There were about half a dozen buses parked. I went into one of the shops and I ended up buying a little bright green fluffy Nessie and thought I've got to give this to Sam and I understood everything I needed to know about Nessie there and then and what a brilliant marketing idea this was for Inverness. It must make the town millions every year from tourists. You only end up there because it's at the top of the loch and then you're trapped and you spend money. The guy who created the myth should have been knighted or given the keys to the city or some kind of national hero status."

Hannah nodded and said "okay, I'm going to phone mum and tell her they must come, they must be here early on the 29th and I have lunch all planned. She always gets her way with my dad."

CHAPTER 11

Hannah's parents arrived by train at Haymarket station and we were both there to meet them on the morning of the Royal wedding. It was a bright and sunny day, perfect for any wedding and I hailed a taxi for the trip back to the flat and we settled into the living room with the castle view and the television set ready to showcase the big day. I was introduced to them both as Hannah's mum and dad, no first names and now I had to refer to them as Mrs Swann and Mr Swann, rather awkward I thought as I was of an age at 22 where first names seemed easier and more comfortable. At work, in an office, fair enough but Hannah's mum and dad? I was waiting for her dad to show some willingness to shake hands but he held them firmly in his pockets as a more than obvious sign he had no wish to. I'd hoped he'd be man enough to accept me as I am but blatantly not.

Ben had agreed to join us from his bedroom for some of the day, Neil was working, covering the news for his newspaper and said he'd try to get off early, while Susan, Hannah's older sister would be joining us later when vows were about to be taken. She had little interest in the event and seemed unconcerned about any of the fuss about her mum and dad arriving for the day. I thought she had the right attitude but I must admit I had been looking forward to meeting them and finding out how formidable an opponent her dad might be.

Mr Swann was a big man but her mum was shorter than Hannah by quite a bit, both parents, grey haired and immaculately dressed. We laid out snacks in the form of peanuts, hazel and almond nuts, potato crisps with avocado dip, cherries and raisins and a large pot of tea. No drinks of any other variety on offer as instructed by Hannah. Mrs Swann said she loved the view of the castle and asked Hannah to show her around. The flat we lived in was bought by my dad before we left for Canada. He reckoned it was the least he could do when he left his eldest son to fend for himself and he thought it would be a good investment. It had three bedrooms, a large living room, decent sized kitchen and a modern bathroom with the best shower set up he could buy. Its major feature was a side on view of the west side of Edinburgh Castle and everyone who visited for the first time commented something or other about how good the view was. After a while you stop looking out the window.

Hannah's mum marvelled about how well she was looking. Her dad was a man of few words. Hannah had arranged a roast chicken with potatoes and peas and would be spending time in the kitchen, leaving me alone with her parents. Fortunately for me and my cunning plan, Ben would be alongside giving me a bit of back up and vital support. Mrs Swann was remarking from time to time about how well dressed members of the Royal family were, her favourites being the Queen, the Queen Mother and Princess Margaret and it was an experience to watch events unfold, the masses of onlookers, hundreds of thousands of fans lining the streets of London.

I was engaging in polite conversation talking about the great weather there in London and here, the street parties happening across the entire country in the villages, towns and cities and how much I admired Diana and how at such a young age, today must be a terrifying experience. This wasn't just about a young woman just getting married, it was doing so in front of hundreds of millions of people worldwide and everyone wanted to see her. All the hype was about Diana. They didn't seem to share my over enthusiasm about her but Mrs Swann did acknowledge her beauty and charm and thought she was a perfect match for Prince Charles. I knew from talks with Hannah that she didn't share that view at all and that she thought Diana could have done better. I had laughed at the comment and said that I thought all young girls grew up dreaming of being a princess, not only that, she'd become a Queen. I was joking around of course and agreed with Hannah.

I was about to get up and check on Hannah when Mrs Swann turned to me and said "you seem awfully fond of Diana. Are you attracted to her?"
"Attracted" I asked. "No I'm not attracted in the way you might mean. She's very pretty. Not as pretty as Hannah. I like her. I like her shyness and the way she laughs. She's a breath of fresh air for the royal family and I think a lot of us can relate to her. Maybe I've got a soft spot for shy

people. Nothing wrong with being shy and a lot of us just mask it anyway."

"Are you shy? Is Hannah shy" asked Mrs Swann.

"I don't think I am and Hannah's got some shyness. She never shows it to people she meets in the shop but I see another side of her and she's good at hiding it but she's a lot like Diana and she's beautiful inside and out and everyone loves her."

Ben had finally surfaced from one of his deep sleeps and he and Hannah joined us in the living room and the introductions were done to Ben and her parents. Both gave him a slight nod of acknowledgement and Hannah sat next to me and took my hand. I thought that was a good sign for her dad to see and he could see her happiness was all that mattered and should matter to him. I asked him about his gardening and vegetable patch as I'd been primed by Hannah and he replied in a few words, helping himself to a handful of nuts. Seemed relaxed enough to me. Nobody had to say much at all as we listened to the build up to the wedding play out and watched the hysteria in the crowded London streets. I was thinking to myself, nobody could do this like Britain can and there was a complete coming together of millions of people, what a great institution the Royal family is after all. The BBC too, everything about the event was astonishing to watch live. It was a help yourself lunch and would have to be eaten in front of the television on our knees and the kitchen table was out of the question. Hannah had prepared a perfect celebration feast and we'd have ice cream with fresh strawberries later on, followed by two or three pots of tea.

As we were watching the sea of union jacks in the crowds lining the procession route to St Paul's Cathedral, Mr Swann turned to me and said "I hear you're a Rangers man, I'm a Celtic supporter myself."
"Yeah I am," I replied, "you've got a good team and they were worthy winners this season. Hannah and I watched the Cup Final on television and I thought Rangers were brilliant on the day. She told me she'd never even watched a match before."
He then asked me if I had any friends who supported his team.
"I knew a lot at school, well quite a few were and a few of us still keep in touch. Not everyone from Edinburgh supports Hibs or Hearts. Celtic are always very strong. I missed a lot when I was in Canada but got into ice hockey, baseball and American football there. Canada's got Canadian football, it's like American, slightly different rules but the TV coverage of sport there is phenomenal. A dozen or so live channels of sport on weekends, is that about right Ben?"
"Maybe not as much as that but it's wall to wall stuff and I actually prefer ice hockey and baseball to football here now, or soccer as it's called there. Mr Swann, you've got to go to a live hockey match to believe it. It's fantastic to watch. Our local team's the Toronto Maple Leafs but Tom and I support the New York Rangers."
"I suppose you would" replied Hannah's dad.

I interjected saying "it's not because of the name. It's just their style of play, their fans."

"And because of the name" said Ben, "you can't deny it Tom, when we first started watching it was all because of the name and the colours. Mr Swann, they even wear red, white and blue."

I of course knew this but was trying to steer the chat away from the subject of football and onto something neutral sounding but hey, if he's got a problem with the team I support, I couldn't care less. As it was, the subject quickly changed to Diana as she first appeared on the screen for the day with her father in the Glass Coach surrounded by half a dozen policemen riding horseback and the Household Cavalry front and back, the noise of the crowds rising on The Mall. She was wearing her wedding veil and her father seemed pretty happy as they both smiled and waved their way along the streets of London packed with adoring fans screaming and cheering as if caught up in the complete euphoria of watching a fairy tale play out. It was a fairy tale in real life and it was all because of Diana.

Not long before Diana entered St Paul's Cathedral, Susan arrived and I was half expecting her boyfriend, Ian too but it was Susan on her own. She hugged her mum and dad and sat on the couch on the other side of Hannah and I offered her a cup of tea.

"Christ no,Tom. Don't you have something decent to drink? It's not every day you get to witness a future King and Queen."

I glanced at Hannah and replied "beer, wine, gin but I don't think we've got any tonic water left. I could nip out for some. We've got lemons."
"A glass of wine would be great, a large one."
I returned with Susan's wine and offered anyone else anything to drink. No one did and Diana was approaching the front of the cathedral where Prince Charles was waiting.
"Oh well, I think I'll join you Susan I said. Ben are you sure?"
"Alright, beer thanks" he replied.

Watching the vows being taken with a cold glass of wine was a much better idea. Everyone seemed okay. As I was listening to a very nervous Diana stumble a bit accepting Charles as her husband, I was thinking how come Susan was able to be so much more relaxed and mature about being herself in front of her parents. What's up with Hannah, pretending to be an angel? She'd love to join Susan, Ben and I and I thought it quite sad that she felt wouldn't or couldn't. Hannah's mum turned to me and Susan and said "I love the colours. Her Majesty looks beautiful in pale blue." Susan replied "I like the Queen Mother's green outfit and that hat made out of those fluffy feathers would look good on you, mum. They have great taste in fashion, real style, I'll give them that. Look at Princess Margaret in peach, they're all beautiful."
Hannah turned to me and smiled and said "and Tom, what do you think?"

"I like Princess Anne's yellow hat. Diana's fringe looks a bit odd and why does the train of her dress have to be so long? It goes on forever, never seen anything like it." I managed to keep a straight face long enough before bursting out laughing. Hannah grabbed and squeezed my ear.
"That's how high society does it" replied Hannah's mum. "We shouldn't sit here and be critical."
"Since when have you become an expert on fashion, Tom" asked Ben with a smile. He started laughing and then burst out into a giggling fit and he could get the giggles.
"Since I got to know Hannah" I replied. "You wouldn't know, Ben. In Canada it's only jeans or jeans." I was tempted to respond to Hannah's mum but Hannah's squeeze told me otherwise and I kept quiet.

Charles and Diana left the cathedral arm in arm after the vows were taken. The church bells began to ring out amidst the loud cheers and screams of thousands of spectators outside and we watched the whole horse drawn carriage procession back to Buckingham Palace, the waving to the crowds on the balcony, the kiss that the newspapers had predicted and the aerial flyover. Dessert was served by Hannah, drinks poured by me and the noise level in the room was rising. Ben was having a long chat with Hannah's dad and I think his beer had something to do with it and the fact that he wasn't screwing his daughter and Susan was deep in conversation with her mum when I heard the sound of the front door closing and Neil entered the room. "Sorry I'm a bit late but I got away

as soon as I could" he said. "Hannah, you're looking beautiful as usual. Introductions please."
"Of course" said Hannah. "Susan, you've met, this is my dad and this is my mum. Dad and mum this is Neil, Tom's older brother.

"Great to meet Hannah's dad and mum but first names would be good." Neil held out his hand towards Hannah's dad and said "very pleased to meet you, I'm Neil."
"I'm Bill and this is my wife, Rhona" replied Hannah's dad as he stood up and shook Neil's hand. Neil asked if I could grab him a beer from the fridge. "To Prince Charles and Princess Diana" said Neil opening his can of beer.

"I've written my article for the paper and wrote what the readers want to hear. They're all part of the adoring masses you watched on the streets today. I did it reluctantly but the editor's the guy I answer to, pays my wages and the newspaper's audience expect it."
"What would you have said or written differently Neil" asked Susan.
"Two things I'd like to say, which I didn't write, are that firstly the marriage won't work out and this comes from a friend of mine at The Times who knows friends of theirs and secondly this virgin bride thing is an insult to us all. Why the hell does Diana have to be a virgin and yet the boy wonder Charles not? Anyway, virginity is over rated and on that subject I want to add that if you apply the biblical version of waiting till you're married until you lose it then the monarchy can't have its cake and eat it. It's

plain and simple suppression of the woman. I said I had two things to say and have said them. A third springs to mind and this one is personal. That young man there, Tom, loves Hannah and I see them together every day and Bill and Rhona, you should feel happy that Hannah has him in her life. Yes he's my younger brother but he's one of the finest people you'd hope to meet and I'm damn proud of him. What we have in the room right now is real, what you watched and celebrated on the TV is farce. Please the masses. let them lap it all up and keep them down and wanting more. Cheer and yell with happiness for two people you don't know because one's a Prince. When are we ever going to grow up?"
"Neil, you're crashing the party" said Susan. "All's good here. Mum and dad are enjoying themselves and it looks like you have had a bit too much of enjoying yourself."

I suspected that this wasn't Neil's first beer of the day and that he and his pals at the paper must have been at their local earlier by the sound of his voice. "We're royalists, we love the Queen!" shouted Hannah's mum. "Today is a special day for us and you're not going to spoil it for us. My husband doesn't like your club but it's because of people he knew in the army, not because we have any claim to be Irish."
"I'm not trying to spoil anything for anyone," replied Neil. "As a journalist I try to tell the truth. Today I didn't write about what I wanted to. Bill, what do you think?"
"Neil, I don't know what to think. Is this about Diana or Hannah? We're set in our ways, Rhona and I and know

what's best for our daughters. We've left our younger one at home and maybe when you're a father of three girls, we can talk."

"I look forward to the moment. You have to excuse me but I'm a writer, I deal with different versions of the truth from people every day, I meet some of the biggest liars and evaders of truth you'd ever hope not to meet and my job is to make sense of it all and inform our readers and at times it's not easy. It's like navigating a maze. Tom is not the person you should be angry with and I know him all too well that he wanted to meet you today and make a good impression and for you to like him. He doesn't want the drama of the last week and there's been plenty in the flat and none of it has done any of us any good. It's the first time I've overheard them arguing. Hannah's like part of our family now and she and Tom make a great couple and I see no reason you shouldn't be anything other than happy for her. I'll leave it to you to fill in the blanks."

Susan held her empty glass up and said "Tom, can I have a top up? I just want my dad to know that I think you're great and good for Hannah and I'm glad that Neil said what he said. Our lives are what matters, not what Prince Charles is doing or not doing, who he's in love with or not or whatever that means as he says about Diana. Dad you must listen to what Neil said. I watched you smiling as Diana was sitting in her carriage with Charlie next to her as if you were genuinely happy for her. Why aren't you smiling for Hannah? Look at Earl Spencer and how proud of Diana he is, be proud of us. Hannah's got big dreams and they're bigger than yours for her. She's changed a lot this year and she loves her life." I was beginning to think 'in vino veritas' and wondered if another glass of wine was a good idea. Hannah's dad replied "I love my daughters equally. I'll not hear a word of anything different. You and Caroline can take care of yourselves. It's Hannah who can't." This surely was Hannah's moment to set the record straight and tell her father the truth and I squeezed her hand this time. "Dad, I love Tom. I just want you to be happy. I'm okay. I can look after myself and I've grown up a lot in Edinburgh. Please don't worry about me because I'm happy and feel safe now." Hannah grabbed my arm as I got up off the couch to get Susan her glass refilled and said "I'm coming with you" and led her into the kitchen and closed the door.

Hannah put her arms around me and we kissed. She was getting pretty passionate when she pulled herself away and said "thanks Tom. I don't know if some of that stuff should've been said but maybe it's time it was. I couldn't tell him the truth and I'm sorry. I was thinking about it when Susan was speaking but my heart was beating so fast at the thought that I just couldn't. I hoped mum would have said something but I knew she wouldn't. Dad seems alright about things but you can never tell with him and mum's happy. I think they've had a great day and will never forget it. The fact that he talked to you was a good sign. He doesn't usually say much and today's the most I've heard him speak in ages.

"I don't think he said more than a dozen words to me in the entire day. If that's him talking, I'd hate to think what his company must be like when he's quiet. I tried to talk to him when you were cooking lunch but it was awkward. He's got a hang up about you and he doesn't like me. Neil let him have it. I'm just glad that you had the day you wanted and that you're happy."

When it was time to say our good byes it was all very friendly and Susan and Hannah decided they'd walk back to Haymarket Station with their parents and see them back on the train to Glasgow for their connecting one home to Stranraer. Susan pulled me aside and told me she was going to buy Hannah a drink after and she'd only be back much later. It would just be Neil, Ben and me for a couple of hours and that meant we could break open a few beers and shoot the breeze a bit, as Canadians call it. The wedding day was officially over.

CHAPTER 12

The Edinburgh Festival in August is a great time to be in the city. The weather's warm and sunny and tourists from all over the world descend in their tens of thousands and Princes Street is packed with them. The Americans stand out as the most colourful, the loudest and the happiest. A lot of them have Scottish ancestry and the Festival is a chance for them to experience Scottish culture for the first time in Scotland. Hannah and Marion were going through brochures on upcoming events and selecting plays they'd like to attend when Marion noticed a Fringe Festival theatre production from Toronto and asked if we'd like that one. I said I thought it was a good idea and the following evening we were sitting in a strangely lit room full of tourists watching two Canadian actors performing a type of 'Waiting For Godot' play with the main feature, a couch, with empty bottles of Scotch standing upside down on it, dominating the stage. It was riveting at times and I wondered how two men could take an entire audience into a different world and do so remembering each and every word for the best part of two hours. At the end and to rousing applause I noticed Hannah crying and Marion squeezing her hand. "Let's get something to eat" I said and we headed to a restaurant in the Grass Market below Edinburgh Castle nearby.
"That was the best thing I ever saw" said Hannah. "I can't believe the talent of those two actors. What were those bottles there for?"

"They were out of money and out of booze" I replied. "The bottles captured their plight as the dregs slowly emptied into the caps and they could then fill part of a glass to drink from. It was clever stuff. I agree the actors were brilliant." Marion took Hannah's hand and asked if she was okay and noticed her tears at the end of the performance. "Marion, I was sitting there with you and Tom and everything in my life just made perfect sense. I was crying because I don't think I deserve this happiness." Marion smiled and I could see the friendship between the two of them and I felt relief that Hannah had someone other than me to lean on and confide in. She was far from her parents and friends from the past and she needed more than me in her life and Marion was becoming someone she could hang out with and talk easily to. She needed a close female friend and I sure can't provide that. There were times I felt I had to be everything to Hannah, her parent, her friend, her lover and I knew I couldn't fulfil all roles and Marion and Hannah's growing friendship was key to taking some of that pressure off me. I felt lighter just watching them talk and laugh with each other.

We ordered a bottle of wine and three bowls of mussels in a garlic and tomato sauce and dined as though we were in France and promised each other that one day we'd visit Paris together and visit the Moulin Rouge and act as though we were sophisticated and cultured travellers of the world. A play like the one we'd just seen has that effect on you. Marion grabbed Hannah's arm and said, "let's go shopping tomorrow, the whole day. I want you to help me buy a dress and I need your eye for style."

"Of course, that would be great. I don't know if I can help but sounds wonderful. I want to see more plays. Tom, more plays please."

"You don't need Tom for everything Hannah. You and I are going to arrange things ourselves and have as much fun as possible. The Festival has just begun and we've got weeks to look forward to."

Hannah and Marion spent almost every evening together during the first two weeks of August and attended around a half a dozen Festival performances. Hannah always came home radiant and happy to the point of delirium and there were times I thought she might be a bit involved in the weed but she insisted she wasn't and it was all about her experiences of the Festival and Marion's company. She was simply happy. There was no doubt that their friendship was doing her a lot of good and she was losing her childlike naivety and becoming the woman she was meant to be before that brute interrupted her life and I was glad I was due part of the credit for it. Just a part. I still wondered at times why she didn't see the beauty I saw in her and asked her once what she saw in the mirror and she replied 'not bad now' and when I asked her why she was so undeniably slim without any effort she replied her doctor back home had said she had a high metabolism and that explained why her body was so red hot when I held her at night. All that time I thought it was me being the cause but no, just pure nature at work. She was born that way.

After one of the last events they'd booked for they both arrived back late in the evening worn out and asked Neil if he would open a bottle of wine and we could all relax a bit. Neil was all too willing to oblige and went into the kitchen. "Tom, it's impossible to walk around town with your girlfriend every day. The looks she gets from men drive me crazy. I'm thinking to myself 'hey, I'm here too!' She's got so many admirers. Hannah, how many times have you been spoken to and asked out these last ten days?"
"It's not that bad, you're exaggerating Marion. Okay I admit that guy next to me asked for my telephone number tonight but most of them just chat and I've only had to tell two or three that I have a boyfriend but they're just being nice to me. I got it in the shop all the time and I know how to handle myself anyway. I'm not that stupid."
"It's not that bad!?" shouted Marion. "Tom, how do you cope with it?" I laughed at the expression on Marion's face and said "I get where they're coming from. That's how I deal with it. I'd look at Hannah too if I were them and I'd do the same thing and I completely understand that men find her attractive and when you see her you do want to look again. It's all a compliment to her and there's nothing wrong with it. The asking out bit, well I've got to trust Hannah and I do and so that's no problem either really. I knew what I was getting myself into when we got together and I don't doubt Hannah for a second. I might be fooling

myself or completely deluded but I think I know how she feels about me. Not so, Hannah?"

"You know exactly how I feel about you and so don't get funny" replied Hannah, looking a bit miffed. Neil came into the living room with the wine bottle and four glasses and poured until the bottle was empty and said "what have I missed?"

Marion replied "Hannah's too damn good looking, that's what you missed. I was asking Tom how he deals with all the admirers and he says he takes it in his stride, or words to that effect. Neil, where do you stand on all this? Rate Hannah for me, you know the scoring." Neil was pretending to look concerned and raised his right eyebrow as if puzzled and keeping the most deadpan face he could, said "eight and a half."

"Where did the other one and a half go?" asked Marion. "Nobody can score ten and so the highest has to be nine and Tom told me that Hannah was very clever, very smart and so I took half a point away for going out with him. She can't be that smart if she chooses Tom and can't score nine. It's simple common sense and a bit of maths." Hannah leant over and smacked Neil on the arm and said, "how can you speak about your brother like that, that's cruel. Tom's the best man any woman could hope to meet."

Neil feigned an injury to his arm and said, "because he's my younger brother, that's what older brothers do."

We were all laughing about Neil and his pretended hurt and his joking around and as I was looking at my empty glass and Neil got up and said "one bottle's not enough, I'll be right back."

"Can't I have my say before you get that bottle, Neil?" said Hannah. "I walk around town with Tom all the time, arm in arm and it's obvious I'm his girlfriend, how can anyone passing by not know? Of course they do. The number of women looking at Tom and he pretends he doesn't notice. He pretends all the time. I know they're all looking at him and it's got nothing to do with me next to him. I'm a hundred times more jealous and it drives me mad."

Hannah squeezed my hand tight and kissed me and turned to Marion, "I don't care how many men look at me or ask me out or try to chat me up, I'm with the only one I'd ever want to be with. I saw you get quite a few looks by the way, so don't act all innocent now. You know and I know the truth and you're a very pretty woman. Tom let's have one more glass and go to bed." Marion and Neil said goodnight and I was alone with Hannah.

"If you could invite three people, who have lived or are still alive, to a five star restaurant for an evening, who would they be" I asked Hannah.

"I don't know. I'd have to think about it. Who would you choose?"

"Let's write it down and swap and read our choices at the same time" I replied and tore two pieces of paper from the notepad by the telephone and handed Hannah one of the pens next to it. We sat looking at each other and Hannah wore a very thoughtful expression before giggling and writing. I wrote down the three names I knew I'd like to invite and when Hannah raised her page above her head, we handed over our selections to each other. Looking at Hannah's answer I knew straight away she'd be disappointed in mine.

"You picked Socrates, Jesus and Raquel Welch." "Raquel bloody Welch! What kind of choice is that?" Hannah shouted and looking anything but impressed. Hannah had written Jesus Christ, Mary Queen of Scots and Tom Miller. "I think you misunderstood the question. I meant three people under normal circumstances in life you'd never get the chance to dine with. You can have a meal at a restaurant with me any time you want. We both chose Jesus didn't we and can you imagine sitting with him for an evening and asking him any question you like and him telling the truth about the bible? Socrates could get a bit heavy on the meaning of life, which I'd like to hear about and so I chose Raquel Welch because she was my favourite actress when I was younger. You know, the One Million Years BC movie and the evening would be more fun. You can't have it all serious. It's a silly question anyway." I looked down at Hannah's handwriting and its artistic style and my name and felt a warm blush across my face. "I didn't expect you to put me down as a choice and the only reason I didn't write your name down was because I meant the question differently."

"Okay" replied Hannah "I'm off to bed. You can sit here and fantasise about Raquel Welch all you like. I bet you'd want to invite her back to a hotel after the dinner was over and you'd said your goodbyes to Jesus and Socrates. I wonder what she'd say."

"Come on Hannah, it's just a bit of fun. We're just having a bit of a laugh here. Don't take it so seriously". Hannah got up off the couch and left the room, closing the door hard behind her and I sat feeling embarrassed and foolish. I'll have to make this one up to her I thought and maybe right now was not the right time. She'd be fine in the morning and would realise it was just harmless joking around I hoped.

CHAPTER 13

It was late on a Sunday morning and almost a month had passed since the Royal wedding, I was lying in a bed reading one of Neil's books and Hannah was asleep next to me. I'd long given up checking on whether she was alive or dead in her sleep. She rolled over, scratched my chest and said "you awake?" "Yeah, just doing a bit of reading and no, it's not your book." "Very funny" she replied. A few nights ago, lying on my back in bed, my heart beat settling back down from sex, and Hannah's too, she rolled on top of me and with one of the biggest smiles I'd ever seen on her, told me that when she was sixteen she caught a bus into Stranraer and from a book store, bought a copy of the Kama Sutra. She said she and Jimmy read the whole thing, well she read it and there were drawings illustrating the different positions for sex and they did every one over the following few weeks. Every bloody one of them and there are lots, I thought. Some of them weren't easy to do she assured me as if I'd respond enthusiastically to the thought of the two of them trying them out. One thing Hannah was good at was planting the image of the brute back into my mind at times it was fading. I really didn't think I was the jealous type and that history's history but there was always a dull pain gnawing away in the pit of my stomach when I thought of her having sex with him.

"Where exactly is Venezuela?" "Why, did you have a dream about it?" I replied. "No" Hannah said, "Simon came into the shop yesterday and asked if I'd like to go to

Venezuela with him. He's going there to visit his dad. He's working there on an oil project for a few years and Simon said he's paying for his ticket and he'll swap a business one for two economy ones. He's going for two weeks and says there are great beaches and the sea's beautiful and the water, warm. I said no of course and he said he only wants me to go as a friend and nothing more, no strings attached. I told him I don't even have a passport. He said it's near Brazil. He said he just craves my friendship, that's all. I still said no and that you wouldn't approve of it and he stood, staring at me angrily and then burst out laughing and said he'd set Alison on you again. I asked him what he meant and he said he'd put her up to it. He was the one that employed her and he told her to put you in your place. He said you weren't supposed to react the way you did and Ian was pissed off with him when he heard you'd quit. He didn't think you'd do it and Alison said she wanted to resign afterwards but Simon refused to accept it."

"I thought he was behind it" I replied. "He craves your friendship does he? The only bloody thing he's craving is your body. It's not up to me but yeah of course I wouldn't want you to go anywhere with him. It's in the northern part of South America, that's all I know. I can picture a map of it but not exactly sure. I suppose the south of it must border Brazil. There's no end to the guy is there? Why doesn't he just accept your rejection of him and get on with his life? If a girl turned me down once, I'd move on. You've rejected him a hundred times. The guy's not normal. As a friend only and for two weeks in a tropical paradise? Where are you going to sleep? Separate rooms,

a shared one with twin beds? Not a chance in hell is that part of his plan. You'd get there and there'd be one room with a double bed in it and he'd expect you to play his game. Hannah, I paid for your ticket and you owe me. I feel a bit sad for Alison. I thought she was a complete bitch but the whole story makes a lot more sense now. Anyway I'm glad to be away from that twit and just sorry you have to see him in your life still."
"I can resign too" said Hannah. I don't know if I can take it much longer. He comes into the shop every day and sometimes just stands at the front and stares at me. It makes me feel very uncomfortable. He doesn't talk to the other girls, just me and they all think he's a bit creepy. They don't like him."
"I like your reply that I wouldn't approve. That must have pissed him off. Good. And I wouldn't. I wouldn't approve of you going anywhere with another man, least of all a nutcase. He's probably a dangerously disturbed type, the type Neil has to write about and the day he got you into bed was the biggest and best in his life. What a damn pity but yeah, I know it was before you met me and it was only once and you were fragile and upset at the time and you regret it all. I know all these things and it's okay now. Why don't I take you somewhere? Where would you like to go, always wanted to visit?" Hannah lay there looking at my open book and said "I've always wanted to go to Arran. Can we go there?"

Hannah had been working at the shop for well over a year and had only taken five or six days off and she told Janet she wanted a week's holiday and that she and I were going away. A week later we were on our way to Arran and the first time Hannah had been on a ferry. We arrived at Brodick and the crossing was shorter than I expected. No big waves or heavy swells, all quite calm and uneventful. We went into a local tourist office and found a pleasant looking cottage on a farm to book for a week and caught a bus towards the west coast and the village of Blackwaterfoot. The driver stopped in the middle of nowhere and directed us in the direction of the farm, a ten minute walk from the road. The farmer was very friendly and showed us to the cottage, handed us the keys and accepted the week's payment in full from me. The place was clean and well looked after and had a small kitchen, a large living room and a large bedroom with a very basic bathroom next to it. Everything looked great and exactly the type of place where we could make a week's holiday together an unforgettable one. The first thing we tried out was the bed and we sunk into the centre of it, Hannah almost on top of me. The mattress must have been about a hundred years old. Not great and we'd no doubt be spending quite a bit of time in this room but we'd paid and we liked all the rest that the cottage had to offer and we unpacked our clothes and the food we'd brought, stocked the fridge with some wine, cheese and milk and went outside for our first countryside walk together. I'd been to the isles of Skye and Mull before but never knew what to expect from Arran and hadn't heard of anything about it but it was beyond anything I pictured. It was astonishingly pretty and I was happy to be here.

Hannah and I went for long walks each day, spent hours in that old worn out mattress and cooked up meals with the meagre food rations we brought with us and shared a bottle of cold wine in the evenings together. I said to Hannah that it must be great to grow up here, the farmer tending to his vast farm, never having to leave the island, not caring about the outside world, it was like living a fairy tale but it was real. No stresses, no crowds or noises, no traffic, just surrounded by beautiful scenery and quiet. The colours of the hills and valleys were the most spectacular I'd ever seen and we found a spot of land we both liked, next to a small river on one of our walks and visited it each day and put down a picnic blanket we found in the cottage and lay there reading or just lying, looking up at the sky and talking and sometimes sleeping. Hannah had said that one of her fantasies was to make love in the open so we did that too. We were too far away from anywhere and anyone to be spotted or disturbed and too isolated from anything to care.

On our fourth day we walked into Blackwaterfoot as the farmer had advised me and bought some things to restock the fridge to keep body and soul together and found bicycles to hire for a pound a day. We took two and said we'd be back in three days and the owner of the shop didn't even ask for a deposit of any kind. I loved the place, this is how the whole world should be. We made good use of the bikes and Hannah was a lot fitter than I expected her to be, astonishingly so on up hills and never out of breath, unlike me, and I had to call her often to slow down a bit but she rarely listened. She said she cycled a lot in her younger days and loved the freedom of it and the feeling of speed and the wind in her face and liked racing me and winning. The two bikes brought us a lot of fun and we were able to see more of the island on our own and take in more views of the sea up and down the west coast than if we were on foot.

On our last evening on the island we were sitting outside the cottage eating, fittingly, cottage pie and drinking our last bottle of wine and talking about what we thought about when we were growing up. Hannah had asked the question of me and I said I didn't really give it much thought. I knew I wanted to do well at school and go to university but didn't think too much beyond that. Later on I did think that I would just go from there into a company and like what I was doing and make money from it, get into management and buy a nice house in a nice area and have a wife and children and a dog or two and go back to Kenya sometimes and see wild animals like I did as a kid. I thought my family would be together though and I didn't see this separation of it happening, some of us living here and others in Canada from east to west. I worry a lot about my mum because she didn't buy into this and she misses her sons badly and never meant any of this to happen. Now we're all 3,000 miles away here. She's just got Sam and maybe Ben will go back next month but that's it. I'll tell you a crazy thing about my mum. She had four kids and she said she had her tubes tied after Sam was born and then couldn't stop crying for days after because she couldn't have any more. How crazy's that? You think if you do all that's asked of you at school and university that you get the rewards but you don't. Look at me, look at all the graduates we know who get their degrees, then nothing. I know a guy I went to school with. He studied biology at Edinburgh University, why I don't know, ended up not knowing what to do and took up mountain climbing for fun. He told me when I got back here that the most dangerous part of climbing was finding a safe place to sleep at night, you know on a ledge half way up a cliff. I was reading the paper one morning and his name was in it and he'd fallen off a cliff somewhere in the Highlands and died. He fell something like a thousand feet and I wondered if it had been at night and he rolled over in his sleep and maybe woke up half way down in mid-air. It must have been the worst nightmare imaginable for his parents. I never met them but I know his dad was a lawyer and a very rich man. I wonder if he'd have been climbing if he had a good job he liked after graduating. There was nothing for him but an emptiness in life and he filled it by climbing mountains and the bloody Highlands."

"I'm so sad to hear about that friend of yours. That's terrible. What was his name?"
"Sebastian. He was crap at sport at school. A skinny guy but grew a lot stronger after school. He told me he climbed the north face of the Eiger. The funniest thing he told me about climbing was a trip to South Africa. He was hiking with a friend and they got lost in the mist. They

didn't have a tent or proper clothing and a massive thunder storm was approaching them. They had no way down as they were surrounded by cliff edges they couldn't see. He said he could barely see the length of his arm. They heard laughter and decided to try and walk towards the sound and keep in a straight line. His friend was convinced they were always one step away from falling off a cliff. They made it to a group of people in a cave, minutes before the storm hit and there were two Irish climbers cracking jokes to three South African girls and it was their laughter they heard. He said he bedded down deep in the narrow cave and was woken up in the middle of the night in pitch darkness by what he described as a primal scream. He heard a woman screaming but more frighteningly, the two Irishmen screaming. He'd never heard the sound of a man screaming before. Convinced they were under attack, he said to himself he didn't want to die in his sleeping bag and tried to get up and fight and in doing so, smashed his head against the roof of the cave where he was. It turned out a rat from the bottom of the cave had run across the South African woman's face and her screams had woken the Irishmen up from a deep sleep and they woke thinking they were about to be killed. They were at the entrance. The scream set off a chain reaction. The worst, frightening screaming he'd ever heard in his life and to be woken up to it made it a hundred times worse. He said he thought he was having a nightmare and then realised it was real. Anyway, one of the Irishmen picked up a rock and threw it towards the sound of scuffling he heard and he killed the rat. Sebastian said he could have bled to death that night but for one of the girls being a nurse and she had decided to hike with a first aid kit and was able to stitch his head up under a torch light. He had fifteen stitches above his eye and a really bad scar. Made him look quite scary and tough, which he certainly wasn't."

"That sounds horrifying. I'm terrified of rats. I feel for the poor girl with the rat on her face. I'd have had a heart attack. And your poor mum. I'm dying to meet her. I just used to think about how I could make my mum and dad happy because they never looked it. I wanted to be a nurse and I wanted to get out of the village and live somewhere where there were lots of people and places with cinemas and restaurants and music and I wanted to meet a boy who was kind to me and would look after me. I was, well still am, scared of a lot of things and I wanted to be this great nurse who saved lives and looked after people and made them smile. I love making people smile. I think growing up is a lot harder than I used to think and that we aren't prepared for it. Nobody teaches you or tells what you are doing is the right way or the wrong way. I never thought about making money. I'd leave that all to my husband if I found one. Someone just like you." We talked late into the night about our childhoods and Hannah wanted to know what my first sad memory was. "I was five and I saw an elephant shot dead and I didn't cry. I just remember the terrible sadness I felt. I went up to him lying on his side and I stroked his trunk and prayed he'd get up. One of my dad's friends was a hunter and Neil and I went on the trip. I remember the noise of the gun

shot and the elephant's breathing and its eyes open and staring. It was staring at me and I thought for years after that the elephant thought I did it. That was worse than the shot. I felt guilty and condemned by the elephant."
"You didn't shoot it. Why did you feel guilty?"
"Because the elephant thought I did. I could see it in his eyes. He looked sad. That's all I remember. He was looking right at me and blinking and then stopped. He was dead."
"That's cruel, Tom. You should never have been put in that position. You were too young and should never have been there. It scarred you. It's not your fault. I shouldn't have asked such a stupid question. I'm sorry."

The next day after returning our bicycles, catching the local bus and Hannah making a quick call home from the telephone booth near the pier, we caught the ferry back to the mainland. We were standing at the front of the ship, the sea breeze in our faces and Hannah turned to me and said "I told my mum and dad about our holiday and how great it's been. Dad was shocked when I told him about you hiring the bikes and he said it was a waste of money and you're obviously a spendthrift and not a very wise man. Mum was happy though. Can we go out tonight to the Indian place when we get back? Let's ask Neil and Ben and Marion too."
"Okay, sounds good. I'm sure Ben will and hopefully Neil and Marion. Think about how much fun you had on that bike for three days and all the things we were able to see which we'd never have seen otherwise. Your bike cost three pounds. I think it was worth three hundred pounds

but I'm not going to win that one am I? He's got a hate on for me and life goes on." Hannah grabbed my hand and looked out towards the approaching land and said "you think much bigger than my dad and I wouldn't pay any attention to what he says if I were you. He doesn't like you and probably never will. He's stubborn about things and he's been like that all my life and probably all his too. He says you're too middle class, you're feeling like you're above us. I know it's my fault."

Neil and Ben did join us later in the evening, Marion was out of town and Neil said he felt so privileged to be seen at a table in a restaurant sitting next to Hannah and have people looking at him with envy that he was paying the bill. Maybe he could see a three pound deficit in my eyes and thought he better help me out. As the eldest of four, he used to say that he carried the greatest weight on his shoulders and the rest of us got off easy. He'd say it jokingly but always with a suggestion of truth about it. He was a good elder brother to have and I always looked up to him and held huge respect for him. He was a great writer of news and had spent a summer in his mid-teens in Bonn with one of our uncles, a journalist with the Express newspaper, a foreign correspondent who wanted to stay in a foreign country for good. He had said that Neil had talent at the age of sixteen that he could only dream about and I believed him and still do but for Neil, he finds the frustration of working for a small local newspaper almost unbearable. He broke up with a long term girlfriend a few months before meeting Marion and decided he needed a break or a holiday as he termed it, from relationships. Not women, just relationships. That's a lot easier said than done he assured me and it seemed to me he and Marion were well suited and in a near perfect one.

The following week I took Hannah to see three movies on three nights at our closest cinema on Lothian Road after I thought about the comments she made about when she was younger and I realised we'd never had a date at the movies together. In Canada, that was usually the first one. The one thing we couldn't agree on was the popcorn, she loved it and I hated it. I told her the popcorn in Canada was salted and this sweet stuff was inedible and she couldn't imagine the taste any different. Strange how taste preferences are formed. To me the Yanks and the Canadians had it spot on. It was a good feeling to sit in a darkened cinema with Hannah next to me and hold her hand, knowing she was happy. Happy with me was the thing that made me the happiest about each passing day and I had not the slightest doubt that I wanted to spend the rest of my days with her by my side. It doesn't matter how good a friend is, how close your family are, no one but Hannah sees me stark naked, no clothes to shield me, no words to hide behind, no pretences in any form, nothing but the total truth of who I am and she's okay with it. All of it, the good, the bad and the in between and she's that to me too. We were deeply, deeply connected and were less than nine months into this journey together. My mum and dad never had this, not that I ever saw any part of and my mum had told me she never had what it was I was looking for in life. Marion's friend Linda had told me a year ago that when she walked down the aisle she knew it wouldn't last, that she wasn't in love and I thought to myself how many people do that, marry someone they don't have this kind of connection with and who settle too easily for someone who's just okay. Okay doesn't do it surely and now I'm wondering about the whole Royal wedding and the great show and thinking to myself, is it about the title for Diana and the looks and the virginity for Charles? That must be pretty sad if it is and yet it can't be when I think back to the smiles and the laughter on their faces that day. No, what we have can't be that uncommon and most of us have the same emotional experiences when we fall in love and we're just like every other couple sitting here watching the movie.

Hannah was having more thoughts and worries about working at the shop and she was losing the joy she used to feel about getting up in the morning, making her breakfast and getting ready for work. She adored her regular customers and the thought of meeting them all at some point during the week inspired her. Then of course new ones would walk through the door and by sheer luck or by choice they'd too meet her and want to meet her again and they'd all let her know how special she became to them and how much they looked forward to coming into the shop to see her. Simon's presence had shifted everything for Hannah and to use her words, when he walked into the shop he 'turned the air grey' and she felt a deep unease. I had said that I was happy to speak to the guy and let him know the effect he was having on her and to back off or risk losing her for ever but she assured me that she was old enough and ugly enough to look after herself and she didn't need a big brother to sort out her fights. I thought Susan could advise and help her and she must have a huge influence on Ian to do something but Hannah didn't want Susan to know anything about it. Another strange family flaw I thought and the secrets and half-truths and the lies that flowed between them didn't help, didn't serve a single purpose and just didn't do any good at all.

I gave all the reassurance I could to Hannah that I would back whatever decision she made, that she was safe with me, that she had my family's friendship, the flat with the view, I'd be working soon and all that mattered was her happiness. She went into work and told Janet that she was leaving.

CHAPTER 14

Hannah was back in a job with a clothing company owned by the husband of one of her favourite customers' within two weeks of leaving the shop and working in sales and was asked to attend weekly design meetings. She was pretty thrilled about the whole thing and I was amazed at the ease with which she handled the transition from one business to a totally new one but it came as no great surprise because of who she is and how she is with people and it reinforced much of what I had learnt in a classroom that business is fundamentally about the interactions and relationships between people.

I had sent out over fifty CVs and letters to companies I'd searched for from newspapers, the telephone directories and the library, where I was becoming a more frequent visitor. Harry had run a very imaginative advert in the local paper promising quality gardening services from trusted university graduates, having completed his time at St Andrews and Ben had gone the other way, starting his degree there. There was a lot of change happening and autumn was setting in. One morning, going through the papers I came across a page on sporting fixtures and followed up on two of interest. I phoned an old schoolmate and asked if he could organise two tickets for a rugby match in December at Murrayfield where Scotland would be playing Australia and explained I hadn't been there in five years. I then went out and arranged two tickets for a Rangers, Celtic match to be played at Ibrox at the weekend. That should excite Hannah I thought. The new job she had meant she no longer worked on Saturdays and had the whole weekend free. I phoned my grandmother, my gran on my dad's side of the family, known to everyone in the family and on her street as Granny Miller and told her I'd pop in and see her for a visit after the match. She lived about a mile from the stadium and I hadn't seen her in almost a year.

I just got back into the flat when the phone rang. "Tom, it's me, I've got a proposition for you." It was Harry. "I know you're busy job hunting but come and work with me in this gardening idea of mine and let's make a few quid. I've got five bookings from the first day of the ad and I can't do it alone. I thought Hess might help me out but he's not interested and says it'll screw up his dole money. You're not in that position and so what have you got to lose while you're waiting for replies to your letters?"
"What do you want me to do and anyway when did you ever pick up a gardening tool in your life? I'm not getting involved in any con. If it's about doing it the right way and we both pull our weight, I'll help you out. When do we start?" Harry laughed "It's no con, there's a gap in the market and I'm going to fill it. You might even learn a thing or two about business and use it later in your stellar career. We start tomorrow morning. I'll pick you up at eight and we'll see all five callers and their gardens, give them quotes and decide on who's first and when the rest will follow in the week."

"Okay, I'll see you tomorrow. I won't be here on Saturday by the way. I've got plans for the old firm match and am taking Hannah through for it. So if you've got gardening then, you're on your own for that one." "So you are in love" replied Harry.

I told Hannah about the weekend plan and she was less excited about it than I expected but said she was going to phone her friend, Mary from back home and tell her and make her jealous. She was Celtic mad and had never been to a Glasgow derby and always hoped to one day. Hannah was more enthusiastic when I mentioned the rugby match against Australia in December and said she preferred rugby players to footballers. "They've got more brains" she said.

Harry had a motorbike and an extra helmet for me and we got to see all five gardens and their owners by lunchtime. His quotes were all thumb sucks, higher than I would have gone and all accepted and we gave each a date for starting. We decided to begin with the largest garden first and the smallest and lowest paying last and tomorrow would be the day to begin our love affair with gardening and this would be all about cutting grass and hedges and weeding and laying paving stones and nothing about planting and all the beautiful and creative aspects which proper gardeners love doing.

It was as tedious and uninspiring and back breaking as I expected it to be and the first garden we attended to was larger than we'd given real consideration to when we first gave our less than expert opinion and we'd be spending at least two days longer on it than planned and all the other dates would have to change. At times we'd work apart at different ends of the garden and other times next to each other and talk. Harry was using the garden hoe on a bed of weeds while I was digging up an old tree root and asked "Tom, I've been giving something a lot of thought recently and want to know if you think the same way as I do." I was expecting it to be about Rachel and Hannah when he went on "I'm terrified at the thought of dying. The very thought of death, your body stops working and you cease to exist is too much for me to bear at times. Are you scared of dying?" "I don't give it any thought, Harry" I replied looking at him a bit puzzled. "I mean it's just part of the deal. If you're going to live it means you're going to die one day. Maybe by the time you do die you won't be afraid and so you're just wasting your time with things that aren't worth thinking about."

"I know all of that. It's not the enormity of the idea of dying, it's the enormity of mine. When I hear of someone dying I don't really get affected by it but the thought that it would be my own and that I'd cease to exist is too horrible a thought and it's bloody terrifying. Come on, you must think about it, it must scare you, the thought that there's no more Tom in the world, you're just replaced by an emptiness that will exist for millions of years."

"Think about what you're saying Harry. So you're afraid of dying and that's fair enough but you've just turned 23, you're young and fit and able to do all the things you want your body to do. So let's say you don't die any time soon and you get to do all the things you want in life and you have a great life and because you don't die, you get old and too old for your body to do the things you want it to do. Then you're tired, worn out, seen it, done it and your mind starts shutting down saying you need a bloody rest. You're about to die and you're ready for the idea, you're okay with it. It seems to be you're not afraid of ceasing to exist, just that you are right now. Don't think about it. You think you're the centre of the bloody universe."

"I am. I'm the centre of my own universe. I can only think about it right now as the person I am right now, not as some old codger sixty years from now. I don't know that person, I only know this one. I don't have any other reference point but the one I have today and tomorrow."

I was digging deeper and deeper into the ground around the root of the tree and beginning to get some leverage on it and said "it comes back to the same thing. You're afraid of the Harry you are today ceasing to exist, not the one in sixty years. Accept that and you'll realise that the chances are that you are going to grow old and then you can confront these exact thoughts when you reach that age. You don't seem to care too much about him dying and so leave it till then. Anyway it sounds like you don't believe in the soul or anything spiritual from what you're saying. I don't mean religion. Have you ever had a spiritual hunch?"

"Nothing. I don't believe in that stuff." If you can't see it, it doesn't exist."

"So radio waves don't exist then?" Harry laughed and then added "The idea's great but there's no proof. Prove it to me Tom and I'll believe it."

"I can't but that doesn't mean it doesn't exist does it? It doesn't say if it can't be proven then it one hundred percent doesn't exist. My grandad's neighbour used to say when we were young that he'd see us back at home. We'd all meet back at home or on the way. People we meet in life, we meet on our journey along the way and those we don't, we'll meet them back at our real home when the journey's over. He had no doubts, he didn't go to church, didn't worry about dying. The guy was a happy and content man. That's the way to live, not worrying about something we know nothing about. Remember what we learnt in school about Socrates when he said the only thing he was certain about was that he knew nothing. What did the ancient Greeks ask at a funeral, did he live with passion? That's what counted. Live with passion." Harry replied "I'm more passionate about living than I am about living with passion. If you think I'm feeling any better about my dying now, you're wrong. Let's get this damn job finished."

"Harry, before we do, let's sit down and take a break. I have a couple of questions for you." We were both a bit tired and I needed to share something with my close friend. We put down our gardening tools and sat under one of the oak trees and drank from our water bottles. "What's on your mind?" Harry asked.

"Two years ago a friend of mine in Canada, Mark and I, decided to drive to the Grand Canyon for a visit. I said we should pop in to Las Vegas, seeing as we were in that part of the US and we agreed to spend two nights there first. On our second night we were checking out the night life, there were topless waitress and barmaid clubs, we'd gambled a bit the first night, caught up in the bright lights and action of the place when we went for a beer two blocks from our hotel. There was a lady standing in a short coat with her hands in her pockets and as we passed by and said 'can I show you a good time'? I stopped and said 'thanks but we're having a good time' and she replied 'how good'? If you ask me which Hollywood actress she most resembled I'd say Natalie Wood. She was about mid 30s in age. She was damn beautiful. 'Good enough' I said and she went on 'men come here for gambling, drinking and women and how many of the three had we indulged in'? I replied the first two and she said she could supply the third. I didn't realise she was a prostitute when we first got talking. I tell you Harry, she was gorgeous and classy. Mark said he wasn't interested and I asked how much. 50 dollars was her answer and I asked how does this work and she said give me your hotel and room number and I'll see you in 15 minutes. I gave it to her and headed back to the hotel and she knocked on the door about five minutes after I got there. Mark was downstairs in the bar and I let her in and she asked for the money and the use of the bathroom. She came out stark naked and she was unbelievably beautiful. She said 'no kissing on the lips and take down your trousers to let me inspect you' and I did and she said all was well and for me to get undressed. For such a slim woman she had fairly large natural breasts and asked me to lie down on my back on the bed. Before I knew it she'd slipped a condom on me in seconds and was on top of me, thrusting like you wouldn't believe. It was all over in about 20 seconds. I got dressed and she did the same in the bathroom before saying she had a friend she'd like me to meet for a threesome the next day for a hundred dollars. I told her I couldn't as we were heading for the Grand Canyon in the morning and she gave me a kiss on the cheek and left.

We left the next day and I pondered my opportunity missed for hours. A threesome with her and no doubt another as pretty was a fantasy come true. Flipping idiot I thought. Mark thought I was an idiot for having sex with a prostitute but I'm 20 years old and could never pull a woman like that in real life. 50 dollars was all it took, can you believe it? We slept a night at the top of the canyon in a tent and almost froze to death and were advised to walk down to the Colorado River the next day and sleep there where it was warm. We did and it was great. On the way back up the canyon Mark got ahead of me and he was carrying our water bottle and it started to get bloody hot. Two thirds of the way up, I was having to stop for a rest after every 10 steps or so through exhaustion. I was finished. 10 steps, rest, 10 steps, rest again. I could look up and see people at the top of the canyon but thought I'm not going to make it. A tourist party on ponies coming down the path stopped and noticed my sorry state and gave me water and a bar of chocolate and I thanked them for saving me before practically sprinting to the top and throttling Mark. I was totally dehydrated because of him. He said he wanted to pitch the tent again and I threw it in the car, told him to jump in and said I'd drive as far south as we could into New Mexico into the night before getting out in the desert and camping in warmth. The thing is I missed out on a threesome fantasy. Have you ever had one?"

"I have. A girlfriend at St Andrews was up for it and her friend too. It's totally overrated. One was always in the way. I didn't know how to handle two. One's enough, it was awkward and the truth is I didn't enjoy it. I can tick it off but believe me you did yourself a favour trying to kill yourself in the Grand Canyon instead." Harry rolled onto his back and started laughing loudly and the hysteria of his laugh grew until I thought he was in tears. "What's so damn funny?"

"You are." Composing himself and pulling himself off the ground to face me Harry tried his best to keep a straight face and every time he'd try to talk he'd burst out into a complete fit of giggles. I let him laugh himself out and I was laughing too. "Spit it out" I said, "what's so funny about my story?"

"Only 50 dollars! For 20 seconds!" He was back on the ground rolling in laughter. "Is that the best you could do? 20 seconds of action and it costs you 50 dollars and you think you got the deal of a lifetime. God you make me laugh. I've never heard anything like it. I bet that woman left your hotel laughing as loud as I am. Probably still is."

Harry's laughter continued, he was in hysterics and I stood up and picked up the axe pick to strike some more blows at the remaining tree roots and thought to myself, he's got a point but he's missing the point.

The following days had been far more difficult than we thought and the first job was finished and the house owner was happy with the job done and handed over our first gardening payment. It was getting towards late enough in the morning and the time I wanted to leave to catch the train to Glasgow. I told Hannah I wanted to board it at Waverly Station at the east end of Princes Street rather than Haymarket and get a better chance of getting on an earlier train and a seat together and she was acting very out of character by taking an age in the bathroom. When she did emerge she was looking her beautiful self and wearing a new top she'd bought from work and thankfully blue, under her brown jacket. I was wearing no colours to give any indication of being fan of either club and we set off.

The train journey was busy and full of fans of both clubs but the spirits were high and the forty mile journey covered quickly. We connected to the underground and came out onto the Copeland Road to a sea of red, white and blue colours and thousands of fans heading towards Ibrox Stadium. The noise levels were rising and today was to be a special day with the opening a new stand at the ground. It was now one of the safest in all of Britain. I

knew that of course before I bought the tickets and the days of being pushed, jostled and generally crushed by tens of thousands of supporters were over. There would be forty something thousand seated fans at the game and I'd been to one with almost another hundred thousand added on in comparison, almost all standing. This was child's play. Inside the stadium and seated in the new stand, we had a perfect viewing position near the centre line and not far from the front and like all these matches the two sets of fans were singing their favourite songs and shouting their abuse and threats at each other. There was a huge police presence visible and it was just another derby day. Of course it was loud and to make yourself heard you have to shout at the person next to you but all was normal and the teams were due to appear at any moment. Hannah had been holding my hand all the time and was now squeezing it tightly and I could feel her lips next to my left ear. She was saying something to me and I turned to look at her. She was in tears and visibly terrified. I put my arm around her and could feel her shaking and shouted as loud as I could that she would be alright and the noise would calm down a bit when the teams kicked off. "Five minutes and we'll be able to talk better" I said. "I want to leave. We need to go right now" she replied.
"We can't. The gates are locked. We can't just get out. It's madness to try. I'll look after you, don't worry."
"I've got to leave right now." Her tears rolled down her face and I held her as tight as I could without hurting her and I shouted that we could go at half time as the noise

levels rose still further as the two teams emerged onto the pitch.

The game kicked off and the volume levels continued and I have to admit it was louder than I expected or remembered but then again I'd never given any thought to it before. When half time arrived and Celtic one nil up I asked Hannah if she wanted to leave and she shook her head and told me she was okay. The second half was no better and when Celtic scored again near the end of the match we knew it was all over and the Celtic fans were in a joyous mood with their chants and songs and scarves. It ended and I turned to speak to Hannah properly for the first time when she said "I've never been so exhilarated in my life. What an adrenaline rush that was. It was the most terrifying thing I've experienced and the noise and the bright colours were deafening and blinding. It was like sitting in the front row seat of a 90 minute storm of thunder and lightning. You don't hear or see it on television do you? I'm sorry your team lost but in a way I'm happy for the Celtic fans. The swearing though was terrible. Is it always like this?"
"I think they swear more when they lose. Let's go."

We left and for the first time ever after a derby match I had to leave at the end of the stadium reserved for the Celtic support and that was part of my plan in dressing in neutral colours. Hannah had her blue top covered by her jacket and we set out onto Paisley Road among thousands of vocal fans in green and white. It was a new experience for me too. Quarter of an hour into our walk and with the crowd thinning out Hannah spotted and dashed into a telephone booth and picked up the receiver and slipped coins into the box. I waited outside listening to the jubilant passing supporters singing their anti- Rangers songs and waving their scarves and I was smiling back at them, looking almost as if I was enjoying it just as much. When Hannah had finished she took my arm and we made our way through the still heavy throng clad in green and white colours in the direction of Granny Miller. "I called Mary. She said she's so jealous of me and I'm so lucky to be here. I had to phone her. I told her she could never imagine what it's like. It's an experience of a lifetime. Thanks for bringing me, Tom."

We arrived at the flat and it was now my turn to introduce Hannah to granny without a first name and she was thrilled to meet her. Inside the living room Granny Miller said to Hannah "I heard the score on the television. I was hoping so much for Tom that Rangers would win today but as long as you're both fine, that's all that matters." Granny used that expression all the time we were growing up, that being okay or fine was all that matters and maybe she was right. "My word, but you are a beautiful young lady" granny said to Hannah. Hannah blushed and said thanks. "Tom must care about you an awful lot."
"Yes I think I know he does" replied Hannah. Granny Miller went on " I mean to take you to a game at Ibrox and not just any old game, a Celtic one, oh my, he must care about you very much. Not like him at all. A lot of men won't do it,

take their wives or girlfriends along to Ibrox or Parkhead. It's their own place, a place they like to keep to themselves, it's as if it's a secret part of them they don't want women to see. I've known many men in my time who just refused to take their wives with them and it wasn't to do with their safety, well it's not like the old days when it wasn't always very safe but even now, they just won't allow them into that part of their life. You should feel very blessed Hannah." Hannah looked and smiled at me and I smiled back and took granny's hand and thanked her for her kind words. There aren't many conversations like that going around a living room in the world right now I thought.

We had a light meal with Granny Miller and Hannah and she chatted about the needlepoint and artwork in the flat and Hannah wanted to know all about her life, questions I'd never asked. I wasn't as close to my gran on my dad's side as I was with my grandad and gran on my mum's and I learned a lot just sitting, listening to the two of them talk away for hours. I looked at my watch and said we'd need to head back to the centre of Glasgow and catch our train. I didn't want to get back to Edinburgh too late and I knew that the later we left it the more chance of rowdy fans leaving the pubs and the last thing I needed were any more frights for Hannah today. We both gave Granny Miller big hugs and thanks and headed home.

Hannah and I had to run to catch one of the last trains leaving for Edinburgh and although there were a few fans on it who had obviously had too much to drink and were either slumped in their seats or raising their voices, the mood of the carriage we were in was friendly enough and Hannah lent her head against my shoulder and closed her eyes. I thought about her talk with my gran and how little I had known of her younger days and what kind of person she was. I knew a bit about the German Luftwaffe bombings of Clydebank and how her husband, the grandad I never met, had narrowly escaped the blitz while working as an electrician on the shipyard but not really much more than that and I knew that only from my dad. She had explained to Hannah how she was left a nervous wreck from the war and how friends of hers had lost their sons and how their lives had ended up. She had lived in her flat for nearly sixty years and knew everyone on the street and all about the lives of most of them. I felt a sense of guilt that I'd never asked any of the questions Hannah had earlier and had shown no interest in her life beyond her being my elderly grandmother and that being her role or title in life. Yes she was Granny Miller to everyone in her street as well but she was much more than that name given to her and I wondered why I had never given a second's thought to her as anything but a doting old woman I was related to.

Two years earlier in Canada, I had got the news that my uncle had died suddenly and that my mum and dad would be flying back for his funeral in Scotland, his body having been flown back from Germany and they'd be away for ten days. I hadn't given any thought to the sadness my dad or Granny Miller must have felt losing a brother and youngest son and had lectures at university to attend and a life to get on with. I had liked my uncle and had always preferred his sense of humour to my dad's but when he died I hadn't felt any sadness or loss and hadn't considered how my gran must have felt and dealt with her grieving. It must have been a huge blow and she said as much to Hannah and she shared feelings with her within a three hour period of meeting her which she never had with her grandkids and she described herself as a young woman in a way that immediately changed the image I had held of her since I could first remember. Hannah's interest in a person seemed completely natural to her and she possessed an empathy I seemed to be lacking. I always thought and maybe assumed I had this quality but I was being shown a true and deeper version of it. I was looking at the world through the only view I had and that was through my own eyes and my first thoughts were about myself and how what I was seeing affected me before I interpreted how it affected another person. I was learning from Hannah what it means to put another first and to consider them before myself and not after. It dawned on me that she was seeing life through her own eyes and those of the person she was with simultaneously and she had a far deeper ability to relate to and care for another without expecting or needing anything in return.

As I was looking out the window at the passing lights showing me we were entering the outskirts of Edinburgh, Hannah seemed to be sleeping or at least in a deep rest with her own thoughts and I was beginning to grasp the value of the lessons I was learning. I cared very much about my family. My mum, Sam and Ben and Neil sprung to mind first but my dad, my good friends like Harry and Marion, Hannah of course, but was it because of what they brought into my own life, made it better, more bearable and benefiting me? It didn't apply to strangers or people I held as acquaintances and God knows, I had dozens of those in Canada and that was because I got little out of it. But I did consider a few others as friends and yeah I cared about them when I came to think of it but we rarely made an effort to keep in touch. With Hannah that didn't matter, it never entered her mind that the person's value had to enrich her life in some form. I needed to look at people differently and try this out and see if I could be a better person for it. I would understand people better and quicker and life would be far more interesting. No wonder I'd been carrying this burden of being alone because it was me alone who's separated me from hundreds or thousands of people I'd met in life. They're the people I was meeting on the way before I get back home and their lives mattered just as much as mine. I'd been blind to this realisation all my life and what a gold mine it was. I may have had fleeting glimpses of it before but had given it no more than lip service but it was Hannah who had opened my eyes. I could never be her but I could be a better version of myself. I wanted to see what was in front of me and not viewed from a distance, the flowers in Princes Street Gardens which Hannah saw individually and pointed out to me on our walks when all I was aware of was a sea of colours of pink or yellow as I was lost in thoughts a million miles away. The woman next to me grasped the moment and I didn't.

We got off the train at Haymarket Station and walked back to the flat in a light drizzle of rain and talked about the afternoon we'd had together. Hannah said she thought the Celtic players were much better looking than most of the Rangers ones and their fans were better behaved and I laughed at some of her observations of the game itself. I was feeling tired when we walked through the front door and my offer of a pot of tea was declined. It was late and Neil was asleep in his room and I had the same idea but Hannah insisted we jump in the shower and wash the dust from our bodies and freshen up as she was in no mood for sleeping and wanted a long night together and I'd be lucky to get any sleep before the sun came up. She was going to make it up to me for Rangers losing.

CHAPTER 15

By the end of October and autumn well into season, the gardening orders Harry was getting from his weekly newspaper ads were piling up and the two of us were kept busy every day of the week and often only took Sundays off to rest up. I was sitting in the kitchen of a house owned by an elderly man by the name of John Ferguson and he was telling me about his time in the RAF during the 2nd World War and how he got injured. I'd asked him about it because he was sitting in a wheelchair with a blanket over his lap and no legs. When we arrived to look around his garden and give him a price to cut back and clean up, a nurse had answered the door and shown us around before introducing us to John. She was his day helper and was very friendly to Harry and me and it was apparent that she had helped John find the newspaper ad and arrange for us to meet.

"I was shot down. I was able to fly the plane back to our air field in Exeter but crash landed. I had no proper control of it. I was just lucky to live but lost my damn legs."
"Were you able to live a normal life after the war? Did you marry or have a career?" I asked. "No, I never married and I did work. I worked for the civil service in an office job until I retired. I lost a lot the day of my accident but I lived and most of my friends in the air force didn't survive the war. The only reason I did was because I lost my legs and was medically discharged from the force." I was looking directly at him and knew he was drawing on a painful

memory, his eyes were light blue and a little bloodshot. I noticed the colour of people's eyes now when I met them for the first time. I never used to.

It was a cold day and Harry was rushing the work. He had bought an electric hedge cutter weeks ago and the early days of using the house owner's old hand held garden clippers from their shed were long gone. We were quicker and more efficient and were finishing jobs quicker and making more money but there was still lots to do around gardens which simply required hard work and time. Late in the afternoon he told me he'd spoken to John and told him we'd finished and he'd paid us. It was time to jump on his motorbike and go. I told Harry we weren't finished but if he wanted to bolt I'd catch a bus later. Harry didn't like the idea and said if I stayed on it would seem to the owner that he had lied to him and anyway the job we'd done looked pretty good to him and was good enough. We packed up, put our helmets on and took off.

That evening Hannah was preparing a fish stew and telling Neil and me about a wealthy middle aged customer of hers who had spent over two thousand pounds on clothing that afternoon and how easily some of the women she dealt with parted with their or their husband's money on what Hannah considered frivolous items. The phone rang and it was my old school friend Jeff and he asked if I'd join him for a beer later, his girlfriend's sister was visiting from Ireland and the three of them were going to a pub near us on Lothian Road. I said yes and asked him to come by the flat first.

We finished eating when the doorbell rang and I opened it to Jeff, his girlfriend Gemma and her sister Keira, neither of whom I'd met before. I introduced Hannah, who Jeff had met once and Neil, who Jeff had known for years and we all talked for a few minutes in the kitchen. "Let's go" I said to Hannah. "No, you go" she replied, "I'm a bit tired tonight. I'll see you when you get back. Don't be late." I was a bit surprised that Hannah wasn't joining us as I did mention it as soon as I'd hung up the phone and she said okay to me.
 The four of us went out the door and headed out into the night on a five minute walk to the Lions Head. It was fairly quiet inside and we found a table and I ordered the first round of beers. It was a pleasant evening and Jeff was enjoying talking about the time he met Gemma's family in Ireland and how they spent a weekend pub crawling in Dublin. Jeff and me had been good friends at school and known each other for ten years and he had been one of the school's best rugby players and was almost always top of our class in all subjects. He was working for his family's construction business now and never went to university and owned a very stylish two story flat in one of the city's most expensive areas. He was a good looking guy to women and had always had girlfriends that I could recall since around the age of fifteen. He and Gemma looked a good couple together and I discovered Gemma and Keira had both gone to Trinity College in Dublin and were a year

apart in age. There was no question both were attractive and spoke confidently and happily as Irish people often do. They laughed a lot and it was laughter from the bottom of their lungs and it made Jeff and I laugh. Jeff and I were asked a lot about our school days together and when and why we became friends and how we coped with the strict disciplines of the school, the usual old school talk. We finished our third beer each and said our goodbyes and Gemma insisted that the next time we get together I must bring Hannah along.

I arrived back at the flat just after half past ten, not late and was a bit surprised to see that the living room and kitchen were in darkness and Neil had already called it a night. When I opened my bedroom door Hannah was lying on the bed naked with her arms folded across her chest and didn't respond to my smile. She stood up and came towards me and said "where have you been? You've been away for over three hours and I've been worrying about you. You had sex with Keira didn't you?" I was astonished at Hannah and her accusation and I couldn't believe my ears or my eyes. She was angry in a way I'd never seen her before. "Don't be crazy" I replied, "of course not. What the hell is wrong with you?" She slapped me hard against my left cheek. Damn hard, I thought. There was a lot of power in that. "Is that the best you can do?" She laid a second and even harder slap that stung. I'd never been slapped before or at least not that I could recall, punched plenty of times in school ground fights, on rugby fields and my self-defence classes in Toronto but this felt different and it

hurt. A punch you expect in a fight, a slap from your girlfriend you don't. She turned around and was a few feet away from me when I slapped her hard on her bare bum. She turned around and shouted "don't you know you're not supposed to slap a woman on her bum when she's having her period?" Her face was red with anger.
"I didn't know that. They never told us that one at school. Just when she's having her period is it? Otherwise it's fine?"

Hannah collapsed onto the bed crying. "You always think you're so clever. You think you know everything. Well, you don't. Prove it. Prove you didn't have sex with her. Do it right now."
"How can I prove it? How the hell can I prove to you I didn't touch the woman?"
"Fuck me right now, right this second. I'll know."
"You're having your bloody period."
"I don't care. Prove it to me right now." I took off my clothes and got on top of Hannah and she was thrusting violently with her hips. Faster than I'd ever known and I couldn't hold back. I had no chance and came quickly. I got off Hannah, grabbed a pair of shorts and was about to walk out the room in anger when she said to me "okay, you've proved it. I know how long it takes you to come a second time." I turned back, got into bed and Hannah switched off the lamp and turned her back to me. I lay there for what seemed like hours thinking about what had just happened and I was having difficulty putting the Hannah I just encountered with the one I knew or thought

I knew. It wasn't her, it wasn't the same person. I'd long known that the naivety and innocence I'd first thought of as Hannah was anything but and she had more sexual experience and demands than I had and probably most people I knew but this violent part was a shock to me. The left side of my face was red hot and the burning sensation was giving way to an annoying, tingling one. I was thinking I should get up and run some cold water over my face but I was hoping Hannah was sleeping and I didn't want to wake her up getting out of the bed. She might not be sleeping so deeply right now and the best thing for me is her quietness, no words, no shouts, no slaps.

The next morning in front of the sink, I was surveying the red mark on my face in the mirror. It had taken a good whack alright and was feeling a bit tender to touch, a bit swollen in fact and I was thinking to myself that I needed to hide the evidence of last night from Harry when I meet him soon. I phoned him and told him to start without me and that I'd try and catch up with him at the address we were due at a bit later in the day. Hannah had gone to work early without saying a word to me.

I caught a bus to the southern part of the city and knocked on John Ferguson's door. He was surprised to see me, asked if everything was okay, did he still owe us any money and had a good look at my red left cheek without commenting on it. I told him that all was fine and that he owed us nothing but that Harry and I had realised after we'd left that we hadn't ticked off our entire list and that the job wasn't finished. I wanted to spend the day in his garden attending to the list and that there would be no further charge. He must rest inside with his tea or a scotch and I'd let him know when I was done. He was happy with my suggestion and thanked me.

I spent the morning working as fast as I could on the flower beds still covered in weeds and raking under the hedge Harry had cut yesterday and hoped I'd be finished by early afternoon and still be able to meet up with Harry later. It didn't work out that way and there was no point in ignoring the parts of the garden needing attended to and it was after five o'clock in the afternoon and almost dark when I knocked on John's front door to tell him the work had been completed and to keep in touch with us and maybe meet up again in spring. He thanked me for coming back and asked me to come inside for a glass of brandy. It was a drink he liked at this time of day he said and would enjoy the company.

I asked him where he kept his bottle and glasses and said it would be easier for him if he let me help. We sat in his living room and clinked our glasses together and he said "Thomas, you seem to me to be a competent young man and the advert says you're a graduate. What are your plans for yourself beyond digging up people's gardens and where does that accent come from?"
"I spent four years in Toronto doing my degree in business and I picked up a bit of Canadian. Competent, I'd like to think so and thanks for that but I have sent out dozens and

dozens of letters to companies asking if they're thinking about hiring and I've heard back from a few. Most said they weren't and five have said they'll keep my CV on record and let me know if they decide to start looking to recruit early next year. I'm hopeful but I'm aware that my best options might be in London and I might need to spread the net a bit further than here. The economy's not what I planned for when I came back last year and I've just got to face reality. What about you, John, what keeps your days ticking over?"

"Oh, my days are manageable. My best ones are behind me now and long gone. I have two nurses who come into the house and make sure I'm okay and help me out. I love aviation and birds and I have hundreds of books on both and I'm always looking for new material and reading up on anything new on bird life. I think they're God's most beautiful creation, much better than man has been."

John emptied the last bit of brandy in his glass into his mouth, picked up the bottle next to him and stretched over to refill mine before his. "The air force was quite an experience for me. I was twenty eight when I was shot down. I never expected to get out of the war alive and never thought I'd grow old. I went into it full of excitement and the force ragged, bagged and shagged me and sent me on my way rejoicing. That's how I see the whole bloody dreadful business. Oh but we won the war. Yes we did and that was all that mattered and today's generation don't really care and they're right not to. It was all such bloody claptrap. It could have been prevented you know, from the very beginning. Once it got out of hand, well by then it was too late and there was no turning back but wars never solve the real problems and the talking that comes later should always come first. Sometimes this may simply be impossible but the world wars could have been avoided and should have been. The airmen, the soldiers and sailors, they didn't start it and there were so many civilians who were killed or badly maimed. That's why I like birds so much."

John and I talked about how the country might change under Margaret Thatcher and where politics was going and I left feeling privileged to have had his company and touched that he had cared to share a part of his life with me and I travelled back thinking I'd have missed this if I'd never met Hannah and I had woken up because of her. When I got back to the flat it was after eight in the evening and Hannah's first words to me were that she could smell alcohol from my breath. "Where have you been?" she asked. "Gardening" I replied.
"You have not. Harry phoned two hours ago asking where you were. Why are you lying to me? Are you seeing that girl, Keira?"
"Oh my God! Don't' start on Keira again. I've been gardening. Harry and I did a crap job on an old man's garden yesterday, took his money and ran. He ran at least but I went along with it and this morning I decided to right the wrong. I told Harry I'd try and see him later and I didn't tell him where I was going. I admit that but I was with an old man with no legs from World War Two and he asked

me to join him for a brandy after I'd finished and we ended up having two."
"Are you telling the truth?"
"I am. Why would I lie to you?"
"Maybe because you think you can and get away with it. That's why."
"Well I'm not and you can phone John Ferguson if you like and ask him where I've been. There's an idea. You can tell him you found his number in my book, I'm not home yet and you're getting worried. That'll sort this stupid argument out, won't it?"
 Hannah thought about what I'd said for a moment and then smiled at me and asked me if I was ready to eat. "You or supper" I asked. "Both" she replied.

Late in the evening after Hannah had insisted on great make up sex, I lay next to her as she slept and thought about her sudden jealous outbreak and change in temperament and what could have brought it on. I had been to more than thirty houses in this gardening phase of my life and met with more than thirty ordinary people, couples, families and experienced all kinds of things from being welcomed through their front doors and into their gardens. There was a woman in her forties who told me all about her husband, how he had been a school teacher for a number of years after they had met at university and he'd turned into a shrivelled up little man who wouldn't say boo to a goose and then got out and started his own advertising agency and transformed himself but didn't satisfy her. Another in her mid-forties said her husband was always away in London on business and she knew that most of it was being done in a hotel room, flat on his back with his pretty young assistant and she was looking for some revenge sex and another, I'd say mid-thirties, came into the back garden one morning and told me I was covered in dirt from the garden and would I like to join her in the bath tub.

There were two others I could think of where the invitation for sex was a tad less obvious but the hint of invitation was there if I took up on it and on every occasion I gently manoeuvred my way around the subject with humour, not once, not for one second considering it. I definitely would have with the bath tub lady if I was unattached but I'm not and that's what I bought into with Hannah and it's easy to deal with and I wouldn't do anything that would hurt her or damage what we have together.

I met up with Harry the next morning and told him about his evening phone call getting Hannah all worked up and that I had been back to see John and he told me that he was glad I did in a way but that he just had to get away from the property. He said he can't be around people with limbs missing and that it makes him physically ill and that I can but he's never going back to that house again, no matter how much he'd get paid. I think his compassionate button was switched off.

CHAPTER 16

The days were getting shorter and there weren't a lot of hours in one to finish a proper day's gardening work and I was spending more time at the library reading or sourcing leads for companies I might be interested in applying to and I was beginning to think about Christmas and my first one with Hannah. She'd gone home for a weekend with her parents and had met up with her younger sister, Caroline, in Glasgow where she had started a nursing diploma and had been suffering from homesickness. She'd made friends with some of her class mates in first year but was missing home and Hannah thought it was the ideal time to help her and spend some time together with her mum and dad.

I met Hannah at the station early Sunday night and went back to the flat where I'd cooked a pasta meal for us to warm up later and made sure I had a good white wine in the fridge. She was only away for two nights but I'd missed her. I opened the wine and poured a glass for ourselves and sat down next to Hannah on the couch. "How were your parents and Caroline?"
"They were all okay. It was great being back in my old bedroom and bed and I was thinking of you a lot and wishing you were there. Nothing's changed and I think it did Caroline a lot of good being back because when I said bye to her in Glasgow this afternoon, she actually looked quite glad to be back and she saw that she's not missing

anything back home. I told her that she must come through to Edinburgh on her day off and Susan and I can take her out for lunch and show her the town. She's never been to Edinburgh and she'd like to see it."

"And your dad? He was okay was he?"

"Yes, but I didn't talk to him much. He didn't say anything bad about you but he did remind me about the coffee table Jimmy made for us two years ago and how good he is with woodwork. He might be a carpenter on houses and buildings but he can do other stuff like furniture quite well when he puts his mind to it. His mum still speaks to my mum quite a lot and I bumped into her at the shops. I couldn't believe it when she told me he'd gone to New Zealand. I never thought he'd leave. He has an uncle who moved there in the sixties and he's helped him hook up with a job and everything and he's working on a building site. His mum says all the workers on the site are alcoholics and so he doesn't socialise with them after work and hasn't made any friends but that he's glad he moved and sold up everything here. She told me that I hurt him very badly and she always considered me like a daughter to her and that I should have married Jimmy."

"Interesting news. She considers you as a daughter and wants you to marry her son. I'll give him credit for New Zealand though. I never expected to hear news like that. New Zealand? It's a couple of islands with great rugby and weather like here. I seriously doubt all those workers are all alcoholics. They probably all go for a cold beer at their local after work to unwind. That's all. That's what I'd do."

"Well you would wouldn't you" Hannah said laughing.

"Anyway" she continued "I'm happy for him and I hope he does very well there and finds himself a girlfriend."
"Doubt it" I replied.
"Why, do you think he's that bad?"
"Listening to all the things you've said about him, yes. He hasn't a clue how to treat people and I can't see a Kiwi woman accepting his bullshit and control freak ways and not drinking Fosters or whatever Kiwi beer they've got there and not wearing lipstick to make him happy. And to top it all, she never gets to orgasm. I can't see a Kiwi putting up with that."
Hannah looked a little miffed at my answer to her question, took a sip of her wine. "Maybe he's got a point. Maybe I shouldn't be drinking this. I hardly had a drink before I met you and now look at me. I drink wine at least three times a week and when I meet Marion I take a puff of her joint. You could say you're a bad influence on me."
"You could" I replied "and you could say you are on me. I'd never had all night sex before I met you. Didn't think I was capable of it. I'm practically a vegetarian now, you eat so little meat, my clothes are too baggy and don't fit me anymore and I hardly read these days. I definitely think about other people more, I try and show kindness to strangers and would go out of my way to help one if I could and I'm sleeping better than I used to. Hang on a second, those are good influences you've had on me."
"Well because you're such a bad influence on me and I'm such a good one on you, let's have another glass of wine and take it to bed."

We were in the last week of November and Hannah was meeting Caroline off the train and she and Susan had planned an early lunch and an afternoon on Princes Street with her. Hannah was carrying out her plan to help Caroline get over her nerves of being a first year student in a strange city and with us being only a short distance away by train, it made all the sense in the world to visit and hang out with her two older sisters. It would be like the old days but just in a different setting. Susan had broken up with Ian and had more time on her hands to spend with her sisters. She told Hannah she was bored and told Ian she'd had enough of their relationship and wanted some adventure in her life, what that would be she didn't know but she was certain she wouldn't find it with him. I'd been surprised by the news because I thought he was a thoroughly decent guy and they did look a good couple together. That plus the fact that he was likely to end up stinking rich I'd have thought must be an appealing quality.

Hannah and Caroline arrived at the flat around 5:30 in the afternoon and the plan was for Caroline to catch the nine o'clock train back to Glasgow. I was watching television with a cup of tea and got up to be introduced to Caroline. She'd turned 18 a few weeks ago and she had a similar family look to Hannah. Caroline was slightly shorter and slender built, she had long hair the same brunette colour as Hannah and she had noticeable breasts. They were fairly large and very apparent in her lamb's wool jersey and although she didn't have the astonishing prettiness of her sister, she was an attractive 18 year old. I shook Caroline's hand and told her that I'd heard hardly anything about her and that I had been looking forward to meeting her. We talked in the living room for over two hours and I said I'd go out and get us a pizza to share and left the sisters in happy animated conversation. I ordered an extra pizza in case Neil was interested when he got back and when I returned we had an evening of pizza and beer. I wasn't going to offer anything but tea, but by the time I'd returned with the meal in hand, Hannah and Caroline were already on their first beer from the fridge together.

The evening was good fun and Caroline loved joking around and making us laugh and telling us funny stories about the hospital she was attached to. Since getting together with Hannah I'd hardly spoken to a woman outside of Marion and Rachel and I found it to be quite a refreshing change to be able to chat with Caroline, knowing that it was all good with Hannah being her sister. Everything seems much easier when it's family. Neil arrived just before we were due to leave for the train and sat with us for a bit with a couple of pizza slices and his story of the day about a drunk doctor on a hospital ward added to the flavour of the evening.

We saw Caroline onto the train and Hannah seemed ecstatic about her day and how happy Caroline was. It had all worked out well and we'd all be seeing a lot more of her. We were walking back under the lights of the shop windows with all their Christmas decorations when

Hannah pinched my arm and said "Do you think she's prettier than me?"
"Who?"
"Caroline. You know who."
"No. Nobody is" I replied.

Our birthdays were two days apart in December and I wanted to organise a big get together of friends and family for Hannah's 20th. It would be kissing her teens goodbye and my turning 23 was no big deal and I hadn't done anything on my last birthday anyway but Hannah was insistent that she didn't want a party, she didn't want anyone over and had only one plan in mind. We'd give each other a card and go for a drink at the Rose Street pub we went to on the evening after our day at the zoo and that day would be the one between the two of our birthdays. We would end up celebrating neither birthday on its day but she felt the one in between would be special because it tied the two days together and this was a sign for us. It seemed an odd choice but I thought about it for a while and agreed that in a funny kind of way it made sense. This way we'd be killing two birds with one stone and maybe it was a good idea not to make a fuss and not to have others around us and just celebrate the moment together in the spot that was to be our secret place after all. It can't be our secret if twenty other people around us know all about it.

On the day of Hannah's 20th I waited for her to wake up and gave her a box with an emerald ring in it. I'd told the jeweller that the ring had to be small as Hannah had very slim fingers. I even took a photograph I had of Hannah along to show him and he had taken a good look at her hands in it and figured out that he was going to be very accurate sizing the ring for her. She opened the box and smiled and slipped the ring onto her engagement finger and said it was perfect. She loved the colour and I told her when she asked me how I managed to get such a perfect fit around her finger. The ring and my card to her had made her perfect morning and she had to get ready for work. I wasn't comfortable that there would be none of her friends from the health food shop or her sisters or my brothers to get together to at least wish her a happy birthday and although I couldn't care less about mine, the day after tomorrow, the day in between plan wasn't sounding as good an idea as I'd been talked into. But the more I thought about changing our agreement the more I understood that I had to respect her wishes and do it her way. What I would do was go out and buy a bottle of champagne and keep it in the fridge for this evening and Neil, Marion and I can toast her birthday to her and recognise that the day is a very special one for her.

We had a great evening together and drank a little too much and listened to Neil talk about some of his latest assignments and Marion about her dreams of travel. I asked him if we were cramping his style in any way and he assured me we weren't and that an old colleague of his had written to him inviting him to spend Christmas with him in London. He said that he was going to take him up on the offer and use the week after to talk to some of the newspapers down there and spend a bit of time on Fleet Street. Hannah glanced at me as if to read my reaction and I kept as straight faced as I could, knowing full well that the mere mention of the city by name could spark a fiery argument.

The following evening we went out to celebrate our joint birthdays and remember our first time here on Rose Street together. We sat at the table we were at that day and drank the same drinks and we talked for hours about the changes in our lives since agreeing to be boyfriend and girlfriend and laughed at how silly sounding it must have been to anyone listening in. Hannah said "I remember you saying something like oh what about the one you have and you wouldn't want to share me. That's so funny. You're sitting there in front of me wondering if I'm proposing that I sleep with you from Mondays to Thursdays and Jimmy from Fridays to Sundays. You must have been thinking what kind of girl you're with. I've thought about that moment and when I do it makes me laugh. There was that look on your face for a split second and I'll never forget it."
"What was my expression like?"
"Just for a tiny moment, a split one, it was shock. I think you were surprised I came out and asked you but shock first. It was so funny to see it. But I was also caught up in the moment because there was a big part of me that thought you might say no and I would be devastated if you did. I knew you liked me from the moment we were sitting on Calton Hill but I thought I'd lost it all later when you

know what happened. I told Jimmy the next morning that I hated him more than anything in the world and for the first time ever I pushed him away when he tried to hug me. He put his tongue into my mouth and I was nearly sick. He grabbed my arm tight and I kicked him as hard as I could in the shins and he backed off. He's a very strong man and I told you he beat people up. One day he took on four thugs at the same time and two had to go to hospital. People were scared of him and that's why I always felt safe out with him. If anyone looked at me he'd go crazy and threaten them. It was horrible and embarrassing at times but I felt safe. With you it's completely different. People look at me and you don't notice or don't care or you pretend you don't and I like that feeling. I don't look down when I'm with you, I look up. You've got a gentle and handsome look about you and nobody wants to cause trouble with you. Not because they're afraid of you but because you don't attract looks from people who want to cause trouble or to have a fight. They know you're not working class. You're too posh for them to bother about. I laugh when you say you've been to a self- defence class in Toronto. It sounds so girly and it wouldn't do you any good in the real world."

"Wouldn't it?"

"No it wouldn't and you know it. Not against people like Jimmy it wouldn't."

"I don't know about that. It works. It's simple when you get the hang of it. Well maybe not simple but you develop a muscle memory and you react quicker to certain things and it gives you confidence in yourself. You know you're not going to go down quickly if you're attacked but a fight could go badly wrong. The thing is to avoid them in the first place if you can and that's the best advice. You can talk yourself out of a lot of fights. The other person is human too and it's better to calm things down before resorting to the last resort and if a fight happens then self-defence is valuable."

"Ben said you were taught by the best. Who was he?"

"A guy in a club I used to play football for. He was in the same team as me and we became quite good friends. He's a lot older than me and he's a stock broker and in fact he's still got some money of mine in a gold mining company in Canada. I don't know what it's worth. They were doing quite well when I left but who knows, I haven't checked since. His name is Alex and he's an Israeli and been in Canada about twelve years now. He ran a self- defence club at night and he talked me into going one night and I ended up going along for quite a long time."

"Is it karate or judo?"

"No" I laughed "nothing like that. You don't have to be fit or get belts. It's fighting like they learn in the army. Well the Israeli army anyway. You won't have heard of it, it's called Krav Maga and it's about learning to defend yourself in a real fight. A really, really bad fight, the type you say Jimmy would give me. If I got it right I should be able to stop him in a few seconds. If I get it right. Most of these street fighters might be tough thugs but they never learned how to fight properly. They taught themselves, but you can learn a lot more from a professional. Lots."

Hannah was staring at me with a very serious expression on her face and said, "My God Tom, I had no idea."

We spent almost three hours at our table and sometimes in silence just watching people and promised we'd be back soon enough. The barman, a friendly amiable guy shouted as we left "don't leave it too long. Make it sooner rather than soon enough."

The next morning I woke to my birthday and a card from Hannah telling me how much I meant to her with a silhouette drawing she'd done of a tall, longhaired woman in high heels. She said she was taking the afternoon off work and I should try and be back at the flat around mid-afternoon and she'd wish me a happy birthday. Harry and I didn't have a lot in the way of bookings with the cold weather front hanging over the city and I told him to handle a small order he'd got on his own and I'd spend the day at the library. I was reading the business sections of the newspapers when I noticed an elderly man who had been one of the first to book Harry's gardening services and who asked us to diarise every second Friday of the month to return and maintain his sprawling lawn, flower beds and massive hedges on four sides of his acre sized property. He looked up from the newspaper he was reading, waved at me and I went over to him to greet him and shake his hand. Harry and I just knew him as Mr King and his property in the suburb of Barnton was the finest of any we had visited. I hadn't spoken to him about anything beyond his garden and although I knew he was English and lived alone in a large five bedroom house and was meticulous about his lawn and his hedge, I knew nothing at all about his life. I asked him why he had come so far to read the newspapers and he said he likes to drive into town once a week, wander around the library and have a bite of lunch and asked if I could join him.

His restaurant of choice was in the Caledonian Hotel, a grand and sophisticated setting not far from the flat and one I'd passed frequently but never frequented. The bar yes, but never the restaurant. There was a familiar face at the table next to us who I couldn't put a name to but was regularly on the BBC. We were given menus and I was looking for the least expensive option when Mr King leant over to me and said he was paying and that he'd recommend the salmon. Salmon it was and a bottle of expensive wine was ordered. Mr King was smartly dressed in a jacket and tie, he was slimly built and his full head of hair didn't hide the fact that he looked old and frail. He asked me how Harry and I knew each other, how we became friends and what my plans were for the future. I spoke to him about our school days, how we'd kept in touch when we went to separate universities and why I decided to return to Edinburgh and why I spend as much time as I do at the library looking at companies hiring and researching even those which aren't.

Lunch arrived and we were on our second glass of wine when I said "it's my birthday today and thank you very much for this invite for lunch." We touched our glasses together and he seemed delighted at the news. "What about yourself, Mr King, you seem to have done very well for yourself in life. My guess would be in business and a very successful one at that."

"I was in business, I was the chief executive for over thirty years with a private bank in the city, London that is and when I retired I decided I'd retire here where my mother was born and live a quiet life. I've been quite successful at that too. I still sit on boards of a few companies and advise on investment matters and I have to go down to London two, sometimes three times a month for meetings. I have a place in Knightsbridge and so I don't have to bother about hotels and things like that when I fly down there. I keep myself busy during the days with the financial papers and as you've probably heard from the garden, listening to classical music. You haven't lived if you haven't listened to Mozart. And Thomas, do you have a girlfriend?"

"I do. Her name is Hannah. She turned twenty the day before yesterday and we've been together almost a year. We live together now not far from here, a flat that my dad owns but doesn't live in and she's very different to anyone I've ever met. She's exceptionally pretty and when I say that, I mean that's not just coming from me. Everyone who meets her says the same thing. But it's not just that, she has a way with people, all kinds of people, anyone she meets in fact, they all end up loving her. She has a Princess Diana quality about her. I don't mean she's royalty or comes from a rich heritage or blood line, I mean she has an easy and natural way with people she meets. She doesn't fake anything and she sincerely cares about them.

What she's doing with me? Maybe that's a bit of a mystery."

"I don't think that's any mystery, Thomas. You come across as a very fine young man. When I was about your age I came across a lovely young lady, Miss Green, and I had lunch with her twice. It didn't go any further than that but I often wonder how my life would have turned out differently if it had."

The waiter had cleared the table of our plates and we were observing the tables of businessmen and women around us and I was still trying to put a name to the man from my television set and thinking what life must have been like for Mr King. He must be into his eighties and he's recalling a lunch with a woman he doesn't even refer to with her first name. It's as formal and distant as you could get and I wonder if that's as close as he ever got to a woman. He says you haven't lived if you haven't listened to Mozart and I must admit I'm a bit of a philistine when it comes to classical music but you surely haven't lived if you haven't held a beautiful woman in your arms and felt her naked body next to yours.

I asked Mr King about his career and what he thought about the importance of the character of a person in determining success and he went into a lot of detail about his experiences of honesty and integrity and the personalities of people he'd met over 50 years in banking. He'd graduated as an actuary and said it was his qualification which gave him many advantages but not all and I should read up as much as I could on the financial aspects of a company because they revealed a great deal about it and often those involved in running them were blind to some truths which needed to be faced. Although he was biased towards financial figures people and finances, he said he'd met many marketing people far more successful than himself and brilliant in business and he could see why I was interested in that side of business affairs.

We left the hotel and Mr King said he'd like to make this a regular lunch and would love to meet Hannah and that the garden would need some attention after winter but he somehow doubted I'd still need to be doing this kind of work much longer. It was a quarter to three and the sun was low in the sky and I headed back to the flat, a five minute walk away. When I walked into the kitchen there was a tall woman with blonde hair wearing high heels and nothing but a tiny apron standing in front of the stove with her back to me. A moment of shock was followed by my recognition of the perfect long lean legs and bum I was looking at. "You can hold me if you want" Hannah's voice sounded out. I stood there in stunned silence for a few seconds as she stood with her back to me stirring a pot on the stove. I walked towards her and put my arms around her waist and she turned around, putting her arms over my shoulders. "Happy birthday" said Hannah. "This is for you. This is your birthday present, birthday boy."

I'm six feet tall and I'm looking up at Hannah. She was wearing a lot of mascara and some lipstick and a blonde wig and an apron covering her stomach and breasts and nothing else. She looked down at me and started kissing me, my lips barely reaching hers. It was as if I was kissing another woman, I was cheating on Hannah and yet it was Hannah and that's okay to do. She pushed me backwards out of the kitchen, into the passage and into the living room, all the time locked in an embrace and kissing and we stood in the middle of the room caressing one another for what felt like an age until she unzipped my trousers, pulled my clothing down and pushed me onto the couch. She straddled her legs on either side of me, sitting on top and thrusting her hips. It was explosive excitement and almost too much to take and I knew I would come any moment and to my surprise Hannah let out an almighty scream as she climaxed before me. We sat there for a few minutes, her sitting on me and looking above my head out of one of the windows and not saying a word. I was hoping she would stay in that position for hours as I held her bum in my hands. She looked down at me and smiled "That was the best sex I've ever had. I'm not taking my heels or apron off until your birthday's over. I know you've got a thing for Diana. Well I'm Diana today. I borrowed the outfit from work." This beautiful long blonde haired woman looking down at me had given me the best birthday present I'd ever had and there were still eight hours left in the day. Some of them had to be in the bedroom I thought. She said she's staying like that and she will and what if Neil gets back before midnight

CHAPTER 17

It was the morning of the 19th of December and Harry and Rachel had their tickets for the rugby match at Murrayfield and Harry had told me earlier in the week that he had an extra one after his dad bailed out of going and would I like it. I already had my two and when I put it to Hannah that one of her friends from work might want to join us she jumped at it and phoned Caroline. We met Caroline off the train and the five of us walked the half hour trek to the stadium. Only Harry and I had been there before and we'd seen Scotland play many times during our time at Heriots. The crowd is a lot more civilised than you find at football matches and there's never a hint of trouble among the fans and the only thing you might find going on is the two sets of supporters drinking too much together in friendly embraces in the pubs around the west end of Princes Street the night before and the morning of the game. I've seen a lot of drunk rugby fans passing out and on one occasion two young women collapsing in front of me in the stadium but I think that must have been something to do with drugs because the paramedics who treated them were in a panic and looked distressed before they were both stretchered away.

The stadium was sold out as usual and match itself was fairly dull and Scotland won by six points. I was glad that they beat the Australians and the three women with us looked pretty pleased when the final whistle blew. I was thinking to myself I hope the brute in New Zealand had become a Wallabies fan now that he lives near as damn it down under and it occurred to me that Hannah might have a soft spot for them. She did say to me that she liked their colours and it reminded me of the Ibrox match when the Celtic fans were singing 'you'll never walk alone' with their scarves held high and she nudged me and said what a beautiful sight the colours of green and white made. We knew all the pubs on the way back into the city centre would be full and noisy and took the decision to walk in another direction where we knew of a quiet place about a mile and a half away.

The pub wasn't as quiet as we had expected but it wasn't full and we found ourselves a table and Harry and I went to the bar to order drinks. Everyone was in a good mood and it was clear that Hannah, Rachel and Caroline had enjoyed their first experience of an international rugby match. We ordered more beers and the room was getting too warm with us sitting there in jackets and scarves and it was time to take them off. Caroline was sitting directly opposite me and she removed her jacket to reveal a very tight fitting woollen top in what looked like a royal blue colour. Harry turned to Caroline and said "what are you doing wearing Rangers colours?" Harry was a Hibs fan and we'd spent years agreeing to disagree on our two teams and according to him most of the Rangers fans were bigots and it was an argument I'd long given up on continuing with him about. "It's my favourite colour" replied Caroline. And anyway I like Rangers."

"Since when?" Hannah called out above the background noise of the pub. "No you don't. I've never heard this before. You don't even follow football."

"Since I moved to Glasgow" Caroline replied. "And Tom supports Rangers."

Hannah was looking at me as if waiting for me to say something but I just sat there looking at Caroline and took a sip of my beer. I turned to the whole table and said "It's just one of those things here. People seem to either love Rangers or hate them. It's an odd one but very few fall in between. You don't find many football fans who say they couldn't care less or that they're indifferent, they come out with all kinds of insults and abuse." I think half of Scotland supports Rangers and I'm sticking to that. The other half don't and so it sounds like we have another fan in our ranks. Well done Caroline. Rachel, you don't get the same thing where you come from. I mean nobody walks around saying they hate Norwich City, do they?"

" No one I know of" replied Rachel, " maybe some people from Ipswich do but I've never met anyone like you do here but living in St Andrews, you never hear these things. They talk a lot of rugby and cricket up there, the students. The ones from England and there are lots of them."

"Too damn many" said Harry.

"And you Tom, do you like cricket?" asked Rachel

"Not particularly. Baseball, any day of the week. It's a fantastic sport and I got hooked on it in Canada. I think some of baseball must have come from cricket and if it did, the yanks made a better job of the sport. It took me a while to get into it but once I did and got to know about

the players and the rules, I was a fan of it. The Texas Rangers is my team. Hannah, you'd like it."
"I don't think so."
"I would" shouted Caroline throwing her hands above her head and stretching.

Harry was looking intently at Caroline and said "I wouldn't wear it but the colour suits you." I took Hannah's hand and asked if anyone would like another beer and all said they would except Hannah who said her glass was still full. We spent another hour in the pub, drinking and talking about Christmas in four days' time and all the women were going home to spend it with their families, Harry would be at his mum's place and wouldn't see his dad and I'd be spending it with Neil and Ben.

We caught separate buses and Hannah and I saw Caroline onto her train back to Glasgow. We were both a bit hungry and bought a couple of baked potatoes on the way home. Neil wasn't back yet and we sat watching the news on television and I sensed Hannah was being a bit quiet, less than her chirpy self at least. "So was the match as good as you expected?" I asked.
"It was okay. I enjoyed it. I know Caroline did. I saw you looking at her breasts, did you enjoy them?" I was hoping nothing of the discussion in the pub might come up to be replayed and the Rangers fan talk hadn't gone unnoticed by me but I didn't expect this question.
"Don't be silly. I wasn't looking at anything. I might have been looking at the colour of her top but that was all."

"No you weren't. You were staring at her breasts. Yes they're big but you don't need to look at them all the time. Admit it, you saw them."

"I might have glanced for a second. No, not what you're saying but yeah the colour caught my eye. You don't normally see royal blue in a jersey."

"You can sit there and deny it all you like but I saw you looking at her breasts."

"I didn't stare at her breasts, never saw them. If she took her top off and showed them to me then that would have made a lot more sense of what you're accusing me of. Look, I might have noticed I admit that but who wouldn't? I'm sure Harry and Rachel did too. She wasn't wearing a bra and I got caught a bit off guard. I bet Rachel's not interrogating Harry right now and giving him the third degree. She's your sister. She's no threat to you, why are you acting so funny about this? She's a nice looking 18 year old, she's your sister you love and we had a great day out. Isn't that enough?"

"She's my sister yes but I've always been jealous of her. My dad's always spoilt her and two years ago she goes and develops these great big pair of breasts that my boyfriend wants to look at and probably get his hands on and I'm supposed to sit here as if nothing has happened and talk about a stupid rugby game to you?"

I sat looking at Hannah and could see she was upset about this. God knows, I could hear it not just in her words but in her breaking voice and I'm getting flashbacks of the Keira evening. "Well I think you've got the best breasts I've ever seen and you're a lot prettier than either of your sisters. You got the best genes. You shouldn't be jealous of anyone. I'm sure any woman must be jealous of you and wish they had your looks. God couldn't have made you look any better than you do."

"You're just saying that to make me happy, Tom. I'm going to bed. You can sit up and have a beer and wait for Neil but I'm tired and want to sleep. I'll see you in the morning. Goodnight. Don't wake me up."

I didn't have a beer and didn't wait up for Neil to arrive back and gave Hannah enough time to fall asleep on her own before I quietly got into bed next to her in the darkness. I lay there thinking about the talk of Caroline and how much truth there was to Hannah's accusations and concluded there was very little if not none. Yes I noticed her tight blue top and her very obvious breast size and nipples and I don't think Caroline did much to not flaunt what beautiful assets she has but there's no more to it than that. I certainly don't desire her sexually, it never occurred to me to think of her as anything but Hannah's younger sister and I'm 23 years old now, she's only 18. I think I'd lock myself up for that one if the cops didn't. Hannah's jealous outbreaks are a bit suspect. She knew there was no way I'd had the time or opportunity to have had sex with Keira, she knows Caroline was not shy about wearing such a revealing item of clothing and that I've been in love with her at least since the day at the zoo and I show her my feelings for her every single day. I couldn't do more to make her feel as special as I do, could I? There have been occasions when I think to myself what a great moment or day we're having and Hannah jumps in with something which feels like a knife being twisted in my guts. It's usually something to do with the brute, some horrible memory she feels she has to share with me or break some news about him that I wish I knew nothing about. The Kama Sutra was one. Why the hell do I have to know that? All I'm left with are images of him doing things to Hannah that I wish I didn't have. If anyone should be angry lying here it's me, not her. I've never once, well not more than once mentioned anything about my old girlfriend Kristen, never a damn word about our favourite sexual positions or the size of her breasts, which were big, or how she flippantly told me one morning she was going to do a master degree in America after we graduated together and would send me postcards. I had to switch my thoughts off, had to sleep. Christmas would make things better.

Neil, Ben and I spent Christmas day together in the flat. Neil had decided against taking up the invitation to London for reasons he didn't say. Ben had two weeks off and was glad his first term at University was over. He was making friends in St Andrews but said the smallness of the town was a bit claustrophobic and he was missing the wide open feel of Toronto and the ice hockey season. Talking to him about his new surroundings, it was obvious to me that he was missing home too and it got me thinking about our home in Canada, a large beautiful wooden house set in a sprawling garden in a pretty suburb of Toronto and I was reminiscing with him about my bedroom in the basement and the friends we had on the street we'd play hockey with and mum's cooking. I was missing mum and Sam too and Neil wasn't faring much better when he talked about his visits there as we slouched in the living room eating the chicken we cooked for lunch and slugging back bottles of beer.

Ben was seeing a girl he'd met at a student party and she was from a small town in Surrey and told us how difficult it was for him to be hooked up so early in the year as there were so many good looking girls in St Andrews and most of them wanted to party and have fun and he was missing out on a lot of the party scene. "You'd never get this in Canada" he said to Neil, "their drinking age is 21 and lots get fake IDs but it's not the same as here and I've never seen so many girls out at the pubs before. I think I'll just see how things go between us but I already have someone else in mind and if not her, I wouldn't mind being single again and just having as much fun as I can. It's not as if I get this time back again." I asked him about how his marks were in classes and he said they were decent but he planned on working harder next term and I said that listening to him talking about the social scene, I had my doubts.

We decided that after we phoned mum and spoke to her and Sam we'd surprise dad in St Johns and wish them all merry Christmases and spend a small fortune phoning on the most expensive day of the year. We ended up speaking for over an hour to the family in Canada and when we put the phone down, grabbed more beers from the fridge and reminisced even more. I took a break from our talk of the family to phone and wish Hannah a merry Christmas and to her mum when she answered and Hannah told me about the presents she got and asked if I was missing her. She got my card and thanked me, asked if I got hers and said she'd write and phone and was already looking forward to getting back in the New Year. I knew she couldn't talk freely on the phone.

It was my second Hogmanay since being back in Scotland and Ben joined me in going out to some pubs with Harry, Jeff and our other old schoolmate, Ron. We drank too much and saw in the New Year together. We weren't drunk but well on our way and Ron had my ear for great big chunks of the evening. He was always a bit of a strange character going back to the age of twelve when we first met and hadn't really changed much. He was the overly studious type at school and although by no means the brightest, he tried hard and always did his best. He could have gone, but didn't, to university with the marks he got and went instead to college to study towards laboratory work and had become a bit of a technical nerd. He didn't have a girlfriend and I told him he should get himself a decent haircut and ditch his glasses for contact lenses and on the subject of hair, wash the bloody stuff more often. He was always the brunt of jokes at school about his hair, always being a bit too long and the company Shell, drilling a hole for oil in his head and he always responded by laughing louder than anyone else. The pub was noisy and we had to shout in each other's ear to be heard and Ron said "I know I've only met her the one time, but are you still seeing your girlfriend?"

"Hannah, yes I am. She's at her parents near Stranraer for the holidays." I replied.

"Tom, you're a lucky man. I'd give anything in life to have a girlfriend like that. She's the most beautiful girl I've met and she spoke to me like she'd known me for years. I couldn't believe she was so interested in anything I said but she was and she left a big impression on me. When you both left that night I thought you were the luckiest of any of us and I also thought you deserved it."

"Why do you say I deserve it?"

"You were always the kindest to me of anyone at school. Never teased me about the way I looked, you stopped me getting a good beating once, remember and I never have forgotten that and I don't think I'd have the maths marks without your help. You deserve your good fortune and you look good together. You're both good looking and you look just right together. When you introduced me to Hannah I thought here we come, a real bitch, too full of herself, too caught up in her looks and she turned out to be the finest woman I've ever spoken to."

"Hell, Ron, big compliments there. Thanks. I don't remember stopping you getting a hiding from someone. You sure it was me? Hannah's all those things you say and more if you got to know her better but she's human like the rest of us. She's not perfect and who the hell is? We'll get together for a night when she's back."

"My only advice is don't screw it up" Ron went on "If I had her as a girlfriend and she left me, I'd kill myself. There's no question I would."

The five of us saw 1982 in and wound our way home and Ben was in one hell of a good mood with the beer taking effect. As we walked home he said that he saw this year as being our best one ever and predicted that by its end I would have found the job of my dreams and would be married and he would be top of his class and with that other girl he was keen on.

CHAPTER 18

Hannah was back at work and I was at the library writing letters to some companies I'd been doing as much research on as I could find. Mr King had phoned me earlier in the week to ask for my address and said he would be sending me some public papers on some companies he knew well and he thought I would benefit from analysing them and looking for areas of strength and weakness. I had written to a few London based companies with Edinburgh and Glasgow branches and was hopeful on at least two of them responding. The funny thing was that I hadn't exactly been getting the responses I'd been hoping for the past few months and yet I felt I was making progress and not feeling any despondency at all. I was just becoming more and more determined.

I got back to the flat feeling good about a bunch of flowers I'd stopped to buy Hannah from a florist around the corner from the library, the first time in my life I'd bought flowers and saw that Hannah was home early. It happened from time to time and she had simply done all that was needed for the day. I found her sitting on the couch holding something in her hands. She looked up at me as I entered the living room, looked at the bouquet in my hand, asked if I was feeling guilty and handed me an envelope addressed to me and said "I saw this earlier and noticed it was stamp marked London. It's for you. I knew you'd be writing to London and I told you ages ago what I thought of that idea. This is also for you. I'm not going to post it though." I looked at the second envelope and read only the name part of it written Jimmy and the address ending in New Zealand. I felt a surge of blood rush instantly to my face, my heart began pumping fast and I felt an anger I'd never felt in my life and was struggling to breathe. My hand was shaking as I looked down again at the letter. "How did you get his address" I asked.

"I phoned his mum when I was down there and wished her a merry Christmas and she gave it to me."

"What the hell is this?" I shouted at Hannah. "How can you do this?"

"I wasn't going to write it, but if you're going to write to London. I'm not posting it. I wanted you to know that I wrote it, that's all."

"Well if you're prepared to write it then I'm prepared to post it." I was struggling badly to contain my sudden surge of anger and I sounded out of breath. I turned round and headed out the flat, throwing the flowers on the floor before slamming the door as I left. I'd never slammed a door shut in my life. By the bottom of the stairwell I needed to stop and bent over trying to catch my breath again. Adrenaline was surging through my body, the letter in my hand like a red flag to a bull and my body was shaking. I managed to compose myself a bit with a few deep breaths and made my way onto the street. I was walking fast and ran across Lothian Road narrowly missing oncoming traffic and went straight to the teller in the post office and asked for the right stamp. My hands were still shaking as I struggled to find the change and I was getting a concerned look from the lady handing over the stamp and sticker saying airmail. I had to get rid of this letter in my hand as if I was holding a package on fire. I licked the stamp and sticker, banged them both down onto the envelope and tossed it into the post box.

Where could I go now I thought? I had to keep walking, I had to release this adrenaline pumping through my body, had to find a way of calming my breathing. The Meadows and a bit of grass lawn will give me some comfort and it was both far enough and close enough for me to keep my brisk walk. When I arrived I was out of breath and sat down on a bench on my own. I held my head in my hands and looked down at the grass between my feet. What has Hannah done? Why did she do this to me, why did she seek out his address, why write, why thrust it into my hand and why did I post it? I could have read it, tried to steam it open like you see in a movie before sending it, could have read it and not posted it, could have just ripped it up when she gave it to me. I could have done anything but I reacted without even thinking .The letter represented the ultimate insult that she could possibly have given me and she knows full well and knew what she was doing and knew how I'd react. She knew I would take up her challenge and I'd post it.

I was beginning to calm down a bit and my mind's racing thoughts slowing down. He'll get the letter and I'm guessing that she gave our address and he'll write. That's the good part because he's barely literate and the response should be interesting to read. She'll realise the error of her ways and the sheer stupidity of writing to him and of what she's done. On the other hand, maybe I did over react, perhaps she had absolutely no intention of posting it and handing it to me was her test of me. If I tore it up, it showed I cared and if I didn't, I didn't care. But once she'd written it and addressed it, the letter wasn't mine to decide upon, it didn't belong to me and my role in the string of events was to post the damn thing. She must write it and I must post it. I even managed to laugh at myself when I thought of how idiotic Hannah was, what chain of events she's set in motion and what price she could end up paying. Less than an hour ago my life was in complete harmony with the world and everything was happening as it should and in an instant it's gone. What felt right now feels wrong. One moment of misunderstanding about a letter addressed from London, a stupid reaction without rationality or thought and now this. What the hell just happened?

I reflected over and over again about the timing, the handing over of the first letter, Hannah's words, the second letter, her words again. The letter from London, I hadn't opened it, it was to a firm with an office here. It wasn't about moving to London for work, the work is right here. I would never have gone behind her back and secretly arranged for the rest of my life without her in it or moved to London with the intention of finding a gorgeous female colleague to run away with. That thinking of Hannah's was sheer lunacy and I told her in as many words that I'd never be pinched from her, never. I'd calmed down and for the first time noticed I was sitting in the middle of the park in pitch darkness and knew I had nowhere else to go but home and home to Hannah. My anger had gone and was replaced by a deep sadness and I felt it both for myself and for Hannah. I was actually feeling very sad about the thought of her sadness just as I always had and this time there was nothing I could do to take it away. I couldn't tell her it was alright or not to worry because it wasn't and there was a lot to be worried about.

I got up and began walking back and I knew what had happened wasn't just a fight between us and it wasn't something we could brush away, it cut right into the heart of our relationship and it involved the brute once again. When I arrived at the flat, Hannah was in our room with the door closed and I went into the kitchen and took a beer from the fridge and sat down in the living room. There was a single lamp on and I opened the letter from London. It was written by one of the senior managers of the company and thanked me for my interest and said they were unable to consider me for any position in their Edinburgh office due to company cutbacks and the economic slowdown the country was experiencing. I crumpled the piece of paper up and chucked it across the room. I was alone with my thoughts and glad that Neil wasn't back and I knew he'd quickly pick up on the gloomy atmosphere of the room if he did walk in and I wasn't ready to walk into my own bedroom and find Hannah still awake. I was stuck on the couch with a beer in my hand and my despondent thoughts for company.

There were times when my thoughts were great company to keep and I resolved many problems in my life having a mental dialogue with myself but tonight they were going to be of no value and there was no chance of a bright and sunny conclusion on the horizon. It was a desperate situation which made no sense. I listed all the positives which Hannah could derive from how events may unfold and I came up with one and that was giving New Zealand the benefit of the doubt in that its weather was better than Scotland's. I tried to look at things as objectively as I could possibly look at them and I couldn't come up with one positive she gets out of this. I wouldn't come out with one either and if we're both going to lose so horribly what is the sense and where is the logic to this. I thought of every angle I could to find where I could have gone wrong or simply messed things up. I met a friend's girlfriend's sister for a couple of hours and maybe said a dozen words to her and I glanced for a moment or two at her younger sister's bust in a woollen jersey. Beyond that I thought again about London and I gave her no reason to doubt me or worry that we were about to pack our bags and jump on a train to Kings Cross Station. I don't have a career is a definite possibility of motive but surely she can see I've been doing a lot of work to rectify that and it's only a matter of a bit of time before a breakthrough comes. Maybe it's the glasses of wine or the beers and she thinks I drink too much. I have been drinking more than I used to but there are often five days in the week when I don't have anything, I never crave the stuff, I might have two or three glasses and a couple of beers on a weekend but I never get drunk. In Arran we did share a bottle of wine each evening which might have worried her but we were on holiday together for the first time and she enjoyed it just as much as me and it's the only time in my life I've done that.

I sighed at my thoughts and looked at the bottle of beer in my hand thinking it could be you but it's more likely me. She once said to me that I think I know everything but I don't. Who likes a person who thinks they know it all? 'No one' is the answer but I don't think I know it all, I don't think I know much at all. I don't have answers to life's questions and I might have opinions but surely that's okay and if I didn't then that would be ten times worse. I told her I don't believe in the Bible and that could be damning and lurking in the back of her mind. Points against me, but I've told her I respect those who do. It can't be that, surely. Or maybe she feels I've pushed her too much, told her she can be anything she wants and she doesn't want to feel she can. Or maybe it's not me, it's her and she has problems unresolved with her dad and her sister or deeper than that and holds memories of the brute she can't let go, ones she might have had when she was 15 or 16. They would have to be ones she never shared with me in the middle of the night because every single one of the hundreds she did share was either horrific or slightly less horrific.

The sound of the bedroom door opening distracted me from my thoughts and Hannah appeared in her nightgown and asked me if I posted the letter. I nodded and she said I could come to bed whenever I'm ready and try not to wake her up.

I woke early and put the kettle on. I hadn't slept well and felt uneasiness in the pit of my stomach and dryness in my mouth and needed a mug of tea badly. Hannah walked in and took a mug out of the cupboard for herself and asked me if I was okay. "Not really" I replied. "I didn't sleep much."

"It was just a letter. Nothing will come of it. You shouldn't have posted it. I said I wasn't going to."

"Just a letter" I replied. "It wasn't just a letter. It was a knife in my heart and then twisted. To anyone else in the world, yeah it would have been just a letter but not one to him."

"Please don't be cross with me. I didn't mean to hurt you and I can't bear seeing you upset like this. I just asked him how he was doing. I saw the letter from London and got angry with you. And Caroline likes you. I asked her when we were home and she said she likes you and you make her laugh. You don't make me laugh, do you?"

"I don't suppose you mentioned you were living with me in the letter did you?"

"Nothing will come of it, Tom. Please don't be angry with me."

We drank our tea together in silence and Hannah showered and got ready for work. I sat where I was and listened for the front door to close before getting up and going through to the bathroom sink and throwing up the mug of tea I'd just had. I showered and washed the sickness off my mouth and stood staring at myself in the mirror as I brushed my teeth. I looked at the person in it and strained myself to look deep into his eyes to see if I could see any hint of happiness and all I saw was a deep sadness and despair.

The rest of the week passed slowly and Hannah had insisted that we put our differences aside and try harder to make each other happy. She would wake me up in the middle of the night to make love and little by little things settled down between us. It was good having Neil around and although we didn't talk about what had happened I knew he sensed all was not well and the atmosphere in the flat had changed. He took us out for a couple of beers one evening and we listened to a band playing live music and enjoyed each other's company, the sound of the music being played as we talked. The following evening we played cards and laughed a lot at Neil's jokes and the terrible playing hands he was dealt and retired early to bed. It was what seemed like the middle of the night when I was awoken by what sounded like a distant ringing and it was soon followed by a knock on our door and Neil calling to Hannah that there was a phone call for her. She got out of bed and ran to the living room and I could hear her faint voice as she answered. I couldn't hear what Hannah was saying and I was hoping there was nothing serious involving her family.

After what seemed like ten minutes talking, Hannah came back into the bedroom and switched on the light and stood by the door. "Is everything alright I asked?"

"That was Jimmy. He asked me to marry him."

"He asked you to marry him? What did you say?"

"I said I'd think about it." The only thing which registered with me was that she said she would think about spending the rest of her life having sex with him. I started to cry. My crying worsened into sobbing, deep shuddering sobs and tears were rolling down my face. I held my head in my hands and couldn't control my shuddering and heaving sobbing. Hannah sat next to me on the bed and put her arm around me. I couldn't remember the last time I cried and was thinking of a time when I was five years old and it was my first day of school in Kenya and I watched my mum's car driving off, leaving me alone with my first ever teacher. This isn't me, I couldn't recognise this person who was crying and I couldn't stop. I got up and went to the bathroom for tissues and ran some water into the basin and bent over it and wept.

Neither of us slept after the phone call and Hannah thought I should phone Ben and spend a night or two with him in St Andrews and she would think about the call she'd received and answer his next one in a day or two. She needed time alone. I didn't even argue about it, didn't question her suggestion. I phoned Ben and arranged to meet him in the early afternoon at the train station in St Andrews and left with a sleeping bag of Neil's.

The train was full and there were a lot of university students or what looked like students on it and I sat across from a woman about my age and stared down at the floor between us. When I did look up to glance at the passing countryside I noticed her looking at me. It was a look of concern I thought. It was as if she could see my sorrow. Ben met me at the station and we walked back to his digs at the student res and he showed me his bedroom floor I'd be sleeping on. He kept asking me what the hell was going on and I kept telling him I didn't know. We went to one of the student hang out pubs on Market Street and Ben ordered two pints of lager. "What's wrong Tom? Tell me what she said, tell me what's happening."

"Her ex has asked her to marry him. He's moved to New Zealand and he phoned last night and asked her to bloody well marry him." I was looking into my glass of beer, I couldn't look Ben in the eye and I was doing everything I could to calm my breathing and not cry. I could feel tears welling in my eyes and I could feel my throat tightening as if someone had a fierce grip around it. I felt a deep pain like an agonising knot in the pit of my stomach. I knew this was not good.

"What did she say to him?" asked Ben

"She'd think about it. He's phoning her back today or tomorrow."

"She won't say yes, she won't do it. She can't. Tom, she must be off her flaming rocker, she won't leave you."

"I don't know. I think she will. I don't know why and the thought of losing her is too much for me right now Ben. I don't know how I'm going to cope. I gave her everything I had of me, everything and it feels like I'm losing part of me. It feels like I've lost it. I don't even recognise me anymore. It's not me, this person in front of you. I don't know what I did wrong."

"Tom, I've never seen you like this. She won't do it. She'd be mad to. I just can't see it. None of this makes any sense. Am I missing something?"

"No. You're not missing anything. She worries that I might go to London and she thinks I've got something for her sister, her younger one. I don't and never gave her a reason to think that. If I had to go to London I'd only go if she came with me. I'd have asked her to marry me but I can't do that now. I can't ask her now. It would just seem

I'm doing so because he did. I couldn't now. I couldn't go through the rest of my life wondering if she's wondering what if she married Jimmy. I couldn't live like that, I couldn't live with myself. Every plan I had has gone. I thought I'd spend the rest of my life with her and I didn't even make a year. Tomorrow's the anniversary of our first year together and I miss it by a day. Exactly a year, can you believe it? You couldn't make it up. A year ago she asked me to be her boyfriend and phoned this guy up and dumped him and on exactly the same date tomorrow I'll phone her up and she'll dump me and say to him she'll marry him."

I looked up from my beer I hadn't touched and could see the tension in Ben's face. "There must be something we can do Tom. Neil can speak to her. Marion can call her or go round and talk to her, I could phone her. There must be something we can do before it's too late. Can't we try and see her tonight. We'll catch a train back."

"It's no use Ben. Thanks for your offer of help but it won't help. She says she has to think about it but I know her mind's made up. She's already decided and she'll say yes and no one is going to make a difference to her decision. It wouldn't be good if a year from now she and I aren't getting on because of all this and she says Ben talked me out of it and it's what I wanted, would it?"

"You're right. It wouldn't. I see your point. There's no solution. It's out of everyone's hands but hers. She's making a terrible mistake and she'll regret it for the rest of her life. Why does she want to go back to him? It's absolute craziness. I can't believe what I'm hearing. Let's leave our beer. I've got some extra gear back at my room. Let's go for a run. One like we used to in Toronto. Come on, I'll beat you again." We went back to Ben's room and put on some shorts, old t shirts and I got a pair of his old running shoes a size too small for me and we headed out onto the streets jogging until we hit the main road north and started running. We turned back five miles out of town and did the same thing back, sprinting the final two blocks to the res. Ben did finish first and I sat on the ground completely and totally shattered. I hadn't run like that in over a year and my legs and chest were in agony. I was breathing heavily and after a few minutes with my head between my knees I could feel the first pangs of deep pleasure and noticed the ache in the pit of my stomach gone. I gave Ben the thumbs up as he stood next to me leaning against a garden wall catching his own breath and clearly, totally spent.

We went to a party in the evening and I met Ben's girlfriend, Cathy from Surrey, a very friendly young blonde haired girl with beautiful blue eyes and the three of us got together with a group of their friends. The flat was packed out and the students were singing along to music, dancing and all having a great time like students partying do. I was introduced to a few but the noise around was too loud to have any kind of a conversation and I stood back from what was happening around me with a beer in my hand and watched the joy and happiness and drunken fun unfold around me. I was suddenly aware that I wasn't part of it and that those years were behind me and I needed to get away and sit somewhere quiet. I told Ben I'd see him back at the room and left. I went for a walk towards the golf course and onto the beach. It was a cold night and there was a bit of a breeze but it didn't bother me. I sat down and looked out towards the sea and thought of the day I'd be facing tomorrow and wondering how I would be able to deal with it and I compared my fate to those happy, smiling, fun loving students at the party I'd just left. That was me two years ago and it suddenly seemed like another lifetime.

Ben never came back from the party and I slept in his bed rather than in Neil's sleeping bag on the floor and when I awoke I thought immediately of the call I'd be making to Hannah and wondering if she had received another middle of the night one from New Zealand. Doesn't the brute know the time difference and account for it? Surely he has enough brain cells to figure out a decent time to call instead of waking someone up in Scotland at three in the morning I thought to myself. Whichever way it goes, today would define the rest of my life. It would change its direction one way or another. It was as if I was standing at a cross road not knowing if I'll take a left or a right turn and not knowing what lies down either. It would probably be the most important day of my life.

I couldn't eat any breakfast and hadn't eaten anything yesterday when I thought about it and I was surprised that I didn't feel any hunger but I thought I could manage a cup of coffee somewhere in town and found a small café to sit for a while. I bought a newspaper and read through the headlines and sports pages before going to the finance ones and looking for any positive signs. Ben had suggested a game of golf today but I told him I wasn't in any mood for it and would probably hit shots into the sea, the way I last played. My thoughts drifted back again to mum and Sam and I wished I was back there. I wished I could be sitting in the kitchen talking to mum about my university lecturer, my football games and car engine troubles like a teenager again. This grown up world came too fast too soon and I don't think I'm up for it. God, I thought, imagine if mum and worse still, Sam, had known I cried the other day. How embarrassing must that be? I couldn't even understand it. I don't know where those tears came from or why. I didn't think I could cry, didn't think I was capable of it and yet it just happened. It was like turning on a tap. The humiliation of the whole thing and there was Hannah to see it for herself, first hand, how weak she must have thought I must be. I was a pathetic specimen of a human being and felt deeply ashamed. Who is this person who is me?

I went back to see if Ben was around and the town was beginning to wake up from a long night of partying and recovering hangovers were passing me in the streets. There was no sign of Ben and so I sat on his bed and found one of his books to read and spent a few hours immersed in one of his first year business studies journals and it was good enough to take my mind off the troubles I had. It was early in the afternoon when my brother pitched up and he apologised, saying he'd spent longer than he planned with Cathy. I brushed it off saying I was the intruder and shouldn't be dumping my problems on his young shoulders. We went for a walk along the beach together, not saying much and occasionally trying to push the other into the surf and laughing. It helped pass the time and it felt good to be together again. We both felt it. It was getting dark and I said I'd call the flat and find out if Hannah had come to a decision on her marriage proposal and the direction of our lives and Ben said he'd wait for me in the pub we were in yesterday.

My hand was shaking as I dialled our number and Hannah answered almost straight away. "Hello Hannah, it's me. Did he phone" I asked her.

"Yes" she replied. "What did you say to him" I asked again.

"I said yes."

I turned my back away from the pedestrians passing the telephone booth and wept. I was welling up badly and tears were running freely and I couldn't talk. Hannah went on "I phoned my mum and told her and she said I must come home straight away. She said it's not fair on Jimmy for me to stay here any longer. I phoned Caroline and she's coming through after college to help me pack. She says it's silly for you not to be here to say goodbye. She wants you here to say bye to us. I'll cook lunch."

"I'll pick up something and I'll cook" I replied. "You'll be busy. I'll catch a train in the morning."

I found my way back to the pub Ben was at and we sat together drinking a pint of the same lager I didn't drink yesterday in silence. There was a tear in his eye too and his only words were to say how sorry he was for me.

I cooked a meal of rice with onions and tinned salmon while Hannah and Caroline packed in the bedroom and we ate lunch together with Neil. It wasn't nearly as sombre as I had expected it to be and Neil was excellent in guiding the conversation onto mundane matters and news is always a good subject for that. We'd just put our plates down when Hannah asked if she could speak to me privately in the bedroom. I closed the door behind me and turned around to see Hannah take off her dress and underclothes and standing naked said "make love to me." She lay down on the bed and I pulled my jeans and shorts down around my ankles and got on top of her. It wasn't making love, it was quick, pure sex and I came quickly. Hannah didn't. I pulled my jeans back up and sat on the edge of the bed while Hannah dressed and held my head in my hands and silently wept. She sat next to me with her right hand between my legs and kissed me on the side of my face. "I'm sorry Tom. I'm really sorry. You'll be fine" she whispered to me. She opened the door and called

Caroline to say her good bye to me and they collected Hannah's packed bags and left.

CHAPTER 19

The week after Hannah left was what I thought would be the worst of my life and it was bad, but it turned out things got worse with each passing day. I lost my appetite completely and when I tried to force myself to eat I would be okay for a few minutes and then retch horribly. My stomach was in a constant grip of pain, far more painful than the knot in the pit of your stomach feeling and it felt as if something was choking me and my throat felt raw. My mouth was dry and I had to carry a hiker's water bottle in my hand most of the time. I couldn't sleep properly and when I did it was a light one and lacked the depth my brain and body required. There were mornings I woke in a pool of sweat, the sheets drenched and my heartbeat racing as though I'd just run the four minute mile and more than once I thought I was having a heart attack, the ache in my chest was so severe. I thought of Hannah all the time and missed her touch, her smell, her words, her body and her smile most of all. My God, how I missed her smile. I missed her company and lying next to her in bed in the middle of the night. I always slept with my left arm over her and now there was nothing there but an empty part of the bed and my life. I craved proper sleep because that was the only part of the day I could find any peace but the harder I tried to sleep the more I stayed awake. It was a vicious cycle I couldn't break and I knew that my mind was being affected badly. I tried counting my blessings and being grateful for them and rationalising all the good my family gave me and how much I owed each and every one of them but it all failed. I just saw no point in tomorrow. It wasn't just my mind I was worried about, my body wasn't getting the nutrition it needed and my ribs were becoming more prominent by the day.

I discovered that my best therapy was walking and I found it almost impossible to sit still in a room. I needed to move. I had to get outside and walk and I developed a five mile plan with a route which included Princes Street Gardens, Holyrood Palace and the Royal Mile and did it once and often twice a day, sometimes in the middle of the night when the entire city was asleep. There were moments when the pain would subside but they were brief and the pain would always return. I tried to fix my problem by trying to make sense of why Hannah had left and wished every day that the phone would ring and she would say it was all a mistake and she was catching the next train back but when the phone did ring it was never her. I remembered how good I felt after my run with Ben in St Andrews and decided I'd run three times a week up and around Arthurs Seat, a difficult and long uphill part and the flat and downhill allowed me to generate a bit of speed and kick in the endorphins I wanted to flood my bloodstream. Most of all, I just wanted to experience a different kind of pain, ones in my legs, my lungs, anywhere away from the pit of my stomach. The problem I had with my recovery plan was that I wasn't getting the food I needed and my energy levels were falling each week. I couldn't drink a glass of wine and even the thought of beer made me queasy and my only real sustenance was my Earl Grey tea and my water.

I was alone in the flat one afternoon listening to Springsteen's The River. My thoughts were that my future had no hope at all and I couldn't see a way out of my life's crisis when the phone rang. It was Hannah. She sounded happy and told me she and her mum had been to Glasgow to see some Home Office officials about her passport and travel documents and she had her ticket paid for by Jimmy and would be leaving for New Zealand in four weeks' time. The words and the news didn't make me feel sadder than I already did but I was surprised that I felt a little better just hearing her voice. We talked for around quarter of an hour before she said she had to hang up but before doing so said if I wanted to, I could phone her on Wednesdays at 3 o'clock in the afternoon. Her dad was always out of the house having tea with his brother, a regular occurrence of the past five years. My mood had lifted slightly and I thought that maybe the idea of making a weekly call might help me.

Within hours of the call I was feeling as bad as ever and decided to take one of my twice daily showers. At my worst ebb I'd sit under the shower and let the warm water wash away the salt from the tears covering my face. I couldn't believe that crying could happen so easily and so spontaneously and I wondered where all the moisture for them came from. Surely it must run out and the source dry up but it didn't. In the shower I was safe and hidden from outside world and the sound of the running water drowned out any evidence of my desperate plight. The shower became my sanctuary.

Neil was getting increasingly worried about me and could hear me awake most nights and see before him that I was losing a lot of weight I couldn't really afford to and he called Marion to come around and help. She arrived one morning without letting me know beforehand and walked immediately into my room. It was a mess with clothing strewn around the floor and the first thing she did was rip the bedsheet and covers and pillow cases from the bed and bundle them into a bag. "They need washed and they're covered in Hannah's scent. Put all those clothes into the washing machine right now Tom. Open the window and I'm taking these photographs with me." My framed one of Hannah caught in the early evening sun at the top of Arthurs Seat was my favourite and I asked Marion for it back. She refused and said she'd keep it safe for me. She got out the hoover and vacuumed the floor before saying she was taking the bedroom linen to the laundromat and would be back in the afternoon.

When Marion arrived back, she remade the bed with the fresh linen and asked me to join her in the kitchen for a talk. "I've mixed these shakes for you to drink. Just try a few sips at each meal time and work your way up each day until you can manage a full glass. They've got everything in them your body needs. You have to get the nutrition into your system Tom, there are no arguments. You have to do it. Please tell me how bad things are, how you're trying to deal with this."

"Look Marion, thanks for all of this. I'm feeling pretty low, that's all."

"It's not just low Tom. I'm shocked at how thin you've got. Neil says you're not sleeping either and that's a really bad sign."

"Not sleeping but disturbed, yes. I've been doing a lot of walking and running and I'm bound to lose weight. The eating problem is worrying me, I admit. I've got no appetite and I've tried to force myself but I just bring most of it up. There's something wrong with my stomach and I know it's not a bug or flu. That part I can't understand but I know a doctor can't help with words of 'there's plenty of fish in the sea'. I couldn't bear to hear that bullshit from someone who knows nothing of what it's like, who's never gone through this. A doctor who married their childhood sweetheart could never understand. No book teaches this. A prescription won't help. I know medication won't solve my problem. I don't give my heart away easily to anyone and I did to Hannah and she broke it and she knows she did and I'm now paying the price and the price is a great one. I can't sugar coat it and pretend anything other than it's a price I have to pay and I don't know if I'm strong enough to face it. When I go to bed at night I don't know how I can get through tomorrow. I was lucky enough to meet Hannah and unlucky enough to lose her. There's not a moment in the day I feel any form of happiness and it's a lonely feeling, just pure physical and mental agony. As for appetite, it's like asking a person who's just had a three course meal to eat again an hour later. They can't. I don't know where my feeling for hunger has gone. It's not there." Marion spent the afternoon talking with me and when she left I felt a surge of relief that I was able to talk to someone and let them know a little of what I was feeling.

A week later I was sitting on the same bench in Princes Street Gardens I'd sat on the day of my resignation from the shop last year and looked at a cover of a book I had been carrying with me but never read and reflected on my phone call to Hannah the day before. I told her I wasn't doing too well, not coping with life and that I was troubled by the thought that this somehow wasn't supposed to have happened and she replied to me that if we were supposed to meet and be together forever, then it would happen. I didn't really want to respond but I told her that I had lost almost every shred of dignity I had and that my dad had always told me and my brothers to go through life with self-respect and that I had to try and cling to that little bit I had left. We'd never again be together from the day she landed in New Zealand, whether it was written in the stars or not, whether we were supposed to be together or not. I asked her to understand that after she had been to bed with the brute that there was no turning back and we would never be together again and that I had accepted this and hoped she would respect my feelings on it. I told her I'd never be able to live with myself if we did, that the last sliver of regard I held for myself would be flushed well and truly down the drain. She said she understood and changed the subject to how she had counted the past few days in the hope of my phone call and how she longed to hear my voice and I thought, does Hannah maybe have something wrong with her and she's delusional? I know she can be volatile and go crazy but she sounded out of touch with reality now.

I noticed an elderly women sit down next to me and smiled at her. She asked me what I was reading and we chatted a little. Her eyes were almost a silver colour and she wore a friendly warm smile. She introduced herself as Mrs Williams and asked why I wasn't working or in class and where my girlfriend was. I told her I had neither a job nor a girlfriend and that I had recently gone through a breakup. She wanted to know why and said she had a family living all the way in Southampton which she saw twice a year and she loved to talk. I explained that my story was a long one and she responded by saying she had all the time in the world to listen and so I began to tell her about Hannah and how beautiful she is and how people warm to her and as I talked it felt as if I was talking to myself. The words flowed and I concluded over an hour later that my greatest fear now was my future and that there was no hope in it. I told her that on a normal day it was like sitting in front of a black wall with a glass of water in my hand and on a good one the wall was a dark grey but still with my glass of water in hand. There was neither colour nor flavour left in my life.

Mrs Williams sat quietly the whole time and after allowing me to suppress my tears said "oh my, what a dreadfully sad story, how dreadfully sad. I'm so terribly sorry to hear that. There is hope. Life has a way of giving it to you. You might still be together again one day." "No, I couldn't do that. It would be a lie" I replied.

"Why would it be?"

"Because it would never be the same, it would always be less and I would have to go through life living a lie to myself that it was okay to live with and I can't do that. Maybe it's pride but it's all I've got left and to be honest there's not much of it remaining. If I lose that I lose everything." I looked at the elderly lady next to me and thought to myself she's like Granny Miller, she had youth and beauty, did she ever experience anything like this ?

"And you Mrs Williams? Did you ever face sadness in your life, the feeling that you can't go on?"

"I did. My fiancé died in the war, the first war. I was 18 years old at the time. His body was never found and I went through a very difficult time. But I met a man, years later and we married and he was very good to me and we were married for nearly fifty years before he passed away."

"I'm sorry to hear that."

"I still think of that young man, even today. The heart's a very sensitive thing."

We talked for over another hour and I offered Mrs Williams help to her bus stop but she assured me she was fine to do it on her own and we promised each other to look out for one another on the park bench each time we visited the gardens. I walked back to the flat abandoning my daily walking route and noticed I felt a little better. It felt so easy to talk to her, a complete stranger and I told her feelings I had I'd never have told a friend or my brothers about. I didn't try to hide things from her and she understood how truly bad I was feeling. I knew no doctor or pill could fix this and just being able to share some of it with a kind hearted stranger had done more good than all my walking and running put together.

Marion continued to be a great source of help to me and I managed her nutritional shakes easily now and although still in discomfort, I was coping. Hannah had promised to send a letter after I wrote to her to say that it was funny that people react with understanding if you suffer a broken leg but think a broken heart can be cured with a cup of tea and a jam scone. I said I probably did too not so long ago. The post arrived and I opened her letter with some hope and read it.

'Dear Tom

What can I say now? But I do love you. I do want you still so very much. I know I'm not good at writing letters, especially when I want to say so much but can't find the words. What we shared was wonderful, we shared many precious and beautiful moments and I'll never forget them. You were everything I ever dreamed for but perhaps it was too good, too dreamy. When I think of the times we made love, every time I kissed you it meant so much. They were always so deep and exploring. I've never kissed anyone like I did you and we were both perfectly natural together.

Then we started to argue, I became suspicious of everything you did. We were around each other too much. It was hard for us to stand back and look at the situation and discuss it cos we were too deeply involved. I had (still have) a quick temper but you were always so calm and collected, always willing to talk about it but I got myself so worked up I just couldn't be rational. And all that business with Caroline, God I was stupid and immature. I knew you loved me but there seemed qualities about Caroline you admired and I of course envied them. I was so convinced you'd leave me I even told Marion. I think the poor girl thought I was mad!

Then there were times we made love and it seemed to be over too quickly and I assumed you were losing interest in me. I was really confused Tom. When we went to Arran - I never told you – but I was so worried about what was going to happen to us when we got back to Edinburgh. I was really scared. I know I still love you and what I'm about to do might be a disaster – but what can I do? I do care for Jimmy you know but if it doesn't work out God knows what I'll do or where I'll go. I might not stay long enough to get married though my parents would kill me. Me married? I always imagined the two of us like that.

What has happened my darling? I would so much like to see you but if I were to touch you again, that would be it! The other day when I asked you on the phone what we'd be doing if I were with you and you said one of those hitting the ceiling together moments – Tom , my love we always accomplished that - I've never loved anyone so much and when you said that I almost climaxed on my own. Sometimes when I think of you in my bed, I really ache to hold you, to kiss you, to have you come inside me and for us to reach heaven together. My God, that would be wonderful. Please keep on loving me Tom because I do you. A day doesn't go by that I don't want to make love to you. I've just been looking at your pictures – you really are beautiful and to think that you were once mine. I know I'll never love anyone like I do you. It's impossible for me to love even a drop more I love you so much but I have to do this Tom. You know me. Think about it, you'll understand one day. Remember one night you were worried when I thought I might be pregnant – well I didn't care. I would have loved to have had your baby- that would have topped everything we had together.

Be happy. I might be going to the other side of the world but you'll always be with me.

Take care, love

Hannah XXXXXXX

I put the letter down and felt pure, total sadness. I don't know why she says she was worried coming back from Arran, we'd just had the most beautiful week together and the pregnancy bit? She told me her period was late I recall and I wasn't worried. I do remember saying it would be great to have kids one day but I better get my career started first. She says I'll understand all this one day. I'll never understand up to and including the day I die.

As time was slowly dragging by and my mood neither improving nor worsening, I saw each day as a monumental challenge to get through and I kept the routine of walking and running as basic to my survival. I accepted my fate as one without recovery and a return to the person I was before Hannah was never going to happen. A hundred clichés about it ran through my mind and I thought of the one about having run my race many times but it was close to the bone and I did think that I'd run a hundred metre sprint only to be told at the finishing line that I'd lined up for the marathon and I was a spent force for the rest of the 26 miles to be run. I had nothing left to give anyone and if someone lined up all the miss world finalists and said take your pick, no better still they're all yours, it wouldn't have helped one bit and I'd have chosen none. Hannah had even said to me that I should go out and get another girlfriend and she just doesn't get it either. You can't click your fingers to it and switch off your feelings for someone just like that. The truth was I was still in love with her and although I didn't want to be, I couldn't find the button to switch off. I told Ben one night on the phone that it felt as if my soul had been concussed and he laughed at the idea. He might have thought I was joking but I wasn't. Part of me was missing. It was far greater than missing having Hannah in my life and seeing her every day. It was a part of me gone. It felt as if I'd lost one of my senses and I was certain this deep, powerful love I'd experienced was like a sixth sense. It's too real to be anything else. I'd discovered it and lost it.

If I gave myself any credit at all it was that I kept going to the library and still clung to some semblance of faith in the future when a large part of my brain was saying all hope is gone and I had none to look forward to. At times my sheer mental fatigue overwhelmed me and reading financial papers and taking Mr King's advice on analysing companies' strengths and weaknesses was beyond me and I admit that I thought of giving up more than once. At night I'd think so what to have made it through the day because it just meant tomorrow was waiting and how could I face a week, a month, a year of this? A lifetime seemed an unbearable thought. I picked up and put down my pen to write a letter to mum a dozen times as I looked at an old one of hers telling me to take care, a term she never used and I recalled smiling at the words when I first read them. I wish I had taken care. I couldn't get past 'Dear mum' as I couldn't think of anything I could write that sounded good and the last thing I wanted was to send bad news or news that would worry her and I thought if I told her the truth it would break her heart. The only person I'd told is Mrs Williams, a complete stranger who I met once in a park.

I pulled out a piece of paper from my desk drawer, one I had carried with me since given to me by my dad on my 18th birthday and re read it. It was Kipling's 'IF' poem and truly for the first time I got his message. Yeah he's remembered best for Jungle Book but what kind of writer writes the greatest poem ever written, thinks up a remarkable title for it and calls it IF? A genius does. The part that struck a chord most, ' If you can force your heart and nerve and sinew to serve your turn long after they are gone, and so hold on when there is nothing in you except the will which says to them hold on'. My heart and nerve and sinew have indeed gone and there's nothing in me but a will to somehow hold on. My life is broken and worn out tools is all I've got left to rebuild it. God, the sheer agony of this is too much to bear. How did this man know so much about life I wondered and capture it all so simply but sadly in a few lines. He talks about 'meeting with triumph and disaster and treat the two imposters just the same'. Falling in love with Hannah was surely not an imposter. I know I'm not alone in feeling this level of complete and utter despair. Won't be the first, won't be the last. It made me think about my dad and I hadn't given him half the credit he deserves. He gave this poem to me because he cares. It made me think about Sam. She's my driving force to hold on. She often told me how proud she was to be my little sister, that I was her hero and that she prayed for me every night. I'm clinging to a cliff edge by my fingertips and but for her I can't let go. Neil was right that I doted on her all her life and she still needs me in it.

It was two days before Hannah's flight and I'd called on the Wednesday as I had the past few weeks and spoken to her very briefly. She told me she was nervous about getting on a plane for the first time in her life and then telling me that she could never decide if I had more green eyes than blue or more blue than green she said she had to go and hung up without saying bye. The phone rang three times this morning and Harry asked if I was ready yet to put my back into a large garden he was working on and after declining, asked me to join him and Rachel for a beer at his local in the evening and I told him I'd see him around seven. I hadn't been out in weeks and I felt I couldn't say no to him after saying no to gardening. I was about to hang up when Harry shouted "Tom! Before you go, I've got an idea that'll help you forget about Hannah."

"What is it?"

"Do you remember Angela? I've still got her number."

"Angela who?"

"Angela. The woman we did a job for and she asked if you wanted to have a bath with her. Phone her up and ask if she wants her roses pruned."

"Harry. You want me to phone her out of the blue and say 'hi Angela. It's Tom Miller here, your gardener and I'm just phoning to check if you want your roses pruned? You're a sick man, Harry. You need help." I could hear the giggle building up at the other end of the telephone line before his bellowing laughter broke out. I told him I'd see him later and hung up.

Mr King phoned shortly after I put the phone down and asked if I could go over to his place as he had uncovered some very interesting facts about one of the companies I'd written to and researched quite extensively and I said I'd be there at noon. Then Marion phoned as I was about to take a shower and asked if I needed that photograph of Hannah back and as I hesitated to answer said she'd promised to keep it safe for me but she didn't have it anymore and hoped I still had the negatives. She explained that her friend Linda had been around at her flat and had seen the picture and asked about it and when she told Linda about it Linda had asked for it to show to her boss at work. Marion had thought Linda's work was all about advertising and Linda had told her it was more about the production side of shooting commercials and she worked with photographers and modelling agencies. I was losing track of the story and told Marion that I didn't care about the photograph any longer and she could keep the frame.

When I arrived at Mr King's house he already had papers laid out all over his kitchen table and was sounding overly excited as he put the kettle on. He had his favourite paper, The Financial Times open and old editions piled high on the kitchen counter and we sat together drinking cups of tea and I listened to him as he explained his analysis of the company Fox Elliott and news items he'd found of interest at the library. He complimented me on a few of my observations and notes I'd brought with me which I'd been taking over the past few weeks during my own library visits but Mr King was able to show me things from his perspective as a former CEO and actuary which I wouldn't have considered as important. It was no surprise to me that despite his age he was still sitting on boards of companies and advising them. He had Mozart on in the living room and would wave his arms in the air as if conducting an orchestra and we spent the entire afternoon at his kitchen table until he was satisfied that his work was done. Feeling like our time was up I turned to thank him when he said, "don't take life too seriously. You come across today as a young man carrying the weight of the world on his shoulders. Something's troubling you and although it's none of my business you can talk to me about it."

"You're right about being troubled but I'm doing the best I can. I don't want to be a burden to anyone and I'm coping, I'm managing to stay focused on what it is I have to do, to get up each morning and still believe in myself despite everything. I'm unemployed, now unattached, feels like un everything at times but I cling to a glimmer of hope that I can dig myself out of this hole I find myself in and make something of my life. What it will be I don't know but just a moment like this helps, to sit and talk about a career with someone of your success helps beyond anything you can imagine. You'll recall my Princess Diana like girlfriend. Somehow I managed to mess that one up completely and she left me, decided to marry her ex in New Zealand and the pain I feel at times is indescribable. It's my problem, no one else's and it shouldn't be anyone else's anyway. You're right though, I am too serious and I need to shed a bit of that. If I could just learn to smile again and maybe have the occasional laugh, I'd be okay."

"I can see and hear your pain. If I can give any advice it's that this life we're given is full of ups and downs, totally random and unexpected events and it's how we deal with them which measures us all. I carry many regrets in life and am all too well aware that hindsight is a great thing but I've learnt a great deal from what I'd say are failures and used them. My company sent me on a business trip to Canada some time ago, 1963 to be precise and I attended a function in Montreal before I was due to address a group of stock brokers in Toronto. My taxi got caught up in a traffic jam on the way to the airport and I ended up missing my flight and I can tell you now that I was damn annoyed, never missed a flight in my life. I couldn't book an alternative flight at the airport and went back to the hotel I'd just checked out of to phone our office in London and explain that I would miss the meeting. The receptionist looked at me in shock and told me there had been a terrible accident with the plane I'd missed. It had crashed and all 118 on board had died. I should have been one of them and but for an accident on the motorway holding up my taxi I would have. That day changed my life and the way I saw myself and my future and everything I did after was, dare I say, less serious. I decided I wanted to have more fun, count each day as a blessing and take more risks. Yes it did make me a rich man by doing so but there was a lot of luck involved and luck plays a big part in life. I've had a good life and when I look at you I see a young man of great potential. As an employer in my day I would have selected you. Don't let this episode in your life destroy your ambition."

I thanked Mr King for his concern and advice and told him how glad I was he'd missed that aeroplane and as we walked slowly up his driveway I complimented him on his newly washed, shiny Jaguar parked on it and thanked him for his help and I thanked him even more that he cared. Walking down his driveway I thought to myself why would an old man who's achieved the level of success he has in his career care for one second about me and whether I succeed or fail or live or die. I didn't deserve his kindness. I knew he was a compassionate man and kept his humility despite his riches and recalled Hannah asking me what I thought were the two most important virtues of character. He had them both.

I pitched up at Harry's local pub a few minutes late and found him and Rachel sitting at the bar in conversation with two other women who I was introduced as friends of theirs from their St Andrews days and I was conscious of the fact that I hadn't had a drink of anything stronger than tea for weeks and would have to carefully nurse any beer on offer and I'd buy my round next and get that out the way. On the way in I noticed a public telephone at the entrance and thought it could come in useful later in the evening. Harry was staring at me oddly as I took my first sip of lager and it was a small sip and Rachel grabbed my left arm and said "Tom, how are you doing? You're looking thin. You've lost a lot of weight. Are you okay?"

"He's on a starvation diet" shouted Harry above the din of background noise in the pub.

"I'm fine Rachel. I've been doing a bit of running and I've cut down a bit on beer but I'm training hard and just trying to get my fitness levels up. Harry's talking rubbish."

"What on earth is going through Hannah's head? Harry has told me what he knows about the two of you breaking up but I've told him that it doesn't make any sense to me and she must have been very upset about something we don't know about. I told Harry that I thought you handled the evening after the rugby brilliantly and paid no attention to her sister's flirting. My God, it was outrageous. Caroline was wearing a top two sizes too small for her and she just bought it. It's not as if she grew out of it, she was practically popping out of it and trying to show the whole pub, but you in particular, how fabulous she looked."

"Was it as bad as that? I didn't see her flirting. I saw her top, yeah, but I liked the colour. She's got a nice shape but she's Hannah's sister and I don't think she'd flirt with me. I'd be the last person she'd do that to. Hannah was a bit pissed off later but I thought she was over reacting. Obviously not, listening to you now. No, it's got nothing to do with that evening of the rugby, she left because the biggest arsehole in the world asked her to marry him and she said yes. There isn't much to say beyond that and I never did or said anything to get her upset."

"Do you think she was waiting for you to ask her to marry her and she maybe thought you never will?"

"She can't have thought that Rachel. She knew how I felt about her. Even if it was that, she didn't need to say yes to the first one who asked her to marry him did she? Imagine Harry saying to you I love you Rachel and want to spend the rest of my life with you but if you're not too keen on the idea it's no big deal because I've got someone else lined up behind you just in case?"

"Don't try dragging me into this" shouted Harry again. Harry was half listening to my conversation with Rachel and talking to the two young women with him at the same time and I could hear him mentioning my name to them. The last thing I wanted was anyone talking about me and what a sorry soul I was. I knew I'd turned into a big failure but nobody could be more disappointed in me than I was in myself. I was more than capable of being the judge on that and I'd found myself guilty of being one total almighty flop.

I tried changing the subject a couple of times as the evening wore on and managed to drink my first pint and had ordered another round but Rachel was tenacious in trying to tease more out of me on Hannah and a lot of the talk revolved around her. It was coming for nine in the evening and I told Harry and Rachel that I had one last thing to do on the subject of Hannah and that was to say my final goodbye to her and the phone at the entrance was the place I'd do it. Harry implored me not to phone her and Rachel interrupted him saying she thought it was a good idea and that I should and it was the right thing to do.

I knew I was taking a bit of a risk because of the time and that she had said only to phone on a Wednesday at three in the afternoon but I had planned to say goodbye and this moment just felt right. There were no more Wednesdays left to phone after all. The phone rang and Hannah answered, "Hello."

"Hannah' it's me. I know it's a bad time but I just wanted to say bye and wish you all the best and thank you for everything and wish you all the happiness in the world. I'll miss you and remember you. That's all. This is the moment. It's come and I'm saying bye now."

"Oh my God Tom, don't say that. I was hoping you would phone tomorrow. It'll be my last day and I thought you'd phone tomorrow. Please don't say bye now, please."

"It has to be now Hannah. I won't be here tomorrow. I need to go away for a while. It's right now I'm saying bye and I wish you to be happy. I hope I did you some good."

"You did more than that. You gave me so much that was good."

"At least he won't be able to say no one else would have you anymore."

Hannah started laughing and then crying. She was laughing and crying at the same time. I heard a noise and Hannah saying 'no, it's okay, it's okay' when a deep voice came over the phone shouting "What did you say to my daughter? You're bloody well upsetting my daughter, what the hell did you say? I'll put you in the hospital, I'll bloody well do it!" I hung up the phone and walked out onto the street. What did I say he wants to know? That I wished your daughter happiness you old fool. What a shocking crime that is. He'll put me in the hospital? The hospital? Which one you old fool? Is there only one with it being the hospital? He probably thinks there's only one hospital in all of Scotland and being the tough guy he is, he'll put me in it. I walked back into the pub and told Harry and Rachel I'd said goodbye to Hannah and wished her well and I could now relax a bit and finish my beer. "You were so good to her, I really don't understand" said Rachel. Harry laughed and raising his voice shouted "you know the old saying. No good deed ever goes unpunished."

Hannah had gone, the point of no return had passed and a letter arrived in the post. I hadn't expected a final one and sat down on my bed and opened it.

Dear Tom

I'm sitting in bed reading your letters and I don't mind telling you that I'm in a bit of an emotional state! I've been asking myself, do I really want to go to New Zealand? I don't think I do. After you phoned me from the pub I phoned New Zealand (honestly) and I was in a terrible state and it just all came blurting out when Jimmy answered the phone. Do you know Tom, I actually told him I didn't want to come out to him and I really meant it – but he never listened (as usual) and said I was stupid (as usual)!

I'll never forget the times we shared and what we felt for each other and I don't ever want you to forget us. I did truly with all my heart love you Tom and if I never truly love again I know that come certain times, we'll stop and think of each other- and know.

I know you'll be fine Tom – it'd take more than me to break you. I know you won't break, you won't be broken by me, you'll be fine I promise you, your heart will mend, I broke it and I'm so sorry Tom but you won't and will never break. You're the gentlest soul in the world but you're strong, please forgive me – but I also know and I truly mean this that I will always miss you and miss what we shared and planned for ourselves. I shared with you 12 perfect months of my life and if I never find happiness in New Zealand I shall always remember we had it and felt its tingle.

I know I've let you down badly Tom and I think you depended on me as much as I on you but it was much harder to detect in you. Why didn't we promise each other never to let go. I know I want so much to come back. You are so beautiful to me still Tom. I'm crying now – maybe you won't believe but I do still love you – it hurts me terribly – I feel so much pain and emptiness.

But my darling , whether I'll be happy or not with Jimmy – I must go now - I've given him my word and somehow I've pledged my life away. I have no say anymore. You know, that's exactly it Tom, my life isn't my own anymore, it seems as if it has been mapped out for me and I have no say.

Please don't hate me. I loved you very much and I loved Neil and Ben too in their own way and I really miss them. If only I hadn't come back for Christmas – this might never have happened. We were so good together. I think everyone noticed how happy we were together and our arguments were always silly petty things. You have given me a great deal- not just knowing and loving you – but I have learnt a great deal from you and I don't mind telling you that I was pretty damned proud to be your girl for a while cos I think you're really special and very smart. I always felt really chuffed telling people how clever you are cos it always gave me something to brag about. You might never have guessed it but I listened to everything you said and absorbed every word and I discovered a different world to live in. You made me feel beautiful for the first time in my life – you made me feel so special.

I will respect your wish Tom and not try to contact you. I know how much that line in the sand means to you, your dignity but I promise you this Tom, I shall never forget you and I shall keep your pictures and letters safe with me wherever I go and I shall always remember us.

Now don't you forget me- keep something to remind you of us. I'll say goodnight now but never good bye – that was my biggest mistake ever. I will miss you Tom. I promise I'll try and be happy and make the best of my life. Be happy Tom. I'll never forget. Always and forever your best and true friend – love you with all my heart

Hannah XXXXXXX

CHAPTER 20

Spring had definitely arrived as I looked out the living room, admiring the view of the castle. It was almost the middle of the day when the phone rang. It was Marion and she sounded excited when she said she had news for me. "Remember when I told you about Linda and Hannah's picture?"

""Yes" I replied.

"Well, Linda phoned me five minutes ago and they're dead keen to meet Hannah. They want her to go to London and get some photographs taken by a professional photographer of theirs. They'll fly her down for the day. You were right Tom, well I was too, we said she should be on the cover of magazines. She also said you took a very good photo that day. You got the light just right. We can stop her. When is she planning on going?"

"She's gone Marion. It's too late. She left two days ago."

"Oh, no! You didn't tell me. What the hell! Just makes it worse. I'll have to tell Linda. Okay, while I have you on the line, I was thinking, I'd like to you to spend some time at my family's house in Glen Aig and I'm going up there tomorrow. It's empty and you've got your pick of four rooms. Are you going to come?"

"I'll think about it but thanks for the offer."

"Don't think about it. Just do it. It'll do you the world of good to get away and you've been there before, it's a beautiful place and you can go for nice walks and it'll take your mind off of things. You need it and you'll be helping me out by coming. I need to do a few things up there and Neil can't get time off. Please come."

"Okay. What time do you want to leave?"

"Great. We'll catch the nine o'clock train to Glasgow and I'm not sure of the timetable for Arisaig but let's meet at the station just before nine. I'll see you there."

The train journey up to Fort William and past Glenfinnan is one of the most beautiful in the world and it felt good to be out of Edinburgh. I was sitting facing Marion and the carriage was quiet with only two other passengers in it sitting five or six rows back from us and Marion had been staring at me for some time. I looked at her and she said "what's the worst part Tom? Why don't you open up to me? You're going through hell, I know, but it helps to talk and you can tell me anything. I won't tell Neil." I sat looking out at the passing glen we were in and thought that maybe Marion's right and maybe she could share with me what other women would think what's normal, what's beyond any limit of being okay. I looked at Marion and said "the worst part is I think I was addicted to her and it must be like coming off heroin. How many people get woken in the middle of the night by their girlfriend to tell them she's getting married? The things he did to her and she'd wake me up to tell me and cry her eyes out and I'd comfort her but it killed me at the same time. He had sex with her while she slept and she'd wake up at times in the middle of a nightmare screaming and he didn't stop, he took her to a farm one night to hunt for rabbits and told her to run for her life across the field and fired shots above her head as she ran. He threatened her if she refused sex, they never kissed, she had to see her doctor when she was 17, she had severe pains she said in her woman parts and was told she was being abused and the thug wouldn't listen and kept on having sex with her even on the day the doctor said she needed to abstain for weeks or months. She stopped doing her homework because he didn't like it, he told her what clothes to wear, that only tarts wore makeup, wasn't allowed a beer, didn't want her having friends. She believed him when he told her that no other man would go near her or would ever have her and if one ever did he'd kill him anyway. All of it's the worst part and the worst of all is that even after it all adds up to how bad that beast is, she dumps me for him. What does that make me? She told me that when she was younger that all she ever wanted was to meet a boy who was kind to her and would look after her. I was and I did." I couldn't look Marion in the eye any longer, my sense of shame was too deep and I looked out the window at the rugged mountain scenery passing by.

As Marion was listening she never took her eyes off me and when I stopped she got up and sat next to me and put her arm around me and said "it's not what to make of you, it's what to make of her. To put you through what she has is not normal and you're going to get through this. She's made her bed and must sleep in it and I can't answer for her but I can tell you I don't know any woman who would have done what she has done to you and no one I know would have spent a single day of their life with that guy. He's a monster, the worst kind of man imaginable. You'll get over this, Tom. You really will."

"Marion, it's not as simple as that. It's not a getting over thing. Ignorance really is bliss. I didn't know what love felt like. I know the difference now and I was happier before I met Hannah. Not happy but happier, happy enough. Losing her will be something I'll carry with me for the rest of my life and the regrets are killing me. I should have let her know how much I loved her. I thought I did. The funny thing and there's nothing funny about it all, but to call it a funny thing, is that I'll never live in London. It was her crazy fear about me and about us and it'll never happen anyway. So living in Chelsea is the worst thing imaginable? I really just don't get it. She told me she loved me and I thought that meant as much as I loved her. I was wrong. I wish I was the person you knew before I met Hannah. God, I can't even laugh anymore. I don't deserve your kindness or comforting words. There are times I just want to fall asleep at night and never wake up. I dread tomorrows."

Marion grasped my hand tightly and said "Tom, please don't speak like that. You need a friend and I'm here for you. Nobody wants to go through what you're going through. You're stronger than you think you are and better than you think you are and I'm looking after you this week and we're going to have lots of fun together and you are going to laugh again. That's my promise to you."

We got off at a small station before Arisaig and one of the locals was waiting there to take us on the fifteen minute drive to the house. It was a beautiful old white house set in acres of land and Marion's gran owned the entire valley of crofts and cottages dotted around the coastline and there was a small Inn and hotel for good measure. She owned all the hills and valleys around for miles, including a large pine forest which took up an entire mountain side. I thought if you're going to live and grow old there are worse ways of seeing out your days and some of us are just lucky enough to be born into it. The rest of us have to face our own fate and struggles. Marion had told me though that the family makes very little money off the estate and at times it seems more hassle than it's worth.

I chose one of the four bedrooms and threw my bag on the bed to unpack while Marion switched on the mains power and took the white sheets off the furniture in the main living room. There were two large living rooms and a dining room, a massive entrance area and six bedrooms, four of which were for guests of the family and two large bathrooms. The kitchen was the size of Marion's flat in Edinburgh. The garden itself was set in about two acres of land and not very well kept by the local whose job it was to maintain the place but it was pretty and there were over a dozen large oak trees in it. Marion said she was going to get a lift to the small grocery store nearby and I said I was going to go for a walk and she reminded me to take a jacket as rain was expected later in the afternoon and evening and it could get heavy.

I was half a mile into my walk when I suddenly realised I'd left my jacket at the house and I thought for a brief moment about turning back and getting it but I thought to myself that I had my jersey to keep off any chill wind and I'd be back well before I saw signs of rain anyway. I made my way out of the valley towards the sea and I planned on walking along the rocky and sometimes sandy beaches which stretched out for miles around the peninsula. I'd only been here once before and spent a few days with Neil and Marion but I had a fairly good grasp of the geography and which hill was where and thought it would be a good idea to see parts I hadn't seen before. As I was walking I thought of Hannah and wondered how she would have reacted to the news about the picture of her and if she would have followed up on a modelling shoot in London and laughed at the thought that it would have been in her least favourite mentioned cities. There's an irony about that. Anyway that has gone and she of course has gone and I bet right now she's getting laid by the brute. I wonder if she's enjoying it I thought to myself, I wonder if she's orgasming with him and if he's treating her any better. It would be hilarious to be there when he first opens his stupid mouth and says she's not good enough for anyone. She'd look right back into his ugly face, tap him on his forehead and say 'hey, I was good enough for Tom'.

That should be an interesting development. I wonder if she'll use my name around him as freely as she did his around me, the constant reminder that someone else had his wicked way with her, as she used to say and the torment of the thought. What a laugh that should be. He thinks he's getting the same woman back and he's not. She was a virgin at the time they met and all that time together he never had to think of any other man with his special prize and later on never knew about Simon getting his hands on her. Well, he knows now all about me. She can't have said she's been celibate for a year. No let me correct that, she can because he's stupid enough to believe it if she does. There's a thought, she can tell him anything she likes, just make it up. Me? No I got the full force of the brutal truth whether I asked for it or not.

I made my way around part of the coastline I hadn't been to before and walked for miles expecting it to wind back towards the mountain I was using as my reference point. It was beginning to take the direction I thought when I noticed the first few drops of rain and looked out to sea to see a fairly dark and ominous looking cloud. The cloud bank was vast and it was heading towards land and the wind was beginning to pick up. I decided against following the beach and thought it would be a better idea to try and beat the approaching storm by going directly inland and over the hill behind me and I climbed up an easy rock face and followed a path which wound around above the sandy beach towards a rockier and narrower one. I followed the path for over half an hour as it got higher and higher and could see the grassy top of the hill it was leading me to. The wind was getting stronger and the sound of distant thunder was now a lot closer to me and I stopped to look at the flashes of lightning going on in the cloud and it was a sight I'd never seen before. The colour of the cloud was a deep navy blue and black, and the lightning wasn't in strikes but in explosions of orange and yellow, not white as I'd seen around Toronto before in thunder storms.

I kept going and the rain started to come down heavily and although the wind was strong, it didn't feel too threatening and I was almost at the top when my next turn on the path exposed me to a huge gust of wind. The path I had thought I was on was now more like an edge of a cliff and I leant back against the rock behind me and held on to a clump of long grass. My best bet was to stay where I was until the worst of the storm passed over and I clung there looking down at the rocky beach beneath and the now black cloud around me. The rain was torrential and the wind was blowing hard enough to throw me off the ledge I was standing on. I was fearful for a moment but at the same time transfixed by the beauty of the cloud and the thunder and the lightning and knew that this was not a normal storm I was witnessing. I looked below my feet and thought how easy it would be to let go. I guessed the drop was about three hundred feet and maybe five seconds of falling and after that nothing. All I had to do was let go of this clump of grass and my race would be run.

I stood wondering about people who have done this and what agony they must have endured in life to do it and felt the comfort in the thought too. It's the easiest thing to do I thought. Just let it all go. It's not the way I want it to be. What would Sam think of me? Anyway I'm far more likely to be swept off by a gust of wind any moment anyway and I had no fear about that thought. I did think to myself that I should follow what part of the path or ledge I could make out and lean as tight as I could to the rock face against my back and see where it leads me. The storm was now violent and the lightning was hitting the cliff and I was certain I was about to die. I edged my way around the side of the cliff and could see grass above my head and an easy climb up to it. I reached the top of the hill and looked down at the rocks below and the blackness of the sea and I knew that had I stayed where I was on the ledge I'd have been blown off it and would be lying in a crumpled mess on the rocky beach. I wasn't shaking or in any kind of shock at all and wasn't bothered one bit by the lightning above and around me and the only annoying thing on my mind was that I was drenched and starting to feel cold.

I followed the hill into a valley and up again and I was in almost pitch darkness when I could make out the nearness of trees and I walked slowly towards them and into the forest. I was walking down hill and after walking into my third tree decided to sit down. The pine needles I was sitting on were almost dry and my first thought was that can't be a good sign for someone wanting to grow trees. The storm was still overhead and the thunder was ear piercing. I knew I had to keep still and see out the storm and I knew too that lightning and sitting under trees isn't a good idea but I figured if it's going to hit one tree, the chances of hitting the one behind me must be pretty slim. I mean, there are thousands of trees in this forest.

Sitting alone at night in a forest waiting to be hit by lightning wasn't an experience I'd have planned for and I thought back to a camping holiday Ben and I took just before I left Canada and that was the closest I've come to this and then it was with a tent and torches and sleeping bags and we were surrounded by other campers. My clothes were soaked through and the cold was making my body shiver and I took my jersey and t shirt off to see if that might improve things. I grabbed a handful of the dry pine needles around me on the forest floor and began rubbing them against my skin and I did begin to feel warmer and so I removed my shoes, socks and jeans and did the same rubbing treatment to my legs and feet. I thought of what lay ahead of me during the night and stretched my arm out in front of my face to see if I could see my hand and couldn't see a thing, it was so dark. I thought of some crazed axe killer with a torch and a bloodhound creeping around a forest at night looking for victims or a rabid fox looking to take a bite out my leg or ghosts, maybe ghosts wandering around doing whatever ghosts do or some deranged naked man tearing through the forest howling and I thought to myself 'bring it on', I'll kill the axe man with my bare hands and tear the fox apart, the ghosts I'd love to see them anyway and I'm the only crazy naked man around this forest, maybe not howling but crazy enough. My favourite psalm sprung into mind and I could hear myself saying 'yea though I walk through the valley of the shadow of death I shall fear no evil for thou art with me, thy rod, thy staff they comfort me' and I truly felt I was there and yes I was at peace. I knew I'd be up all night and could hear the noise of the storm moving away slowly and the chances of being killed by lightning had passed and I lay flat on my back and closed my eyes and when I thought of Hannah, instead of feeling distressed, my body jerked a bit with a laugh.

I woke up at the sight of the light filtering through the tops of the trees and it looked like something from a movie. I pictured fairies dancing above me. I looked at my watch and it was after eight o'clock. I hadn't slept like this in months and I experienced a moment of euphoria. It was a mixture of pure relief and pure joy and I lay as still as I could and I felt my stomach, rubbing it and prodding it and I felt around my neck and pressed my fingers against my throat and then back again to my stomach and below my ribs and began laughing loudly. There was no pain anywhere. The feeling of the giant knot in my stomach and the tightness around my throat had gone, completely vanished. Staring at the canopy above, I pulled myself up to lean against the tree behind me and noticed a grey object two trees ahead and found myself looking at a rabbit. I was staring at the rabbit and the rabbit was staring at me. I decided to hold its stare till it looked away and we sat like that for over a minute. I thought for a moment that the rabbit was dead but it eventually twitched its ears, turned its head and hopped off. That rabbit was no doubt on its routine early morning run and came across this strange object, being me, lying here naked and thought to itself, what the hell is that? What odd creature do I see before my eyes? It doesn't belong here in the forest. It must have come in here to shelter from the storm last night and it survived. I stood up and looked around at my surroundings and it looked just as exactly as I'd imagined last night. I picked up my clothes and they were damp but not soaked any longer and I dressed and made my way down the hill of the forest. I thought it must be the better direction to go in and most likely to lead to a road or a clearance and it took almost half an hour before I found myself standing in a clearing next to a small stream and I could see the bottom of the valley I was in.

I was thirsty and put my mouth into the stream and drank the fresh mountain water and it tasted good. I put my face into the water and splashed the back of my neck and turned around to sit and take in the view of a perfect spring day. I was about to pluck a daffodil next to me when I thought to myself, no, why kill it, such a beautiful flower and began talking to it. "Good morning, you plucky fellow, I was about to pluck you, my yellow petal friend. Here you are, sitting with one of the best views in the world and you're all alone. Well you think you are but you're not. There is a bunch of your kind just behind that rock by the stream but you can't see them but take it from me, they're there alright. They're minding their own business and enjoying the sunshine just like you. I bet you enjoyed that storm last night. All that water to drink and your roots must be soaking it all up as we speak. You're still growing and each day you'll get taller and you'll see more and more of the valley and the view gets better. It gets much better than the one you have right now. Give it a week or two and you'll see I was right and you'll think to yourself, I shouldn't have doubted my new friend Tom, he knew what he was talking about. One day I might be tall enough to see my family behind the rock. Lots to look forward to but I'll just enjoy today first." I got to my feet, gave the daffodil a gentle caress and made my way down the rest of the hill to a road and I knew where I was.

When I walked through the front door of the house Marion ran up to me and threw her arms around me and burst into tears saying " I thought you were dead Tom, I thought you were dead." She was shaking and buried her head in my chest and I held her tightly and told her I was so sorry to have put her through this. The truth is I'd forgotten to think that Marion may be concerned during my night time ordeal or my chat with the daffodil and it only occurred to me when I was walking up the road about a mile away. She pulled herself away and wiped her tears, looked at me and said "are you hungry. Can I make you breakfast?"

"Marion, believe it or not, I'm famished. I am starving and breakfast sounds great."

"That's wonderful to hear Tom. I'm doing the full English for us both. You look like a hobo. Go and have a bath and you can tell me everything over breakfast. Give me thirty minutes."

I ran a deep warm bath and got in and Marion was right, I was filthy from those pine needles. I lay in it and ran the bar of soap over my stomach again and again and then around my neck and topped up the bath with more hot water and I couldn't get over the sensation of feeling so good. The agony had gone and wasn't coming back. I was feeling happiness as if I'd never had any before and the colours of the bathroom curtains in gentle soft pale green looked spectacular. I dried myself, put on fresh clean clothes and joined Marion for breakfast and told her some but not all of my adventure last night and left out my experience on the cliff edge and conversation with the flower and ate the best meal of my life.

That evening we walked to the local Inn at the bottom of the valley and the bar had a dozen or more of the local farmers and craftsmen with their wives or girlfriends and I knew not to ask which was which because Neil had told me a couple of years ago that a lot of wife swapping goes on here and not to be fooled by the quietness and serenity of the valley. The barman asked what I would like and I ordered a beer. "No, I'm not giving you that" he said. I laughed at him and said "How old do you think I am? Do I honestly look under 18?" He laughed back at me, replying "No beer for you tonight. I heard all about your disappearing act. We all heard you were missing last night in the storm. It's a scotch for you."

"I'm not a scotch drinker but thanks. Beer would be good."

"I'm not listening to you. My finest single malt for Marion's friend and Neil's younger brother, a great man is Neil. I'm not serving up what the tourists order, that's cat's piss and I wouldn't clean my oven with it. No it's my choice of single malt or nothing for you tonight. Let's start again, what's it to be?"

"A single malt please." "That'll be a double then. Coming right up young man" replied John the barman. Marion was listening to our exchange and smiled at me when my order arrived and she took her glass of wine we said cheers together. The taste of the scotch was like heaven's nectar, it was as if my taste buds were exploding and after my two month hiatus from alcohol, barring two beers with Harry and Rachel, simply the best thing I'd tasted. "Everything is back" I said to Marion "my taste, colours, my appetite, my stomach and my throat, my happiness, it's all back. I just can't believe this is happening to me and I can't thank you enough for bringing me here."

Marion had a huge smile on her face and touched her glass against mine and said "strange things happen in this valley. Let's have another." Two of the local patrons got out their fiddles and started playing and some clapped along and a couple danced and I sat there with Marion and watched and laughed loudly and drank some more of that fine scotch. Marion was looking at me and leant towards me and said "Tom, there's something you need to know about Hannah. She confided in me months ago that she was troubled by her dad and that her mum told her she had a choice to make between you and him. She begged me not to tell you but she did say that on the day of Princess Diana's wedding her dad told her to stick to her own kind. She was devastated that the day had gone badly. You told her about a dream of yours when you were young. You were with a girl of your age with long blonde hair and she said something to you. What was it?"

"She'll catch up with me. We were sitting talking in a meadow and I had to leave and she said she'd catch up with me. There were flowers. lots and lots of flowers. That's all. It was just a dream."

"It hurt Hannah. She saw it as the girl of your dreams and she never had long blonde hair, a brunette since birth. She convinced herself that the girl was destined to be the woman of your dreams. I tried to calm her and reassure her and she told me about her jealous episodes, the Irish girl, her younger sister, her tantrums about London, all of it. I said she was trying her hardest to find a reason to mistrust you and prove her dad right and you wrong. You never gave her a reason but could you honestly go through the rest of your life living like that? If her father really cared about her happiness he wouldn't have said what he said. I think he's an evil man."

When I got back to Edinburgh a week later I knew that if I was checked up by a doctor, he'd kick me out of his room for wasting his time and tax payers' money. I don't think I had felt better in my life and I felt better still when Neil handed over a bunch of letters which had been piling up in my absence and straight away I saw one marked Fox Elliott and a London stamp mark. I opened it first and it said that they had received my last letter to them, the first of which was still on file and they wanted to meet with me. They would like me to complete an evaluation with a company in Edinburgh and attend an interview in London and I was given the name of a lady to phone and she'd arrange all the times and train tickets. I opened the rest of the letters and received three saying there were no openings and two asking me to contact them for an interview, one being in London the other one here.

The woman I was asked to contact at Fox Elliott was very friendly and extremely efficient in organising and wished me the best of luck and Neil was a great source of support to me and insisted I visit a tailor he knew to buy a suit for the interviews being arranged. He said I could pay him back when I got my first salary payment from the job I'd be given and I told him that it was a great gesture but I might not be offered one. I was going to phone my old Krav Maga teacher and friend, the stock broker in Toronto and find out how my shares were doing and I knew they were worth more than a good suit. We tried to keep international calls to a minimum and usually only phoned mum at night when calls are cheaper but I didn't have much time left to write and hope Alex would write back quickly enough and so a call had to be done. Alex was surprised to take my call from his secretary and asked how I was getting on in Edinburgh and I told him I was about to go for a few interviews for jobs and needed an image overhaul with a fine new suit and short haircut and was a bit short of funds and wanted to know how my shares were performing, if at all. ""Great" he said "we can convert some into cash. How much do you need?" "I don't know. What are they worth? What's my account at right now?"

"Give me a few moments and I'll call you back. What's your number there Tom?" I said I could call him back but he insisted and I gave him the number and code and he phoned back to say "A little under twelve thousand. How much do you want me to sell? Dollars that is, Canadian of course."

"Twelve! I had no idea. That's great Alex. Let's say half."

"Twelve yeah, my friend. The company's been on a bit of a roll and new gold reserves were found about six months ago. I told you they'd do well with a bit of time."

"Bloody hell!" I thought for a moment and said "Okay make it five thousand. Alex, I owe you a big thanks. I know you had high hopes for the company but this is staggering."

"Consider it done and I'll hand you over to my secretary and please give her your bank account details and we'll transfer the money tomorrow morning. Tomorrow morning, Toronto time. I'll need a short letter from you instructing me but send that off to me and I'll keep it in your file for the records. Before we go, are you keeping up your training, had to use it yet? I hope not."

"I'll post the letter today. This is great news you've given me. I can't thank you enough Alex. No I haven't seen any classes here. I don't think there are any. I haven't forgotten what you taught me and no need for it yet."

"Tom you were my best student and I'm not bullshitting you and you know that. Just remember to stay calm." I gave his secretary my details and put the phone down and yelled 'thank God' at the top of my voice.

I was glad my appointment for my evaluation in Edinburgh with the company Fox Elliott had booked for me was after Glen Aig and not before because I was told it was for a lengthy psychometric evaluation and other tests and would last the full day. God, I thought, could you imagine my scores on depression if I had this two weeks ago? It was a long day and I was exhausted at the end of it and told my results would be sent to London. The next day I visited Neil's tailor and got measured up for the best dark coloured businessman's suit they had and after buying five white shirts I was given a selection of their best silk ties and offered a variety of colours to choose from. I chose two and asked if there were any others as the one I really wanted was royal blue. They didn't have in stock but one would be ordered and ready when I collected my suit at the end of the week.

When I arrived in London the first thing I did was go for a walk past Tower Bridge and along the Thames. I had an hour to kill before my appointment and I wanted to see some of the sights of the city I liked most and most of them were along the river. It gave me a chance to think about the interview but as I walked I found myself thinking once again about Hannah and how she was dealing with life so far away from her family and friends she grew up with and I felt a painful sorrow for her. I couldn't help but think she'd love to be here with me on this walk and she'd see how beautiful this city is. Never did manage that Chelsea match I'd hoped for us both. I didn't think for a moment she wouldn't have done anything else but blow away the photographer who'd be taking her pictures for commercials, she'd be on catwalks right here in London and I'd be right by her side any time she had her moments of doubt. I couldn't figure out what her dad got out of all of this or her mum for that matter. I was sure they loved her of course and wanted only the best for her but wouldn't they have preferred if she at least lived reasonably close by and enjoy her company as their daughter and who knows, grandkids soon and be happier themselves? Now they might see Hannah a couple of times in their remaining lifetime. New Zealand is hell and gone. It's the other side of the flipping world. Hate me yes for taking your daughter's virginity but don't send her there to protect her. And to the very guy who took it anyway. What does the old misery guts think? He won and I lost? Where does Hannah figure in all of this? I knew Hannah better than anyone and she knew me better than anyone had ever known me. I wasn't guilty as her father thought but I probably was of loving her too damn much. I recalled Marion saying to me that it was a father thing going on and that I wouldn't and couldn't understand it and not to try bother to, a bond between the pair and a deep psychological desire to please her dad, make him happy and proud of her and he chose Jimmy over me. Marion did back it up with saying he wouldn't have though if Hannah had just told him the truth and she couldn't without hurting him. I wondered if he'd ever know. Hannah loved the taste of French white wine, orgasming making love, she loved the library, theatre and movies holding my hand, loved Neil, Marion and Ben, she loved Edinburgh and the people she met every single day and I've no doubt at all, she loved me. All gone forever and all her choice and to be replaced by what? God, I'd have loved her to have met my mum and Sam. She'd have loved Sam. Everyone does.

I sat waiting to meet the two directors of the company who would be holding the interview and read one of the magazines on the table in reception. Two men came out and thanked another younger one leaving for his time and asked me to walk with them to their office. The office had a nice view and I commented on it. They introduced themselves as Julian and Richard and we sat down to talk about the company and of course, me. They both liked my tie. After telling me a little about the company they asked why I was interested in joining the firm and how I saw my degree and everything I've learnt from it helping me. I was the last interviewee they would be seeing and they were keen to come to a decision quickly and would let all thirty two candidates know by Tuesday next week whether or not they had been the one selected.

I told them I had done a lot of research on their company and liked their business model. I believed I could increase their private client base beyond their forecasts and without increasing their marketing budget by a single penny and I thought they were quite cautious in their projections. I understood the conservative nature of the firm but I believed it wouldn't be compromised an inch in taking a slightly different angle on tapping into leads from existing long term customers. I told them which of their funds I particularly liked and the ones I had a reservation or two about and why. We talked about some of the newly introduced unit trust funds and performances and how to promote one over another and why. I remembered Mr King's advice to look for strengths and weaknesses and I knew it was better if I talked just about strengths and ones that could be doing with a bit of strengthening rather because the word weakness conjures up a bit of a negative connotation to it and directors of companies like this don't generally like to think they might be architects of company flaws.

As we were talking I was thinking about their earlier comment that I was the last person they'd be interviewing and that they must be a bit bored of the whole business after thirty one of these in a week but they kept up a very professional image and were relaxed in the way they conducted the meeting. Richard was looking at his notes and said my results from my evaluation were impressive and one or two stood out according to the assessor which he'd like to follow up on and said, "All the applicants we've seen are very clever people and the assessment sometimes gives us a better view of the overall picture. You score high, I can see that but on lateral thinking you're off the page and your empathy levels too. I'd like to talk about that but what do you consider your greatest strength?" I sat there for a few seconds and looked at both and let out a bit of a sigh and said " I was hoping you weren't going to ask that one because it's so easily something I could make up or be deluded enough to believe when it fact it's not the truth. A year ago I would have sat here and honestly believed the answer I would have given you to be accurate but the truth is that I would have been wrong. I was lucky enough to meet someone at the beginning of last year and that person taught me so much about how to treat and consider people, people who are complete strangers to you and who might just briefly cross your path in life and I learned the value of them from her. I thought I was a kind and compassionate person and I'd have said a year ago perhaps, one of my strengths is my ability to deal with people and I'd have been fooling myself and you. I won't lie is a strength in my opinion. I learnt to put myself in the other's position and to care about that person and I'll always be honest with a client and a potential one. Every single person wants to be able to trust the person they're doing business with. They want the best advice, they want to make the best and the right decision for their families, not for the company they're talking to. They're really saying, put yourself in my shoes, consider every aspect that I have to and tell me then what I should do. Should I invest with Fox Elliott, which fund is the very best for me and can I have complete trust in this man or woman I'm talking to? It's not friendship they want, they only want to trust and know they were damn smart to do so."

Richard and Julian looked at each other and Richard said "is there anything else you would add?"

"I would Richard and thanks for that. Sadly the same woman I learnt from on what it truly is to listen to someone and consider them first was also the architect of the darkest period of my life and what I learned from that is worth ten of my degrees. I survived somehow but I'll welcome any challenge your firm can throw at me. It's not boastful what I'm saying but in comparison to my journey of having to meet something so difficult and do so and come out of it having met the challenge head on, there is little I'm afraid of now. I know I'm number thirty two and my chances of selection are probably just that, one in thirty two and I'd love to be offered a position but I'm comfortable with your decision either way and know it must be just as awful for you both when you consider some of the people you've met. I've enjoyed meeting you both, your assistant is a kind and efficient woman and I enjoyed my walk along the Thames and I thank you."

The two directors looked at one another and this time Julian addressed me and said "You've just said there's little you're afraid of now. Would you be afraid of some hardnosed Glaswegian businessman?" I laughed at the question and they laughed too. Julian went on and asked "why do you laugh?" I replied "because I'm a Rangers fan."

CHAPTER 21

I was sitting drinking tea with Neil when the post arrived on Tuesday morning and the letter addressed from Fox Elliott was prominent and Neil picked it up and said "should I open it or do you want to?" "I'll do it" I replied and opened the letter. I read it and looked across at Neil. "I've got the position." Neil asked if he could look at it and said "Good show Tom, you deserve it." He read it and looked across at me and said "You'll be on three times my salary. Three bloody times what I earn. And a car allowance. And it's their Edinburgh office. I'm bloody jealous and bloody proud. You're buying the wine from now on. Let's go out tonight and celebrate. I'll get hold of Marion."

Now was the time and I wrote to mum and told her all the good news and said I would sell half of my remaining shares in Toronto and have money transferred into her bank and that she and Sam must come and stay for at least a month in the summer and went out to post it. I decided to walk through Princes Street Gardens and find the bench I knew so well and hoped to see Mrs Williams sitting there. It was a bright sunny day with blue skies and the gardens were full of colourful flowers and I took the time to notice them and wondered how that daffodil was doing in the valley. Mrs Williams wasn't there but a lovely looking, well dressed woman of around my age was and I sat down at the other end of the bench. I noticed she had shoulder length blonde hair and was reading a book and for the first time in a long time I wasn't carrying mine and thought I'd sit there for fifteen minutes and if there was no sign of the elderly lady I was hoping to see, I'd get up and walk back the way I came. I sat quietly for a few minutes when I saw the woman on our bench looking up and sighing. "Are you okay?" I asked and she said she was a little despondent but fine. I had only observed her side on until she spoke and she was a very pretty and had lovely deep brown eyes. "I'm trying to read but I can't" she said. I asked her why not and if anything was troubling her and she said yes and asked about my accent and when I told her briefly about it and the confusion it can cause, she asked me about my old school and how old I was. She told me she went to a girls' catholic school in Edinburgh and was the same age as me and that I must know a lot of the people she knew about my age who had gone to Heriots and she rattled off a few names, most of which I knew, a couple of others I knew of and after a while she paused and told me her name was Ann. I told her I was Thomas and she said I looked more like a Tom and looked down at her book again. She turned to look at me and said "I don't know why I'm going to tell you this but I'm not a little despondent, I'm more than a little. My boyfriend and I broke up a few months ago and it hasn't been easy for me. We were together for seven years. I imagine you have a girlfriend and probably don't know what it's like. It's very difficult to go through."

"He must be mad" I said and she replied "why do you say that?" I hesitated for a moment and said "well, look at you. He must be mad to break up with you. You're a very pretty woman." Ann smiled and said "do you have a girlfriend?"

"No, I don't."

"Well I can say the same thing about you. Why don't you?"

"She left me." I noticed something about fifty yards away down the slope of the garden path and two young men were talking to a guy in his thirties, seemed like a businessman and they were standing over him as he sat on a bench and it didn't feel right to me. The guy in the suit got up and walked away. "I'm sorry Ann. I got distracted by that group of people down there for a second. This is a very strange bench we're on. I came here on the morning I resigned from a job suddenly and promised myself I'd come back to the same bench again and months later I did and there was an old woman, her name was Mrs Williams and I sat here, exactly where you are and I too held a book in my hands and I didn't read it either. I just couldn't and we spoke and she wanted to hear my story and I couldn't share it with my friends or my family and somehow I could with her. She let me talk for ages and listened. As bad as I felt, I felt a bit better after that. For a while anyway. I was hoping to see her today and tell her that my life has got better and thank her for that day. It helped me and if you like, I'm happy to sit here and listen this time if you feel like talking about it. One thing you can be sure of is, I'll understand."

"I'd prefer to talk about you now. Do your family live here?" I was about to answer Ann when I noticed two shapes standing about ten feet in front of me. It was the same two guys I'd seen down the hill talking to the man in the suit. They were both in jeans and t shirts, one had short blonde hair and the other short brown hair and both were about my age. The blonde haired guy shouted "you're in my seat. Get off it." I was looking up them and startled by the suddenness and caught completely off guard. "I beg your pardon" said Ann looking angrily at them. "Shut up tart" he shouted at her and turned to me again and shouted "get off my seat, I'm not going to repeat myself." I could feel my heart pumping faster, blood surging to my face and I said "this is a public bench in a public park and your name isn't written on it" and stood up. My feeling of anger was getting stronger and I remembered Alex's advice to stay calm and I knew this was not a moment to talk my way out of an attack. "I want you to repeat it again. In fact keep repeating it many times" I said to the blonde haired one. I turned to the other one and said "you too."

The blonde guy approached and he was about three feet away and I could see he was clenching his right fist, no knife in it, the way he's walking and too close now, he's not going to aim a kick, he's going to throw a punch right handed and he's about to swing upwards. He threw his punch and I moved my head left, took his passing arm, twisted it and aimed my right elbow into his throat. He collapsed on the ground gasping and choking and holding his neck. My timing was a bit off and I hit him harder than I meant to but he was on the ground and I looked at his friend and said "come on then." He backed away and put his hands in front of him and said "what the fuck did you do to him? What the hell man, what did you do? I don't want any trouble." I told him to pick his friend up and said "you better take him to a hospital. He's damaged his throat. You better take him to one." He helped his gasping friend to his feet and the two of them staggered along the path and away from us. I sat back down on the bench and let out a large breath of air. I was surprisingly calm and Alex would have been proud of this moment.

Ann looked in total shock and was holding her face in her hands and said "are you okay? I've never been so scared in my life. I couldn't move. I froze. Are you a boxer?"

"I'm okay. No I'm not a boxer but I hit him harder than I meant to. I'm sorry you had to see that. I didn't want that to happen but it had to. They were looking for a fight, it wasn't about the bench. The guy wanted a fight and now he better see a doctor and bloody well soon. I could have killed him, the bloody idiot. That sort of ruined things a bit. As I was saying before we were interrupted, this is a strange bench we're sitting on."

"That was the most frightening thing I've seen. I've never seen a proper fight in real life. You were amazing Tom. You don't mind if I call you Tom?"

"No, my friends call me Tom. Please do."

Ann and I spoke for a few more minutes and she said she had to get back to work and this was a day she'd never forget. As we were both standing, about to go our separate ways, I said to her that I get one shot at this and would she like to meet again, maybe have a drink together one day nearby.

I walked west back through the gardens and stopped to look at St Cuthbert's church and looked at the graveyard and thought for a brief moment about the night we spent there and how it was both silly and thrilling an idea and wondered who or what that man in the top hat and long coat was doing. We both saw the same thing and it was real and we never talked about it again. It wasn't as if we ever avoided it, more of a matter of so what, it wasn't worthy of conversation or then again maybe Hannah was scared that night and never wanted it brought up.

When I walked into the flat Neil was on the phone and I could hear he was speaking to Marion and I went into the kitchen and grabbed a bottle of beer from the fridge before going into the living room and waiting for Neil. When he came in he told me that he'd arranged to meet at seven and Marion couldn't wait to toast my new job. I said "I think I've got something you could use for your paper one day. It's a metaphor about life. You know when you're at a match, your team is three nil down and there's ten minutes to go and you see all the supporters, well lots of them, leaving the stadium. You know they're not going to get three goals back, we know that. Once in a blue moon maybe, but you're facing a beating. But what if you then miss getting one back and it's the goal of the season, one you'd remember for the rest of your life. You're not there to see it because you didn't wait for the final whistle to blow. It's like life, you get beaten up badly by it and you think the game's not worth playing anymore and nothing of any good is left and you bail out of it before your own final whistle is blown by the referee. The rest may or may not be what you planned but you risk missing that goal of the season. I learnt a lot. I could've been the richest man in the world, owned all of the gold and diamonds ever mined and I'd have given it all up for Hannah at the time. That's how rich I was and I promise you I would have. Every single one of us will fail or lose someone we deeply love in our lifetime and those we love are worth everything but when it happens we need to keep walking, taking each and every step one at a time, one foot forward after another, need to have hope in our lives. Tomorrow might not be better but the next one after might be. Walking out before full time isn't the answer."

Neil looked at me with amusement and said "maybe I could work something around that." I laughed and then said to Neil "I went to sit in the Gardens this morning. I met this beautiful woman who's split with her boyfriend and we got chatting to each other. Her name's Ann. I told her I'd like to see her again."

"What did she say" asked Neil

"She wrote her number on my hand" and I held it up to show Neil and he said "it's probably a wrong number." I looked at the number Ann had written and said "it's probably not." Neil was about to leave the room when he turned and said "One thing I forgot to tell you when you got back from London was the phone rang while you were away and it was Hannah. A long distance call. She asked to speak to you and I told her you were in London. I didn't say you were just there for the day, just that you were in London and I think she may have interpreted that as being for good. She just said thanks and hung up. All good with that?"

"All's good Neil. Thanks."

I walked out of the living room into my bedroom and looked out of the window towards the castle and thought of the days Hannah and I sat here looking at the same view, her hand in mine, and wondered how she was at this exact moment. Time to open her Christmas card one last time, the one Marion missed spring cleaning my room. One I'd read a hundred times. 'Dear Tom, I miss you. Let's make next Christmas just for us and every one after for ever and ever. Merry Christmas, Love you. Hannah xxxxxxx.' I sighed and hesitated a moment and then tore the card in half, once and then twice and then a third time. That part of my life was over, that dream gone and I looked down at my hand and the ink written telephone number on it and I knew that as good as today had been, tomorrow was going to be better. I thought of the retired nurse holding the hands of all her elderly dying patients and their last words about the beautiful meadow they saw before taking their final breath and I smiled when I thought of that dream of mine all those years ago as an eight year old boy sitting in that garden with the girl with the long blonde hair who said she'd catch up with me and to look at the beautiful flowers and never forget. Ann's last words to me after saying I better phone her and promise I would, were, 'the daffodils look beautiful today'.

Made in the
Middletow
06 June